The Hill Barons' Kitchen
By S. Howard Stockwell

Dedicated to Hideko and

the *Quien Sabe*

Montecito Trilogy: Volume one,

The Hill Barons' Kitchen

First edition, June 7th, 2012, original and unedited.

Preface

Inspired by living on the remains of the Quien Sabe ranch, the story of Paco evolved helped by fascinating conversations with the present owner and others who remember the way this region was in the first part of the 20th century. The current popular image involves its "millionaire estates," which enjoyed a boom around 1920 when the area's shady lanes were traveled by as many as 3,000 cars a day bringing tradesmen to and from mansions in progress of building. America's foremost architects, including the likes of George Washington Smith, Francis T. Underhill, Bertram C. Goodhue and Frank Lloyd Wright were erecting English manor houses, Normandy castles, Italian palazzos, Cape Cod Colonials and incredible marble palaces many sitting like castles on the verdant soft summits of Santa Barbara and Montecito. In 1930 Harold C. Chase, a noted realtor published a roster of over 200 "major" estates.

Among them were McCormick's "Riven Rock," Hammond's "Bonnymede," Bothin's "Piranhurst," Murphy's "Rancho Tijada" (since 1945 the campus of Westmont College), Knapp's "Arcady" (since subdivided), Peabody's "Solano" (later the Center for the Study of Democratic Institutions), Gray's "Graholm" (now the Brooks Institute of Photography), Mine. Chana-Walska's "Lotusland," Gillespie's "El Fuerides," Bliss's "Casa Dorinda." Ludington's "Val Verde," Clark's "Bellosguardo" and may more. The finest gourmet market in the west, Diehl Brothers, is also a location central to the book. Situated on State Street it was a center for superb meats, fresh produce and all the most desired products from around the world. This story reveals a slice of that phenomenal time with a spotlight on the spectacular events and the Chefs with staff who created the fantasies that entertained the region until the terrible downturn of the depression that changed everything.

Table of Contents

Chapter One: The Earth Moves

He had just walked in from stocking the truck with the morning deliveries and

heard the sound of a freight train coming fast toward him. The young man fell

to the floor and held tight to the marble column that supported the front doors.

From there Paco had a stark view of the great catastrophe as it rolled and

revolved through the market. He watched the floor ripple. Small hex tiles, the white turned cream, with black rosettes were actually bobbing up and down. Pots of finest imported mustards exploded, decorating the aisle ahead with sunbursts of ocher and brilliant yellow.

Paralyzed, the disaster suspended for seconds, he saw the event in slow motion. Glossy honey jars vaulted off the shelves crashing into deep ruby jams and blood red jellies finishing on the floor with the mustards. Bins of beans spilled out together, the kidneys, pintos and navies dancing along the tiles with large beige limas. Gripping transfixed, scented waves of cinnamon, cloves, chili, oregano, a multitude of herbs and spices collided smashing to the ground releasing their essence upon him. He noticed the vinegars that lay cracked open and still with limp stems of lavender or fennel, some with onions and garlic, all now pale and exposed, their liquid spreading and rolling around.

The famous pine wood produce stand that presented the Santa Barbara farm's blue ribbon selection of fruits and vegetables had given way and fallen onto Patrice, the manager's wife. He could see her long grey hair and one arm down to fingers grasping under shelves with piles of grapefruit and oranges on the ground. More violent swaying then a panicky feeling of being cut loose, just savagely disconnected from the firmament took him over. Helpless he lay frozen with his mind snatched away for seconds. Then reconnection to life, the freight train sounds disappearing in the distance with an unearthly quietude settling with the dust overall.

A slow commotion began to rise up from all corners. Moans and whimpers, names called out from the anxious and several including Paco headed to help Patrice who by now was immerging from the citrus with a bleeding terrified face. He lifted the boxes and her man, Quincy, held her upper body while a bystander supported her legs. Now all the wailing sirens began and someone was waving for help on the sidewalk.

There is nothing to compare with a crisis like this. Paco saw that his polished black truck with the "Diehls" trademark in gold script on the side was now half on and off the curb, it's back doors still open and softly swinging. All the carefully packed baskets and crates, labeled with estate or family names in Calligraphy, were strewn onto the road. They created an insane pathway, spilling out all the finest gourmet items the world had to offer. There was a case of Mumms, all the bottles broken and omitting their unique perfume, along side the battered tins of Danish sardines and some gold labeled Iranian caviar still safe in it's iced container. All kinds of perfect fruits and vegetables lay scattered smashed and dirty. Paco's prized cargo now lay almost demolished.

He emerged from the doorway, standing tense, stunned at the destruction of segments of Santa Barbara's proud main street. Paco thought about the time. It was 6:46 in the morning and this devastating event would forever mark the year 1925 as the time of the great earthquake. He noticed how bizarre it was to have one building leveled and the one next door standing safe. He dodged a pair of horses that had gone wild, breaking free from their wagon, dragging the reins and seat board. Looking down the way he saw a crippled trolley car had rolled into the front windows of Ott's, a glorified hardware store that sold everything from hammers to Baccarat.

Those were the big observations but there were hundreds of small hazards everywhere. He touched his breast feeling his heartbeat still raging. He felt his forehead with a hot hand and quietly sucked in the staggering magnitude of loss. "Snap out of it kid!", someone yelled, and he spun around to race back inside. There he saw Quincy kneeling over Patrice. She was colorless and staring upward while he petted her hair and called her name over and over. A tall man moved in to work on her as a circle of concerned formed around this couple that everyone knew. Originally sun seekers from New York, they unpacked and soon appeared entertaining daily on their vegetable stand stage with flashy stylish bickering. "Where'd ya get them apples old lady?" Quincy would say. "From your Mama" Patrice would reply, "and they're full a worms". All this was accented in snazzy Brooklyneze that captivated the Californians.

Paco's feeling of helplessness was unlike anything he had known before. The boy had an inauspicious birth secreted away in the beginning since his rolling stone of a father evaporated upon knowledge of his coming. He was the only thing that made his Mother's beautiful mahogany colored eyes sparkle with joy. She sang to him in Italian, fed him tenderly from her large perfect breasts and made him darling baby dresses of vintage lace with satin bows. She taught him to dance and to paint on a big white china platter in strawberry jam with his tiny fingers. Given all this loving attention his eyes sparkled too, just like hers, with an adorable little crinkle at the outside corners that gave the impression he was always smiling. His soft brown curls matched his eyes and sprang out in ringlets that his Mother made by wrapping strands around her fingers.

He was born into a family of noted stonemasons and artisans who had been

imported for their remarkable skills. They came to build the walls of the

millionaire estates that formed the verdant soft summits of Santa Barbara and

Montecito. This breed of super wealthy Americans were called "The Hill

Barons". Made wildly rich by industry and commodities they came from

Colorado and Idaho and many large eastern cities like Chicago and Pittsburgh.

Kings of silver and gold, copper and oil moved in next to coal and tobacco Czars,

even a notorious bootlegger or two found happiness in the cradle of this

California paradise. These were Paco's patrons, the ones, Diehls, his legendary

grocery store handled with kid gloves, searching the world for their requests and

delivering them to their fabulous kitchens to be converted to luxurious dining,

extravagant parties and exquisite events.

The boy grew to a man, still painting now with fine sable brushes, having the

same crinkly laughing eyes but the curls were carefully oiled to lay stark and flat

with a part down the center according to the current fashion. While he worked

he wore a handsome uniform of dark blue lightweight serge with small brass

buttons and epaulets. His trousers were slim tan jodhpurs and he was finished

with a pair of dutifully polished sable knee high boots. He put on a fresh white shirt each day and an Eaton tie peeked out of his collar. His cap was also navy blue with a black patent leather bill.

Paco had a broad muscled back made extra strong by heredity from his stone carrying ancestors. He whipped the heavy parcels and containers with big hands easily from the truck to the fragrant kitchens where the Chefs and cooks played peacock to their underlings. The haughty ones carefully inspected his goods, meticulously scrutinizing and auditing all while he stood waiting for new orders and dismissal by a wave of approval. Every now and then, one of these Masters would strike up a phony conversation with Paco so as to accompany him to the truck where they helped themselves to an ample snoop through the orders placed by their counterparts in the neighboring mansions.

One notorious competition raged for years between Il Brolino's famous French Chef De Vielmond, or Velly and The Bothin's Chef Wilfredo Henriques of Piranhust, called Fredo. The schoolboy pranks and vicious antics of these two provided delicious dirt for days among all of the layers of Santa Barbara and Montecito society. This gossipy networking hit a crescendo when, shocking to all, the two of them were found sleeping together in the Piranhurst pool house.

The he and he liaison was not the center of the surprise but the knowledge they outwardly hated each other so much and yet were secret lovers gave rise to endless analysis. Long conversations ensued about how puzzling it was that Velly, so French, and Fredo, so Austrian could ever become intimate. From then on they were watched closely to see if there was any evidence of affection.

On their days off they had an uncanny way of showing up at Diehls to peruse the inventory at the very same time. Shopping at leisure like that they both looked very chic in fine stylish European gentlemen's attire. In their starched double breasted whites covered with long aprons tied at the waist they were scarcely different save the blousy style of Velly's Toc compared to Fredo's very classical Dodin Bouffant that had 101 ripples to represent the 101 ways a chef could prepare eggs. Each man was impressive in his own way. The short slight Frenchman with dark almost black Spanish coloring and enormous forearms was totally opposite from the extra tall Nordic looking Fredo who was said to have had a Croatian mother that was six feet tall.

While they shopped they would always draw a small crowd that slinked around the market trying to be invisible in order to hear their hilarious yet poisonous interchange.

It always started harmless enough. Looking through the spice shelves pretentiously holding up a bottle of Moroccan powdered star anise, Fredo might say with an ultra aristocratic Austrian accent, "This can be so delicious if you dust a bit of it over fowl". It might appear to a greenhorn to be simply a musing out loud but the experienced knew that some unheard whistle was blown and the games were about to begin.

Shortly Velly would pop up out of nowhere grabbing the same item and glaring in the Austrian's general direction, his Parisian accent so heavy it was sometimes hard to follow, "So amazing one could think this is a good idea, it looks 100 years old. I don't like these at all. I would never put them on fowl only down the toilet", and they would be off to the races.

Then Velly, approaching Fredo and sniffing with a menacing gesture, might remark loudly, "I think we have a halitosis situation here. It smells like 10,000 rotten eggs left out in the sun and then served by your Mother" "uh oh" Fredo would eyeball Velly's large nose closely, "There is a renegade nose hair here, can anyone get it? It's coming out like a pipe cleaner and it's making everyone nauseous." Panning the onlookers now coming forward, he would demand, "Put on your glasses and take a look at this mammoth beezer and you'll see" Sensing he may have gone too far he would retreat but continue, "Ce bon? Are you still serving horsemeat and fooling your distinguished patrons? They will send you to prison next week"

Now the little Frenchman would puff up big, "Fous le camps et morte" which loosely translated was something like fornicate everyone and die. "No, no", he would continue, "not like your Austrian style of serving a roast beef made from a beaver."

Wandering on with an elegant air, pretending not to hear, Fredo conveniently handled the citrus and would pronounce, "These should be wrapped individually in tissue. I want the pink ones here and the orange ones look nice."

Now exasperated, Velly would snap loudly, "You are fondling the grapes? Your hands are dirty? No one will eat them now, you should be fired today and I will take over your job. You are so ugly with that bright orange make up on your stupid face. Your mother is a giant and a fat slut. I'm surprised you can read and write words after all the absinthe she drank while she was pregnant with you. You're a degenerate, a piece of horseshit with 200 maggots eating on your face. Vous êtes une pomme de terre avec le visage d'un cochon d'inde" in English, "You are a potato with the face of a guinea pig" adding, "you are laying your dirty, disgusting fingers on the ground with flies all over you. Tu es betes comme tes pieds", in French he would mean, you are as smart as the bottom of your feet, and winding down to, "you are a sickening beast, a cockroach with the face of a reptile, I spit on you and your relatives all the way back to Genghis Khan. You are an ape, a gorilla with the manners of a wombat. I fart on your revolting suit jacket with horrible cheap buttons."

Only to hear Fredo reply, "Schlappschwanz", meaning, literally, weak tail but it clearly insinuated that the Frenchman was unable to be aroused.

Serious now, both with red faces, they would circle each other with a ferocious demeanor, the huge tall handsome one looming over the swarthy sweating small guy dangerously simulating a crouching black panther. At this critical stand off there would invariably be some surprise movement that would mystically dissolve the situation. A phone would ring, a new customer would ask for help, the market cat, Felix, would rub against Velly's leg, something would give way. Everyone would disburse, the air would clear, the chefs would just leave and the sweet smell of oranges and rosemary would prevail. All this was just a bit of entertainment to boldly spice another beautiful day in paradise.

But paradise lay crushed on this day. The ambulance arrived for Patrice and Quincy followed the stretcher head down as Paco grabbed onto his shoulder, giving him a little push on, as a sign of support. Two firemen came in through the back in full uniform investigating all the damages and since the gas and electricity was out everywhere it was a relief to think that the fire danger might be over. Paco knew them well. Val and Paget played on the same baseball team.

The high walls of the market, except for the Butcher's department in the far left corner, were lined with shelves from floor to ceiling. On the right stood the marble soda fountain with a graceful vintage glass display case and brass fittings for pies and cakes. A mirrored back bar was set into a carved walnut frame that included shelves and in front a row of burgundy leather covered stools trimmed with chrome. Adjacent to these was a line of six tables for two with crisp white cloths that were installed when it was decided to serve breakfast and lunch. Normally, on the counter, there would be perfect pyramids of stacked shiny silver Sundae dishes and taller clear glass versions for Diehls heavenly Sodas that tasted like no others could due to one little secret technique.

The Captain of this bar was the one and only Salvador Rodriguez, a party man with big teeth in a huge smile, making every effort to emulate the esteemed bartenders operating legally in the days before Prohibition. He dazzled the customers with his showmanship and endless supply of creative concoctions. He was hyper since a child so this trait carried him through the day just dancing along the counter tirelessly lining the glasses with whipped cream, scooping on goodness, splashing on flavors, spritzing with seltzer, topping with more goodness, sprinkling with nuts, flipping cherries on top. He loved to bet the newbies that he could tie a knot from their stem with his tongue and of course he could.

His specialties were printed in big letters on a large menu and posted on the back bar for the customer to marvel at the long list of exciting names. It was Sal's great pleasure to describe in irresistible language the ingredients in each creation. "What is the difference between a Black Cow and a Brown Cow?" One little girl would ask and Sal would say in a loud rat tat tat sort of chant, " A Back Cow is two scoops of rich creamy vanilla with America's all time favorite Hires Root Beer. A Brown Cow is two scoops of thick dark chocolate with zippy fizzy Coca Cola and the whipping cream is optional."

"What is in that Boston Cooler?" A large man, his bottom draped over the little bar stool, would ask.

Sal fired right back, "It's for the sophisticate Sir. It is sparkling pale golden Vernors Dry Ginger Ale with a scoop of extra rich creamy vanilla ice cream and the whipped cream is optional".

"I'm not sure if I want a Tango or a Turkey Trot. What do you recommend?" A prim lady in a floral day dress with a tiny hat on top of marcel waves motioned with bright white gloves.

Salvador would pontificate with flourishes; " A Tango is made in an 8-ounce phosphate glass with a dipperful of dark rich chocolate ice cream. Over this I pour 1/2 ounce thick butterscotch dressing and a soda spoonful of finely ground nuts. On this I put a dipperful of extra creamy vanilla ice cream, 1/2 ounce velvety marshmallow dressing, and a dash of ground nuts. Over this a very little heavy chocolate dressing, and I top with a cherry or slice of fresh peach, and one cloverleaf wafer." He stopped for a deep breath. "Or for a Turkey Trot Sundae, I grind together four kinds of nuts, walnuts, pecans, almonds and filberts then pour the ground nuts over thick dark rich chocolate and marshmallow whip and mix to make a pudding. I Place in a sundae cup a dipperful of extra creamy vanilla ice cream, then add the pudding and to finish I put two red cherries dancing together on top."

Sal passionately loved the moment when the customer was confused. It was then he could suggest his favorite always starting with a boring classic like "The CMP Sundae" (Chocolate, Marshmallow, and Peanuts) and holding out hope they might go for his piece de resistance, "The Skyscraper Banana Split. It is my masterpiece little lady", he would say, "In our classy silver boats I put one giant scoop of extra creamy vanilla, one giant scoop of rich dark chocolate and one scoop of fresh strawberry in a line. I cut up a nice ripe banana lengthwise and put on either side. Next I ladle chocolate fudge syrup on vanilla, marshmallow sauce on the chocolate and deluxe strawberry syrup on the strawberry. I swirl fancy whipped cream towers on each one. Sprinkle with candied peanuts and put a cherry on each sky scraper". Sal finished red faced and excited. His innovations were limitless. For the eccentrics he made "The Chop Suey Sundae" that was vanilla ice cream with a brown sugar sauce of raisins and dates sprinkled with flaked toasted coconut and finished with chow mein noodles.

Sal burst into the market shortly after the quake looking scared, rubbing his palms together and shaking his head in amazement while looking at his wonderful fountain still standing. The pies and cakes had made a mess of the glass case and everything was in disarray but surprise to all just the perfect pyramid of tall soda glasses lay shattered.

Filling out the store center were rows of standing shelves with a fine walnut paneled cashier station up front crowned by a gleaming nickel-plated National Cash Register. Seated there, on a normal day, like a Countess, with ample girth daintily spread out over a commanding position, was Esperanza, the cashier, who could intimidate the devil with a tiny lift of one immaculately shaped eyebrow. Her skin was the color of lightly browned biscuits and on warm days it was glossy. She had a grand silky bosom often deliberately accentuated by the cut of a ruffled peasant blouse. Her eyes were enormous and carefully painted with impeccable black lines and heavy mascara. The other features, the nose, cheeks and mouth were large too. She often wore fresh flowers on the side of her shiny black-coiled braids that formed a kind of intricate tiara. Even though a local girl, Espe said she was originally from Spain.

On this day of disaster, right about noon, after Paco and Sal along with two of

his young brothers had just about cleaned the entire place up, the market's

owners, Tahj & Paula came in astonished that so much was still in tact. They

must have passed the mass of barrels filled with fragments of all the most famous

epicurean delights in the world. Smashed to smithereens they could find jars of

Sir Kinsington's Ketchup, Tracklemints Strong Mustard, Yuzu Kosho, San

Marzano tomatos, McCure's pickles, Major Grey's Mango Chutney, American

Spoon Pumkin Butter, Red Bell Pepper and Ancho Chili Jam, Pentelton and

Stockyard Barbeque Sauces, Vaalle Garden's Corn Relish, Rosebud Mint Jelly, a

large selection of Indian Curry Sauce, all the best caviar, Imperial Husso Amber

Caviar, Iranian Caviar, Russian Caviar, Burren Smokehouse Irish Salmon, San

Pedro Albacore, Ortiz Anchovies in olive oil, Danish and French Sardines,

Duck Torchon with Port Wine, Foie Gras de Moulard, Grissini Bread Sticks,

Pain Au Levain, Gache Vendeenne, Sourdough Batards, and a pitiful mass of

Vic's Bagels, to name just a tiny sample.

The little crew came together by the empty produce stand at the entrance and

hugged one another, some wiping away tears. Everyone was giddy now with

relief and gratitude to be spared. Salvador suggested that they put up a sign for everyone to see that they had survived and would be ready for business. Several days later Diehls façade was decorated with a big banner right under "SERVING NOW BREAKFAST AND LUNCH" that said, "DIEHLS CAME THROUGH IN FINE SHAPE ~ COME IN".

Paco slowly walked back to his long desk in the rear of the market. It was simple with a big bulletin board on the wall pinned solid with papers and a hanger with shelves below to accommodate his uniform, shirts and boots that stood next to a small wooden shoe shine box. At the end of his desk he kept a long natural pine box filled with finest watercolors from England and a collection of brushes that he intently cared for by washing carefully in Ivory soap and then making the tips perfectly pointed by forming them in his mouth. He used a white china plate as a palette with the colors of the spectrum built up in hard pools over time. In his spare moments, and sometimes long after everyone had left, Paco painted the handsome fruit and vegetables making little still portraits of what ever suited him. Often he would just paint one orange over and over to get just the right shading and stroke of the brush. He pined a few of his best pieces up on the board and tossed the rest out thinking he was not yet good enough to present his portfolio for entrance to The Art Academy in Italy where members of his family had studied. Further on there were more large shelves on each side of the room

that opened out at the end on the alley where the pristine market truck parked.

There he would prepare the complex deliveries that he started precisely at 6

o'clock in the morning. Just outside the back entrance in a little tin roofed shed

with a big padlock, Paco kept his most treasured possession, a red Model 101

Scout Indian Motorcycle. He had a special nail for his leather pilot's cap and the

goggles with extra green lenses that flipped up to use the clear ones. On cold

mornings he wore his dark brown leather aviator's jacket with a lambs wool

collar.

It was late afternoon by the time Paco vaulted onto The Indian and headed for

home. He had a heavy heart now, all day burdened with worry about how he

would find his Mother and The Quien Sabe. He knew the owners were away in

South America on a cactus buying tour.

The phone lines were down and no word had come to them about how the

Montecito hills had endured the quake. On the way he saw the damages and in

some cases he needed to work his way around fallen trees and rubble. He wound

around the foothills then turned left soon passing the spectacular El Brolino estate with it's spires of neatly trimmed topiaries peeking up over lacy wrought iron gates and high hedges. Following Buena Vista almost to the top, at the little wooden sign hand tooled with "Quien Sabe", he turned into a broad long driveway were he could see a mass of men far ahead struggling with equipment under a geyser of muddy water that gave them an overall sandy brown image almost like sculpture but moving.

Madonna came running to him with Ranger a mammoth collie. They both fell upon him at once. By the look, it was not clear which loved him the most, his beautiful Mother or his equally beautiful dog. Madonna spoke with a musical Italian accent, usually soft and lyrical but now almost shrieking, "You are safe, my wonderful boy, I can't imagine what you suffered? What happened down town? Are you hurt? We are all right except many things are on the floor, we do not have gas or electricity and the pipe from the reservoir is broken." They turned to see the struggle ongoing and the shower of mud constant. They walked on to a series of redwood tables and benches set up under the olive trees. There he greeted Oneda's Mrs., their children and Rosalita with five others, maybe relatives, that Paco barely knew.

They had set up a kind of outdoor kitchen with meat grilling and containers

sitting filled with ice and food. A line of sodas and their Italian family's home

bottled wines, never minding the prohibition, were all set out. Like the rare

giddiness and affection shown earlier in the market, the relief that all were safe

and preparing dinner made for a strange party atmosphere.   Paco's Mother was

the Ranch Cook and home manager. She lived in two large rooms off of the

kitchen where Paco stayed with her most of the time. Oneda, who maintained

with his wife and two children in a tiny cottage near The Quien Sabe entrance,

was the eminent Japanese Head Gardener, a kind of wizard to many who came

into his orbit.

As the murky geyser subsided to nothing, the men disappeared into the water

above to wash and later change to dry clothes, an array of dishes began to appear

out on the central table creating a buffet looking like a crazy quit. Madonna

served what she had in the icebox; meat loaf from veal and pork with garlic, basil

and whole peeled hard-boiled eggs inside, also her sublime manicotti stuffed

with nutmeg laced ricotta cheese and rich wine spiked marinara sauce. She

always had boiled ham and her signature potato salad, dressed with an oregano-

scented vinaigrette including tiny bits of pickled carrots, cauliflower, peppers and celery, on hand for Paco. She was putting out the antipasti with some dill pickles and stuffed olives as Mrs.Oneda, who did not speak English, was gracefully presenting her own Asian specialties. Netsuki simmered halibut came straight from the Hibachi she always used, so preparing dinner this night was not much different from any other. There was a flat woven basket with artfully displayed rows of mackerel sashimi set upon lemon leaves and a large celadon bowl filled with hand collected greens from the mountain in back was dressed with a red miso mirin dressing scattered with roasted sesame seeds. There were neat lumps of steamed rice sculpted from a small sake cup. She made what is called kushiyaki that was grilled meat and fish on skewers with a salty ginger dipping sauce. At the last she presented peaches delicately carved up and placed in concentric circles on a small crackle glass plate along with a bowl of Mitarashi Dango or sweet dumplings that were little balls of firm custard like rice served on skewers in a dark sweet sticky sauce. All this was stretched out alongside a huge platter of Rosalita's extra extra hot, meaty, cheesy enchiladas with accompanying spicy beans and rice. Finally Paco could see someone brought a pile of delicious nut bread & cream cheese sandwiches and a big sack of jelly doughnuts.

The mood began to soar as Rosalita's relatives chased around a large pond with a

Grecian Maiden pouring water in the center. Madonna sipped wine and

blushed with laughter, as Paco and Ranger danced together like sweethearts.

The gaiety halted fast as the earth began to undulate and the trees waved wildly.

The remnants of their dinner party bounced on the tables some falling to the

ground. Everyone felt the aftershock's effects, disengaged from reality, then

exhaled when the motion subsided. Sober now, without a word, they just

gathered everything up and disbursed, surrendering to an unknowable force that

was so much larger than anything they knew.

Inside Madonna and Paco began to check for new damages to the huge

sprawling Ranch house. Taking flashlights they moved warily about the rooms

that were recently renovated with the work of the region's premiere architect,

George Washington Smith. He was a genius with style and the redwood

paneled great room with it's brilliant cathedral ceiling was an example. Earlier

the staff had moved the breakables to the floor foreseeing the possibility of more shaking to come, so the vision was bizarre. Chinese vases, sculptures and

bronzes littered the floor that was covered with several very large Persian rugs,

all intricately designed with a terracotta, cream, pale turquoise, indigo and black

color palette. A rare collection of jade sat in cartons cushioned with tea towels

near the enormous wrought iron fire screen that had molded water lilies

decorating the front. Only the tools had fallen over and the deep golden

Spanish shawl, usually atop the baby grand piano, was laying in a silky pile with

it's remarkable stitched roses in many shades of pink obscured, the long fringe

spread out like capellini. The shadows, the beams of flashlights and the severe

disorder created a ghostly impression that made everything seem sinister even

haunted. They moved through room after room setting a few things straight but

ended the search deciding that all was secure. Madonna busied herself with

dishes and then some knitting, attempting to appear unconcerned, then retired

to her room early. Paco lay on his daybed that was in a little screened porch area

off the main room with Ranger sleeping along side. He was exhausted but still

to stimulated to be drowsy. He took out his sketchpad and made several

drawings of a woman's profile and then her breast with the curve of her arm. He

did a small detail of the curve magnified, loving the sensual line of the

connection. Hours passed and just before ten he arose, went in to brush his

teeth then, oiling his curls flat, he smiled at himself and those little crinkles made him irresistible. He put on his soft camel hair sweater, picked up a bottle

of wine from the cupboard and walked out, Ranger following with interest.

The night was clear and the moon was nearly full. The scented layers of a

California woodland were heavy with citrus, rosemary, bay, olive, roses, gum

tree, avocados, oak, mesquite and even mint all slipping by like a slow turning

kaleidoscope, now featuring the strength of one, then transforming softly into

another. He walked past the olive trees to the grand avenue of oaks that

formed the pathway to the Quien Sabe's famous cactus gardens leisurely

swinging the wine bottle. Ranger followed often preoccupied with unknown

issues that caused him to lag behind then canter to catch up. At the base of the

footpath there was a sizable brick terrace with a fire pit and benches across from

a large table with multiple trays always filled with small plants set in rows and

carefully labeled. Off to the left stood a gateway with two enormous Old Man

cactus sentinels, looming up kelly green with long black spines and crowned by

an odd halo of white silky hair.

The man opened the wine taking a sip right from the bottle then he and the dog

sat patiently by a tiny glowing fire. Soon a purring engine was heard from the driveway a distance below. In the shadows the form of a woman came

breathlessly toward him. The dog raced to greet her as she moved closer and

softly slipped her hands up under Paco's sweater to feel his skin and the

wonderful muscles of his broad shoulders. Reaching down he lifted her slightly

and kissed her mouth with rapture and that was the third time that the earth

moved on that day.

Chapter Two: A Legend Lands

Three jumbo sized women circulated skillfully around the big long white

kitchen of Cima del Mundo (meaning crest of the world), their dark skin

contrasting nicely with starched pink uniforms and tiny white aprons trimmed

in black. They wore peaked white coronets on their heavily oiled and crimped

hair. The trio were all but high jacked several years before when Mr. Knight, the

now divorced husband of the great estate's mistress, Lora, petulant with too

much gin, demanded the owner of Antoine's, New Orleans premier restaurant,

to give him one of his chefs to take home. Since the old tyrant controlled

interests in enterprises like the Diamond Match Co., the National Biscuit Co.

and four companies that eventually became part of United States Steel, the stressed proprietor agreed. Several weeks later Mama Genet, Fayola and Leatrice, each one refusing to go without the others, appeared at the servant's entrance to start work.

Since the Mr. and Mrs. Were both away, they were welcomed in by a puzzled staff and directly set about making rich scented stocks, polishing all the copper pots and shining up the extensive stainless steel counters. They made big market lists that Paco assembled at Diehls and delivered with delight because it was such an event. These ladies always greeted him with rollicking Bourbon Street lingo, a little naughty and so outrageously comical that it tickled him to the bone. "C'mon over here an give ole Mama some sugar" grabbing him and bouncing him onto her big lap. "Whatchall brought me today?" In the basket and containers were the makings for all the spectacular sauces and dishes that made their famous mentors considered among the finest chefs in the world. Exceedingly proud of her sauce making ability, Mama Genet could deftly recreate the important building blocks of Antoine's grand cuisine. These were; "Alciatore", a unique combination of sweet brown pineapple sauce and a rich Béarnaise that was a favorite with lamb or beef, "Champignons", fresh mushrooms in a buttered red wine sauce, "Marchand de Vin", a classic red wine sauce, "Bearnaise", the much loved savory variation of a Hollandaise spiced with tarragon and dry white wine and finally the cooks' best secret culinary weapon, "Demi-bordelaise", a serious reduction of stocks, secret herbs and wine finished with garlic and butter.

Armed with these remarkable skills, the three could produce the very dishes that made New Orleans cooking so acclaimed. They served up; "Poulet Rochambeau", thick slices of roasted chicken breast with Antoine's original style of roux, slow cooked to a deep chocolate brown and a rich Béarnaise over a slice of baked ham. "Cotelettes d'agneau grilles", prime center cut lamb chops grilled and served with mint jelly. "Tips de filet of beef en brochette", sauce Marchand de Vin. "Delmonico Centercut Ribeye" au Champignons et a la sauce au Demi-Bordelaise.

They could also make exceptional versions from the fish menu like; "Filet de Truite au Vin Blanc", filet of speckled trout in a white wine, shrimp, and oyster sauce then baked with a light bread crumb and cheese gratinee. Trout three ways, meuniere, a lemon butter sauce, almondine, with sliced almonds and "Truite Pontchatrain", a signature dish was trout with crabmeat sautéed in brown butter. Mama had lots of styles of pompano and crab available at a moments notice but maybe most glorious of all her dishes were the Pommes de Terre Souffle. These were large puffled balls of deep fried whipped potatoes well seasoned that had a crunchy outside and an inside that literally melted in the mouth. They did almost always accompany her sensational entrées of meat fish or fowl.

And Fayola, dear awesome Fayola, grinning ear to ear with her big pink lips over snow white teeth, could roll out Antoine's complete desert menu without a hitch. She made Pudding de Pain de Noix de Pecan, Meringue glacee, Peche Melba, Chocolat Crème glacée, Cerises jubilee (served flaming), Mousse au chocolat, Creme renversee au caramel, the much prized Gateau chocolat d'Yvonne and a very special presentation of Baked Alaska.

So here they were, out in the middle of forty plus acres in the wooded and flowering hills of Montecito, California, cooking their hearts out, mainly for an amazed and appreciative staff of thirty-six, because their patrons were elsewhere seventy percent of the time. That is not to discount the many times the bosses' offspring blew in unannounced with retinue.

They were living in lovely servants quarters in a sprawling hacienda with seven bedrooms, seven full bathrooms and five half bathrooms. The 22,000-square-foot manor house had a grand hall paneled in teakwood with a hand-painted barrel vaulted ceiling; a living room with a hand-carved vaulted teak ceiling; a formal dining room with a coffered walnut ceiling; a kitchen with a fireplace; a breakfast room with French doors and a sunroom. The master suite had an office, a sitting room and a bathroom with heated towel racks and a fireplace. The estate also had a secret 3,000-bottle-capacity wine cellar carefully hidden behind a tricky trompe l'oeil bookcase in deference to Prohibition, and a butler's pantry with silver drawers and china cabinets; a bowling alley; a billiards room; a gym and sauna (something Lora picked up on her many trips to Sweden); a 15-seat theater and adjoining lobby; a professionally equipped soda fountain; two laundry rooms; four safes; numerous lush gardens, a mosaic pool, and a waterfall. There was also a one-bedroom guesthouse featuring a full kitchen with large living room including a fireplace and that was the real focus for the events that April day in 1927, because only a month prior a certain extra tall lean and exceptionally handsome aviator named Charles Lindberg had just flown across the Atlantic nonstop to win a prize of $25,000 and the hearts of the world.

For the entirety of Cima del Mundo this was earthshaking since, miracle of all miracles, he was flying in to land in the meadow and stay for an undisclosed time with Lora to rest up and avoid the demands of a clawing world thirsty for every intimate detail of his personal story. That clearly was what had Mama, Fayola and Latrice, moving in quickstep to make all the preparations for a festive buffet and any dishes that their hero might want.

Lora Knight was an interesting woman. One curious factor was her preference to sleep on a screened porch instead of in her opulent bedroom. She was in her sixties by now and had distinguished herself with very generous philanthropic efforts in the form of funds for youth who needed money for higher education and as a major benefactor to the Christian Science church. This all dimmed in contrast to her most notable achievement and that was her almost complete financial backing of Lindberg's flight across the Atlantic.

The old lady's life had been tragically marred by the sudden death of her only son at age twenty-five. In her struggle to cope with this grief she had turned to psychics and séances in an attempt to contact his spirit. As coincidence would have it, one of the country's largest centers of spiritualism, a quasi religious movement with the belief that spirits of the dead world have both the ability and the inclination to communicate with the living, was just a winding car ride over the mountains to the sea and the tiny community of Summerland from

Lora's estate. As a matter of fact the experience was still fresh in the mind of

Mama Genet as she hustled around the big kitchen preparing for Lindberg.

Lora Knight had taken to bringing Mama along on these late night trips to

Liberty Hall, the spot where the exceedingly expensive formal séances occurred.

Experienced by growing up in New Orleans where a little gris gris was a

common place remedy for all things, Mama was a reassuring companion. The

medium favored by Mrs. Knight was a certain Harry Allen. He was sprightly,

really hairy with full beard and wild mop. Allen would begin the ritual with a

lengthy, some would say tiresome, lecture always long winded and painfully

detailed on the underpinnings of the faith, punctuated only by his shooting

down glass after glass of Old Grandad. This was a key feature of his technique.

After awhile he inevitably drank himself into a stupor which made it possible to

summon his guardian spirits who could, he claimed, usher in the dear departed

who were wanted at the séance table to communicate with their loved ones. One

especially potent spiritual liaison was a massive black man who liked to play

cards, stood seven feet tall, and had hands that would touch the heads of many

seated there. Mama Genet was sure she knew of him from her background growing up in the most magical and mysterious city on earth. "Maybe a relative of Marie Laveau", she would muse with far away eyes.

Mama recalled this ritual began as always the night before but with new surreal dynamics. Flashes of lights and menacing sounds like animals scuffling made the little circle tremble with fear and the rough shocking antics of an apparently crazed Allen took on a new very physical turn. He fell upon each of the women and fondled them with wild-eyed relish, appearing helpless under his trance-like state. It wasn't his fault that his hands grasped the silky under slip of a pretty big bosomed girl wriggling hopelessly to escape or the way his lips found the lap of Lora sitting stunned. When he made the huge mistake of falling toward Mama Genet, the evening was about to come to a crashing close. With one meaty dark fist she coiled back and let go to actually flatten the drunk mystic onto the big round table where he lay out cold as the little group moved toward the door leaving horrified. Genet recalling it all with wonder stroked her still aching fingers as she worked.

On this momentous day Mama and Fayola were busy producing Latrice's specialties, Pralines, molded sweet potatoes in jelly and something she called "Food for the Gods Salad" that combined finely chopped apples, mandarin oranges, banana slices, pineapple hunks and pieces of marshmallows snipped

with scissors. This all combined with stiff whipped cream sweetened with a

special imported French violet syrup then sprinkled with toasted coconut and

dotted with maraschino cherries. Latrice, traumatized early by some

undisclosed hunger, had taken to stacking and then counting hundreds of cans

and provisions she had taken from the pantries and cellars to almost fill her

room, hoarding so much that there was just a tiny pathway from her door, that

always remained locked, to her small bed in the back. Hiding out in her room, a

habit that typically flared up in times of stress, was usually sympathetically taken

in stride but not today. Mama was cursing Latrice and Fayola looked unnerved,

her big eyes rolling and her wonderful lips pursed when suddenly the roar of a

plane shattered the surroundings. "He's comin now! Get on outta here!" The

girls hiked their skirts and yelling for Latrice they ran out the door to the lawn

where they had a view of the landing strip hastily created in the meadow far

below. Like the second coming, the frenzy multiplied with all the staff, a bevy

of step-children with friends and finally Lora Knight who walked forward to

board the enormous Hispano-Suiza touring car, created to be the most elegant,

respected, and exquisite automobile of all time. It was a light blue grey, a kind of

pale teal, with tan trim and matching glove leather upholstery. Gunnar, the

chauffeur who was imported from Sweden along with many elements for Lora's other great estate, Vikingsholm, a castle on Lake Tahoe, was handsomely turned

out in a dark tan uniform. He escorted the lady in and they were off to pick up a

world weary Charles who stood with a small valise and a dopp kit at the stern of

a glistening Spirit of St, Louis.

Cheers welcomed in the giant car humming to a stop at the entrance of the

manor house. Lindberg alighted and revealed his towering rangy body. He had

a stern yet noble face. His mouth was wide with thin lips that had a hint of a

turn down at the corners. His lack of enthusiasm was excused, everyone just

calling him a bit bashful. He was actually glaring back over his shoulder at the

crowd following him now quietly, some on tip toes, at a respectful distance with

big eyes. Lora walked him toward the guesthouse then shaking his hand left him

to carry on with Gunnar and several others who would set him up in his new

perfect hide out.

The little fan club, frankly puzzled by the icy encounter, broke into groups.

Some milled around the front lawn making up excuses for a strange behavior

while others headed back to their work and Lora, inside miffed, carried on,

heading in to make a change for riding. Part of the young ones decided to go to the pool and the others followed Mrs. Knight for a day on horseback roaming

through the soft sage Montecito hills now in spring dress superbly covered with

patches of blue lupine and bright orange poppies.

Back in the kitchen now, the three cooks went to work heads down thinking

about what a disappointment Mr. Charles Lindberg was. Mama announced

after awhile, "Po child, he is bone weary and juss needs a good dinner to pump

them spirits way up". And so it was that after suitable bathing, powdering and

primping, a big scrub up for the men, a very stylish collection of guests gathered

for dinner on the long candlelit veranda of the hacienda. A quiet twilight had

fallen on the lawn that sloped down to show the lighted doorway of the guest

cottage in the distance. In spite of the inviting long long table with sunny yellow

tablecloths, Spanish style dinnerware, baskets of oranges and small pots of roses

with sprigs of rosemary, all eyes were fixed on the door of the guest house with

expectation. Only when Lora rose to serve herself from the spectacular buffet

amassed on a shelf affixed to the adobe exterior with massive wooden corbels,

did the attention shift.

There marched a dazzling array of the best dishes from New Orleans with a definite spike of Spanish and California influences. First was "Huitres en coquille a la Rockefeller", the famous appetizer of fresh oysters baked in the half shell on a bed of hot coarse salt, each with a secret sauce. Only Mama Genet knew the real recipe because she made it in Antoine's kitchen every night for years. The primary ingredients were parsley, collard greens, strained celery, chives, olive oil and capers all chopped fine then sautéed in buttered bacon drippings with a teeny tiny splash of Pernod. This was spooned onto the oysters with a dash of McIlhenny's Tabasco then topped with breadcrumbs made from stale puffed pastry. Finally it was placed under the salamander broiler for brief minutes and then served to an adoring public. The dish was created in 1889, for John D. Rockefeller, the richest American who would be served with the richest of sauce.

Next on the buffet was the incomparable display piece called "Crevettes Remoulade" that presented a grand tiered silver bowl filled to overflowing with crushed ice surmounted with rows of boiled shrimp and crowned with a small crystal bowl of Antoine's unique Remoulade dressing. Again only Mama knew that it was made from the usual mayonnaise, finely chopped green onions and parsley, fresh lemon, cane sugar juice with chopped celery and the magic

ingredient, a special Creole mustard. This mustard was made by the women

and used frequently in place of the more common French style Dijon created

with blander, yellow seeds. Mama's mustard was powerful, pungent and made

from the darkest brown mustard seeds with a spicy component also found in

horseradish. She added touches of allspice and cayenne along with some drops of

cane sugar syrup. They put this up in graceful glass jars with shiny black lids that

Latrice covered in printed fabrics from flour sacks then tied with red twine.

They were stored in the cool dark cellar to mature for several months before

using.

Moving along the serving shelf there were several entrees of fish and meat along

with a spicy version of Chili Rellenos that used Mama's Creole creamed cheese

to stuff the jalapeños in place of the typical California style with cheddar.

Favorite side dishes were presented including the much adored, puffed and

crunchy, Pomme Soufle followed by the salads where Latrice's "Food for the

Gods" was a stand out simply because she put it in a tall footed glass compote

that beautifully displayed the layers of fruit and cream something like a trifle.

Finally there were Fayola's sweet masterworks, "Creme Caramel" served in little Limoges ramekins and a gorgeous shiny dark "Gateau Chocolat d'Yvonne" standing tall on a china pedestal. She was hidden by the veranda door, watching to see the very moment when the presentation of Baked Alaska with an American flag and sparklers blazing would be wanted to fete the famous aviator with ultimate equanimity. Lora raised her fork and signaled to begin the feast, all eyes darting ever so often to the guesthouse door that refused to open.

Now bored for sitting so long, completely sated and a bit sour the group dispersed passing Fayola who stood eyes down, so disappointed that her glorious moment serving the hero never came. Lindberg as it would evolve never left the cottage during his entire stay but this was not on the minds of the rambunctious gang who gathered now sipping some of the best spirits and wines the secret cellar had to offer. Along about ten o'clock a group of seven, four men and three women, commandeered the oh so willing Gunnar and the Hispano Suiza for a little soiree into the town to have a taste of Café de Seville's naughty back rooms. It was well known that this high-toned restaurant with a notable continental cuisine was a front for the speakeasy hidden below and always guarded by a giant intimidating doorman who demanded the password to enter.

"Lillian, Melly and Corliss enter the Seville Club"

Crossing the threshold that night, leaving Gunnar with the Suisa to forage

around for the leftover wine and almost full bottle of Booth's to keep him

happy, was Corliss. She was small, rosy pink skinned scattered with tiny freckles

and golden red hair in a loose curly bob secured that night with a peach colored

satin headband that matched her scanty dress. She wore a collection of gold and

pink pearl beads that hung to her waist and cream stockings held up with ribbon

tied garters that peeked out when she walked in low heels. Next came Amelia,

called Melly, who was tall with dark hair in marcel waves and a red rose behind her ear with a perfect spiraled spit curl. Her dress, black lace, was far shorter in the front than the back. Carrying a fringed Spanish shawl, she was followed by Lillian done up in a pale grey and lavender evening suit that had a big fox fur collar. A grey cloche hid her sandy blond bob. A matching veil covered her lovely face that was frowning and fearful with trepidation. It was her first visit. Each one, waving delicately in long ecru kid gloves, whispered, "the rooster crows", and was passed through the arched doorway that was glowing red and orange from within. Lionel followed in his eccentric version of evening dress, a brocade smoking jacket with an ascot style tie. Looking European, his hair was slicked straight back and he was smoking a cigarillo from a small tortoise shell holder. Frank and Rennie strode through together in classical tuxedos a little boozy holding each other up and laughing about some inside joke. And last came Oren, quiet by nature, a writer of note in a tweed jacket, jodhpurs and boots, the same riding habit he had on all day. His large sweet blue eyes looked tired.

Lionel, Oren and the girls moved to a table near the small stage where a Flamingo guitarist was playing with facile fingers softly beating out a rhythm on the instrument from time to time. Frank and Rennie headed for the bar. It may be no surprise that the commanding figure working there was Sal

Rodriguez, Soda Fountain Captain at Diehls by day and the notorious Seville

Club Speakeasy barman by night. Here he could really be fully appreciated. His

Peach Daiquiris alone brought the women in. The cocktail menu included

names like, Clover Club, Honolulu, Dubonnet, Sazerac, Old Fashion and New

Fashion, Bacardi Snow Ball, Singapore Sling, Silver Fizz, Golden Fizz, Royal

Fizz, Cherry Blossom and Blue Moon. The most exciting, because they had a

dangerously high percent of alcohol, were Ojen Frappes, made with what they

called the absinthe of the Spanish aristocracy. An additional hazard, the

Suissesse, really did call for absinthe and included anisette, orange flower water,

white crème de menthe, all made frothy with egg white. Always popular with a

dare devil was The Red Death, that was mostly vodka tinted with food coloring

and touches of Amaretto, Triple Sec, Old Crow, Sloe Gin then finished with

dashes of Orange and lime juice. Corliss and Lillian ordered one of Sal's

favorites with the ladies called Death By Chocolate with Dark Creme de Cacao,

D'Artemis Coffee Liqueur, Vodka, Chocolate syrup, 2 Scoops of Chocolate Ice

cream served blended with whipped cream and a cherry. Melly and the men

wanted Martinis.

In the center of the main room was a large circular table where a stunning

platinum blond, appearing to be nude under a skin colored net costume covered

with faux pink diamonds and sequins, stood serving the Seville Club's signature

drink called "Pink Murder" in silver stemmed goblets. Elegant looking and

passed out free, it was actually made with 14 cans of Pabst Blue Ribbon Beer, 1

1/2 liter Gin, 1 liter Raspberry Ginger Ale, 2 liters Pink Lemonade, all dumped

in a giant crystal punch bowl with ice and floating gardenias. Above her and to

the right hanging from the rafters was a flower wrapped trapeze. There, in a

golden spotlight, sat an auburn beauty with giant doe eyes, her lashes thick with

black mascara. The lady's most erotic elements were provocatively covered with

small white camellias and her long gorgeous legs were silky with sheer white

stockings ending in powder blue satin toe shoes that crisscrossed up her calves

finishing with long bows. Her sensual derriere with two perfectly rounded

cheeks hung out over the back of the swing and beckoned as she pumped

gracefully. On the left were three gaming tables and a huge roulette wheel

tended by dark good looking men in modified Matador jackets glittering with gold, touches of aqua and bright cerise. Overall there was a multitude of moving points of light revolving out from the faceted mirror ball in the ceiling, slowly transforming the mood of the room through a spectrum from red to deep indigo.

The place was mobbed with a diverse collection of locals. Mingling together were business owners, shop workers, sports figures, tennis instructors, writers, artists and high-toned society figures, their wives, grown children and wealthy tourists so the tenor was wild but almost sedate by Chicago standards. On this night Paco was helping Sal to move the bottles around. He was watching the action and swiftly refilling everything as needed. It had been almost a year since the earthquake. With a new appreciation for the reality that life is precious, a grateful town still held on to that spirit of celebration. The women, now able to vote, cut their hair and shortened their skirts to go with a new sense of freedom. They were up and dancing, smoking and drinking right along with the men.

Oren, the only sober one in the place was thinking hard, "there must be casualties with this behavior", and as the other six joined the now drunken spree several incidents exploded that ended in their round up and speedy exit. First

Lillian, weaving her woozy way to the ladies room smelling of chocolate, walked into the wrong room to find a private poker game in progress. Nabbed by the giant paw of the one closest to her she was brutishly passed around for a fondling and then dropped to the floor. Her cloche fell off and her grey suit skirt was hiked up to see dainty flowered garters and expensive dove grey satin panties. The men, proving to be finally harmless, helped her up and gave her a big push out the door to join the melee now raging in the main room.

Sobbing in the ladies room Lillian was joined by Corliss who had an enormous chocolate brown stain starting from under her chin and spreading all the way to the hem of her pink satin frock with clumps of unknown material, possibly pieces of Fayola's Gateau d'Yvonne, stuck in the gold and pearl beaded necklace. On the dance floor Melly and Lionel spun to a tango with such violence that it took several nearby to steady them and keep them from smashing into the big wheel of fortune. Melly, her mind blurred with way too much gin, thinking she fell into the arms of a famous Matador, began to nibble his ear then kiss the tip of his large nose. Delicately she brushed his lips with hers then opening his shirt she began to lick her way downward finally to be jerked away by a hysterical Lionel who laughed so hard he cried. Picking her up in his arms her red Spanish shawl almost covering his face he staggered blindly toward the exit. Frank and

Rennie, proper gentlemen that they were, had striped down to their white

underwear shirts and had joined a line of men who were waiting to arm wrestle

the champ, a vicious looking fellow with a pockmarked face, who sat at the bar

beating everyone at the rate of fifteen dollars each. A long line of empty shot

glasses in front of them, they had their tux jackets slung over a shoulder and

Frank had taken two huge pickles out of a giant glass jar. Fingers dripping with

vinegar and dill weed, he passed one to Rennie and the two began to fence just as

Corliss with Lillian, her luminous eyes frozen, grabbed onto them begging, "Get

us out of this place". Oren, now bleary too, quietly herded everyone out to find

the Suiza.

They joined Lionel and Melly who walked dazed and confused a long way until

the huge brilliant car loomed ahead. Everyone was getting in and Lionel began

beating on Gunnar yelling, "Get this thing going! Dam it man get going!" The

stench from all the booze, and stomach acids combined with chocolate thanks

to Corliss, made for a nasty ride. One by one they passed out not noticing that

Gunnar was driving all over each side of the road as if depraved. Lost for

something like an hour he slowly climbed the last segment of the driveway

toward Cima del Mundo's manor house, careening dangerously toward the deep ditch on one side and a fall of fifty or more feet on the other. Coming to the last severe turn, his instincts distorted, he spun out of control and the Suiza did loft it's monstrous body into the air to fall and roll many feet below finishing upside down in a small canyon.

It was about seven the next morning when Paco, delivering his Diehls deluxe shipment of groceries, noticed the giant auto, wheels up, far down from the road. Parking, he climbed down to find Gunnar half in and half out from under the Suiza, barely conscious, just mouthing the word "hjalpa, hjalpa". Knowing he alone could not move the car he rushed to the truck and at the house sounded an alarm for everyone to help with a rescue. Lora called for the firemen and ambulance along with the Sheriff. The entire gardening and maintenance staff, about a dozen strong men, arrived at the crash scene and rapidly set the car right freeing Gunnar but revealing the others. The hideous picture of such pitiful nestled human carnage would be forever in the nightmares of the onlookers.

Chapter Three: The Garden Club comes to Santa Barbara

On the following day, sitting at the delightfully composed breakfast table in a sunlit room flanked with French doors that opened out to a flower studded courtyard, Lolita Armour Mitchell sat nibbling on a deeply-toasted, caramelized and crunchy almond croissant. She was once called, "The richest little girl in America" and now grown up she was the mistress of the El Mirador domain, a property that slowly transformed into one of the most fabulous estates in Montecito. The high points were a 500-foot-long formal Italian garden, with streams cascading down its seven terraces and a fanciful underground grotto with stalactites and stalagmites carved from rocks in a nearby creek covered by a two-story, wisteria-covered pergola that was now in a spectacular pale lavender bloom. A charming tea pavilion was occasionally set afloat on the man-made lake for intimate dinner parties. In addition to the gardens, the estate had an amphitheater that could seat up to 1,000 people, a dairy, a poultry farm, vegetable gardens, avocado and lemon orchards, even a small zoo with two bears, a wallaby, and exotic birds.

She was engrossed in the newspaper that headlined in giant type, "LINDBERG LEAVES WITH LOOPS". Quoting from an eyewitness, the article went on to describe Lindberg's departure after a stay on the estate of Mrs. Lora Knight's Cima del Mundo. He was flying an exact copy of the Spirit of St. Louis when, gaining speed lifting off of the small air strip in a meadow, he left the crest of a rise and dipped down below the horizon, only to reemerge as he gained altitude. Lindberg then performed two loops in farewell to his friends below.

Lolita's eyes moved down to another headline that read, "Prominent Families Mourn". It went on to detail the following:

"A tragic automobile crash in the Montecito Mountains leaves three dead, four critically injured and one missing. The dead are; Miss Amelia Carlyle Addison, daughter of The Honorable Judge George Hardie Addison and Sarah Carlyle Addison of this city; Mr. Francis Dubois Ralph, the son of Mr. and Mrs. C.D. Ralph of San Francisco; and Mr. Lionel Richelieu Holmes of Concord, Massachusetts. The injured were taken to St. Francis Hospital where their condition is unknown. They are Miss Corliss Macclelland, Mr. Oren Jefferson Star, noted author of "How the Bough Breaks", Viscount Renford Combs Fitzroy, Son of The Earl and Countess of Oxford in England and Mr. Gunnar Vernersen of Sweden. Reported as missing is Miss Lillian Hoover. Sheriff Norman Oldman of Santa Barbara County announced, "the details are not available about her whereabouts since the survivors are unable to answer questions at this time".

Lolita turned the pages quickly finding the society section that was covered with stories about an event that had the serious attention of so many. In just six days ninety-nine women from numerous cities across the country would arrive on a twelve car special train in Santa Barbara for The 13th Annual Meeting of The Garden Club of America, an extravagant gala adventure promising fifty-six gardens, four elaborate luncheons, six garden teas and three spectacular dinners over four days.

So it was that months ago Lolita felt obligated to favor the Easterners with a fantasy experience at El Mirador. The invitation described a glamorous entertainment; western-style barbecue prepared by her authentic Spanish chefs in Fiesta costume with sensational dancing and song from the areas best performers. Hundreds of aged and marinated fillets of beef were to be grilled over oak embers and a wide selection of Valenciana styled dishes were planned. Upon reading the Press expectations and imagining the ninety-nine women packed into six compartment cars, two sleepers, a club car, a diner and an observation car for the next six days, she daintily plucked her little silver bell from it's Derby china holder and rang vigorously for assistance.

Aiming to review the party plans with her staff she summoned the lot of them and soon they appeared in a long line. Fresh from the kitchen in perfect Chef's whites with an El Mirador crest monogrammed on the upper front in bright cobalt blue, was the Maestro and head of the line, Juan Del Olmo Pulga, his heavy lidded eyes today a little droopy. He made up for this downturn with a handsomely trimmed and waxed mustachio. The haughty Chef displayed elegant manners for his Mistress but a fierce punishing tongue for the staff that he battered daily with continuous bad-tempered tirades. Next was the Sous Chef Victore Ybarra, a gifted baker whose family came from the Basque region of Spain. He was taught from a small child the mystical ancient techniques that produced a transcended staff of life. At age eighteen he left on a ship bound for California from Barcelona to work in the kitchen of Don Alejandro, a wealthy and influential landowner near Santa Barbara, then on to Lolita's kitchen with the recommendation of a certain Diehls deliveryman. Alongside the Chefs were the women, the hard working cooks who carried the soul of the operation in the persons of Dulcina, Adiva, Trella and her little sister Viola.

Along with the kitchen staff that morning, breathless and straightening her skirt while shifting her brassiere, was Miss Penny, a flawless fresh face, born on a French vineyard in the Layon hills of the Loire Valley as Penelope Elise Lavigne. She was compelled to leave her family and hundred-year-old heritage to find a future free from the suffocating restrictions of her region. Stationed for four years on the spectacular Majestic that served as the flagship of the White Star Line, Penny was initially hired on as a hospitality stewardess for the May 1922 maiden voyage of this maritime temple of all pleasures afloat. Soon after she was promoted to be an important part of the most popular cruise liner in the world. Due to a structural defect in her topsides, Majestic suffered a 100-foot crack in December 1924 and undergoing permanent repairs the crew searched for new positions. A chance meeting with friends of Lolita resulted in an offer the affable Miss Penny, now completely skilled in the art of fine dining and entertainment, could not refuse.

Finally the line of key personnel for the event was ended with Senor Otilio the Head Gardener. Each one was excited by the challenge to compete with the other famous estates, the spectacular Piranhurst and the nationally celebrated El Fueridis, to produce the most glamorous festivity.

Chef Pulga started with the menu adding an embellished description of each dish. Exquisitely rolling his Rs to form an exaggerated trill, a kind of long purr, that gave the food such bravado that everyone continually murmured with pleasure.

"The Lista de Comida Madam will start with the richest red, so delicioso, 'Sopa de Albondigas', con sausage meatballs muy suculento, mais and rice, crema de queso, tortillas superi and chico", he made a gesture of teeny tiny scattering, "cilantro on top." He finished with a big kiss of his fingers and continuing, "We serve the 'Aceitunas', Olives Picante and the 'Gelatins of Tomate et Camarones', the Shrimps Gigantesco. Then, Madam, comes The 'Tamales Argentinos', gordura and tiermo", motioning with his hands fluttering with lightness,

The Diehls delivery truck was pulling up in the rear entrance to what was considered by many the crown jewel of Santa Barbara style mansions, El Fureidis, meaning Little Garden of Eden. It was the creation of J. Waldron Gillespie, the scion of a wealthy New York banking family, and it began an architectural and horticultural revolution.

The Gillespie gardens, with their Arabian-influenced use of carefully placed terraces and reflecting pools took eleven years of planting trees on this exceptional property. Gillespie hired one of the most important and renowned architects in America, Bertram Goodhue, and took him on a yearlong trip to study the buildings and gardens of Mediterranean Europe. Utterly inspired, they returned to build Santa Barbara's finest villa and to landscape what became one of the most spectacular gardens in all of California and the United States.

All this was well known by the ladies of the Garden Club and it was expected to be a highlight of the visit. They were especially excited to see perhaps the utmost rare tree collection in North America. The site of the dinner party had a clear view of the most dramatic element in El Fureidis including the south elevation and its attendant water gardens. Six successive shimmering pools, terraced on different levels of the cascading gardens, linking the main residence with the lower casino would be breathtaking in the twilight. Facing the terrace is the home's symmetrical columned south façade, which features a bas-relief frieze depicting Arthur's legendary Knights of the Round Table.

It would be there that the magical buffet would be presented by a most unusual kitchen staff led by Sepehr Jafar Javeed Foroohar, a Persian Chef of major distinction in his country. Java Sir, as he was called, was forced to flee his home during a bloody political upheaval. He turned up in Turkey commanding the kitchen of a minor Shaw who had taken up residence in a famous architectural treasure on the Island of Corfu. As fate would have it, Mr. Gillespie and Bertand Goodhue were visiting that very estate, spending time eating the Chef's delicious array of Persian delicacies while making extensive plans of the house and gardens to take home to Montecito. It was then they decided to take Java Sir too.

With its high central dome covered with gold leaf in an elegant floral design, the conversation room was the focal point of the home's entry and a dramatic hand-painted gold-leaf barrel-vaulted ceiling by Henry Wadsworth Moore, with a

musician's balcony in the spectacular dining room, provided the perfect setting

for the gifted Persian Chef and his bevy of cooks and followers who were

imported with him.   A vision, this troop of kitchen servants retained their

traditional dress, with many elaborate brocade elements in an exotic rainbow of

colors, each one finished with a turban and sandals.

Paco walked slowly toward the house and out of the corner of his eye saw that,

as expected, the bushes nearby were vibrating and giggling. One brown skinned

shapely arm and then another beckoned with exceedingly graceful motions.

Soon a face appeared with a gold trimmed turquoise veil holding back long hair.

Her eyes were big and black with a very pale yellow where the whites should be.

Thick long lashes fluttered and she leaped to embrace him just as she always did

on the days he brought Java Sir's orders. Her habit was to force him into a small

broom closet where standing cramped inside she would kiss him ardently with

soft warm lips and whisper unintelligible sweet phrases until Paco would try to

become serious at which point she would bolt and run away leaving him weak

and almost too shaky to carry the big delivery into the kitchen.   He would not

see her again until his next visit. He didn't even know her name.

Java Sir always greeted him with praying hands and a deep bow. "Salam dear
Paco. What have you brought me today?" His elegant manners were very
refreshing after the frenzy of the others on his route who always left him hassled
and dazed with their demands.

In the many baskets and cases were the makings for the Chef's extraordinary
banquet with an all-Persian Dinner Menu designed just for the Garden Club of
America. For the Appetizers there would be Maust'Khiar, a combination of
yogurt and chopped cucumber, flavored with mint. Panir Sabzi, a colorful plate
of imported cheese, walnuts and fresh herbs of mint, basil, watercress, tarragon
and radish. Boriani, a medley of eggplant, yogurt, onions, garlic and herbs.

Dolemeh, cooked grape leaves, filled with ground beef, rice, tarragon, split peas, green onions, basil, parsley and fresh herbs, and a splendid service of Iranian Caviar with condiments.

Next on the menu was a Persian Shirazi Salad, a combination of iceberg lettuce, tomato, red cabbage, cucumbers, feta cheese, Greek olives, raisins, lentils, dates and fresh vegetables. The main course entrées would be Albalo Polo, Basmati rice mixed with black cherries served with spicy boiled chicken and Fesenjon, a fried walnut pomegranate sauce. The highlight had to be the grill filled with skewers of Chelo Kebb Barg, filet mignon and Lamb Kebabs done with the finest cut of boneless baby spring lamb tenderloin, all marinated in Java Sir's sultry sauce then barbequed. The easterners would be dazzled! The evening would conclude with the much beloved Baklava, crispy and honeyed with sprinkles of roasted pistachios, served on little golden plates with fancy paper doilies and rose petals.

What a thrilling specter, the Persian water gardens softly illuminated and scented with a galaxy of night blooming jasmine, the sumptuous dinner with all the costumed servers and an entertainment of dancers with flutes and the delicate strumming of lutes. On his way out Paco vowed to bet on El Fureidis to win the prize from the Ladies of the Garden Club.

As it turned out the ladies' unanimous choice was to be the evening at the El Paseo Restaurant. This was a unique complex of adobe styled buildings, wonderful fountains and stairways, embellished with decorative Spanish tiles and big red ones on all the roofs. The floors were an ox blood terra cotta and always kept highly polished. It was created to mimic a street in Spain and was exactly that with lavish pots of cascading flowers and palms everywhere. The main dining room was enormous topped by an open-air roof with sliding canvas awnings that could be drawn in the rare case of some rain. There were huge paintings in sepia tones with touches of color that portrayed all the romantic characters of early California. Pictured there the guests could see a majestic Senorita with her Caballero, caritas drawn by oxen with the bounty of the region as cargo, serape wrapped women with giant baskets of flowers carried on their heads and noble Indians, the woman carrying a little papoose.

Many tables surrounded a grand center fountain and there was a big stage all along one end. It was here that Senor Jose Fernandez presented his Spanish revue that could be enjoyed while dining on a menu of the finest California dishes including authentic versions of enchiladas, tamales and rellenos along with an extensive continental cuisine. Because of prohibition the bar menu was timid but many brought their flasks, some fancy monogrammed silver, to dose the drinks that were served. Overall an evening at El Paseo was like a little trip to a foreign land. It is impossible to omit one detail that would always amuse Paco and Sal who dropped in frequently to sit in the bar and play gin rummy with some of the dancers at a small table in the back. On view, like an extension of her day job, the captivating Esperanza was seated by the door acting as the cashier. She always lifted one perfectly arched eyebrow in recognition as Paco walked by.

The show was already under way with a fine appearance by the great baritone Fortuno Bona Nova with his beautiful arrangement of "Il Provenza del mar" from La Traviata. He was a star who had performed on he Crosby Hour and The Rudy Vallee Program. This was all on the radio so in person it was surprising to see that, although he was handsome, he was only about five feet tall with that huge voice coming from such a tiny man.

Carmen Samaniego, a stunning young Flamenco dancer always followed. Her biography stated that she was abandoned as a child by the Gypsies of Granada and the sister of screen star Ramon Navaro. Her great solo number was "Cadiz" where she wore her breathtaking costume that had an intricately beaded flowered torso with row upon row of white organdy ruffles hemmed in gold thread flowing down onto her train that she used with great dramatic effect. Her castanets were blazing as she tapped out the beat of the music with unusual dexterity.

The audience cheered her off and welcomed the lovely Camille De Montez, known to have a voice of gold. Shouts of "bravo" greeted her. She was a local girl who had made it big. After a short intermission the Maestro himself, Jose Fernandz, appeared with his gorgeous new partner, Carola Alvena, who was Spanish born and trained from childhood in her native dances. It was she who danced The Bolero with him when the Ravel number took the critics by storm. A spirited lovely ballerina her solo number that evening was a primitive rumba that had every heart beating a little faster.

All revved up now the audience was thrilled when Gilberto Galvan performed a fiery whirlwind cape dance that finished with his show stopping comedy bit called, "Making love behind a cactus bush". The crowd was on it's feet, clapping madly, perfectly primed for the next act, Carmela and Gabriel Cansino, a couple coming from a family that went back for seven generations of dancers. Gabriel's mother was the famous Elisa Cansino who played the Orpheum circuit for years. Their routine was almost a clown act. They were dressed as dolls and flew around the stage chasing and phony fighting with each other in an odd combination of tumbling and dancing. The show was finished with the songs of Lupe and Rudy Valesco and the finale where Jose Fernandez and his partner did the all time favorite, "Bolero", with intense sensuality and drama that always led to a brilliant climax. This invariably left the crowd weak with pleasure.

It was the next to last day of the historic Garden Club gathering and a group of well over 100, suitably dressed in their afternoon tea finery, began to taste the blissful collection of Chef Fredo's pastries in the spectacular surrounds of the Piranhurst's mountain top, when a disastrous phenomenon hit the Montecito hills with a wallop. A monstrous black cloud formed overhead bringing a powerful bolt of lightening and a gust of wind that grabbed the marvelous collection of hats from the shocked ladies and sent them skyward, some looping back gracefully to the ground but many never to be seen again. A weather occurrence like this had not been recorded for more than sixty years. The driving rainstorm made mush of the proudly displayed Viennese Tortes while the guests were escorted to safer ground. Mrs. Nellie Bothin and the staff, standing distraught, were wringing their hands with concern, thinking the event everyone had spent so much energy to produce with perfection was hopelessly spoiled. Fredo, imagining his reputation was lost, turned red and then blue in the face, holding his breath for minutes, so as not to blurt out the nasty cluster of expletives he had in his heart. So much imagined, so much destroyed.

To the delight, and for some surprise, of all concerned, The Garden Club of America reviewed the entire visit with the fantastic array of experiences and hospitality in ultra glowing terms. Who would expect, it was noted in a lengthy New York Times article, they especially loved, "the thrilling thunder and lightening storm in the Gardens at Pirenhurst and the memorable service of

such delicious authentic Viennese pastries". Chef Fredo was released from his

melancholy to emerge with an entirely new scenario that named him the

American Garden Club's own star Chef.

Chapter Four: A Forbidden Palace and The Montecito Club

It was later that week that Victore came into the El Paseo bar as planned to meet

Paco and after a quick drink followed him out to the back where their

motorcycles where chained. Hopping on the bikes the two raced to the highway

and almost an hour later they came to the gates of The Forbidden Palace, an old

rancho with a series of low adobe structures. The main hacienda had an

immense façade with arches and an embellished portal. The first impression was

that of a magnificent dwelling, but with a closer look any guest could see the

place was shabby and ill kept. Tonight it was lit up with gaudy pink and green

lights and there were dark figures hovering around the doorway.

They entered into the great room that revolved around a grand fountain now

decorated with nearly nude women, some frolicking in the water while others

were seated drinking and smoking around the base. Almost a dozen painted

ladies were standing on the steps of a staircase waving and flirting behind fans.

Most were wearing bright colored negligees and Chinese peignoirs with fresh

flowered lies of bright cerise bougainvillea leaves and gardenias in their hair.

Paco was drinking in the visual banquet. He loved how the dark stockings

ended high on the girls legs with garters of roses and streaming ribbons. He

wondered if he could sit on the side and paint them and if he did would the work be any good? He worried constantly whether he would ever be good enough. There was a jazz band and a long bar at one side where the two men sat shooting some version of "bathtub gin" and waiting for a hostess that would usher them into a tiny room with their lady of choice. Abruptly someone had a hold of his leg. Looking down under the bar Paco could see a little finger motioning him to lean down. It was Juan Carlos, from Diehls, Salvador's little brother, who urgently forced his mouth to one ear and whispered, "Paco, you got to come now. The lady, she is dying. You know her. She is the one who is missing."

Paco nudged Victore. Moving quietly behind the boy they walked a long way out to a low building apparently without windows. They slithered inside overwhelmed with smoke and the freakish appearance of the room. They crawled along bed after bed covered in oriental rugs containing the bodies of dazed and sleeping people. There were Chinese attendants that filled the pipes or rearranged the bedding and pillows providing more comfort for the guests. A heavy sickening sweet smoke hung like a pale purple cloud over all. The boy pointed to a carved wooden structure that was enclosed by embroidered and striped curtains. Paco found an opening and looking inside he was stunned to find an ivory skinned woman, lying like sculpted marble, covered only with a paisley shawl. It all came back at once. How he had last seen her sitting shattered in the chaos of the Seville Club. He moved forward to lean over her angelic face, carefully lifting one of her eyelids. There were the glittering golden and green flecks in a circle of soft grey now with a tiny little black dot, like a pinpoint in the center. Paco pulled the shawl aside and put his ear gently on her naked breast. He could hear a distant beat. Lillian was alive!

Next he remembered he was grabbed from behind with a hand over his nose and mouth along with a powerful pinch on his juggler. He was out, his head bashed on the solid tile floor. When he came to consciousness he could see he was laid out next to a dead looking Victore with their two bikes in the back of a flat bed truck passing out the gates of the Palace. He heard somebody say, "so that's your kid, Oakley? What the hell is he doing out here? Christ, he's gonna get killed if they find out about him."

Paco blacked out again and awoke as strong arms supported him into his little porch. He lay down with Ranger's long wet nose searching him over and some warm slippery licking on his face that was distressing now with a huge egg-shaped bruise forming high on the forehead. Madonna was at his side and she

rose to face the man who brought him home. He was so tall, well over six feet

and so handsome that he could have been famous. This man with a powerful

body had little smiling crinkles at the outer corners of each eye. He blinked

ashamedly at Paco's Mother, his wife. Every ounce of him wanted to take her in

his arms and beg for forgiveness. Loving her so much he knew this would never

work. He was a marked man and his loved ones would suffer if ever the truth

came out. All this emotion wrapped in a tender glance and returned by

Madonna with tears gleaming she kissed his huge hand and murmured, "thank

you".

Paco spent a fitful night of pain and oblivion. He arose very early and called

Paget, his fireman friend from the team. He needed advise on how to report

Lillian's location and find help for her as fast as possible. He knew that The

Forbidden Palace was purposefully out of the jurisdiction of Santa Barbara and

lay in a county that was sparsely populated without much if any law

enforcement. What there was would be well paid to stay out of business at the

Palace. Paget promised to call in the report to the fire department and then the

Police would be notified. Next he called El Mirador's Kitchen to check for Victore who answered sounding groggy but alive.

Paco exhaled and sank to the chair with his head in his hands and tenderly searched for the huge lump that was now a source of terrible pain. It was astoundingly big so he moved slowly to the bathroom mirror to see the damages. "Oh God" he whispered as he saw the disfigured effect of his wound. From his hairline to his right eyebrow there was a unbelievable amount of swelling but the most shocking was the black and many shades of brown with purple bruising that extended well down below the eye and darkened around the top of the cheekbone. The white of that eye was blood red and a side of his nose was skinned. He was almost intrigued with the vision but so horrified he walked out to dress and get to work refusing to believe what he saw. He covered his damages with his aviator cap, all the flaps down, and gingerly put on the goggles with the green lenses covering the eyes. He found The Indian safely propped against the house and headed for Diehls. All the way he was tortured, thinking of Lillian's astonishing beauty and the tragic way it was used and spoiled. He blamed himself, knowing how he could have saved her as she sat pitifully drunk in the Seville Club.

Entering through the back to his office he moved swiftly to get the phone that was ringing. He imagined it was Paget reporting that Lillian had been rescued. Not so, it was the cook from the Hoffman's estate, the fabulous Casa Santa Cruz, who was checking on the orders for the Gypsy Camp an affair that happened about once a month. He confirmed item after item and set about gathering the final order. He had already delivered an entire lamb butchered for the spit the day before. Sal came over to help him load everything into the truck. He looked closely into Paco's eyes through the green glasses and drew back. "Are you ok? Here, go sit down. I've got it. What happened brother? Did you crash The Indian?" Paco nodded not knowing what to say. They silently packed and he was off.

He had several other stops that needed to be included. The first was the home of George Washington Smith, Casa Dracaena, a sublime structure that made him famous. Created after a tour of Andalusia with his wife, the Hill Barons and their super wealthy friends saw this wonderful home and the brilliant architect with his great assistant Lutah Riggs were hard at work designing upward of 70 more legendary estates throughout the region and beyond. Both Smith and his wife loved to cook so it was always fun for Paco to hear them talk about the dishes they wanted to make and the rare ingredients they ordered from all over the world.

Next stop was for the Hoffmans at their Casa Santa Cruz, a grand mansion that was situated on land right next to the famous Old Mission Santa Barbara and the Seminary nearby. Bernard Hoffman and his wife brought their young daughter who was gravely afflicted with diabetes to Santa Barbara and the brilliant Dr. Sansum who had become a pioneer in the treatment of insulin. They fell in love with the romance of the region and the Spanish influence that made the city so rare. He, along with many city patrons like Storke, Murphy, Malis, and the inimitable Pearl Chase, are credited with the creation and preservation of Santa Barbara style. The sentient event that spurned this movement was the terrible earthquake that left so much devastation. Many buildings were falling down or so damaged that they had to be torn down and hauled to the bay where they became the habitat for delighted sea life. Hoffman set up shop on the grounds of Casa de la Guerra where he made available distinguished architect's plans free for any homeowner who wished to rebuild. The plans were provided through a competition that Bernard held and attracted all the most talented from the region. In addition the plans were available from famous Spanish cities like Seville, Toledo and areas throughout Andalusia. Hoffman and Malis created the Del Paseo Restaurant with Bernard's famous "Street in Spain".

Casa Santa Cruz was huge and rambling white washed adobe style with turquoise green shutters and terra cotta tile roof. Driving into a large courtyard entrance, there was a big kitchen with staff quarters along the right and the main entrance on the left. A charming winding staircase with cascading flowers and plants to the far left led to Hoffman's home office. Paco pulled up to the kitchen door and found the cook who was something of an albino with milk white skin and matching hair that bristled wildly. She wore white garments with a long white apron. The only other color was from a pair of dark brown tortoise rimmed glasses, very round and very dark. Paco was always curious to know if her eyes were actually pink but he never showed her this interest. Everyone called her "Cookie" but that was a comical name given by a very small child to an exceedingly serious and reserved person. She had to adhere to a strict diet for the Hoffman's little daughter who now was skipping around Paco and badgering him with a crochet mallet.

Given his outrageously painful condition the fun and games were off for today. But the little one would not have it and calling her father she demanded to have Paco come to the Gypsy Camp. "Can he come? Can he come? Please Daddy let Paco come to the Camp! He can dance with me and we can throw rocks in the fire and he will help in the garden and, and" the girl was bouncing off her father's knee and stepping all over his highly polished shoes. She grabbed Paco and pushed him forward where he bowed slightly to Hoffman and then moved back so as not to display his bruises. The doting father agreed and issued a courteous invitation with a certain tone that made Paco commit immediately.

The family was one of Diehls best customers and inside he really did want to see one of these Gypsy Camp affairs in person. Bernard and his wife along with an eclectic group of artists, architects and musicians, mainly the entire eccentric creative community that came from all over the world, appeared together in complete costume for the reenactment of an authentic Gypsy encampment including an elaborate Bohemian painted wagon that often housed a prominent fortune teller imported for the evening.

Bernard found large tree stumps and had them imbedded into the ground in a large circle around a huge fire pit. Almost scandalously romantic these soirees included many of the El Paseo entertainers and restaurant staff. They created a buffet with the barbequed lamb that the cooks from the restaurant stuffed with onions, oranges and bundles of rosemary and thyme. They tossed potatoes into the embers and prepared a huge salad layered with chopped tomatoes, red onions, cucumbers, red & green peppers, many slices of avocado, chunks of cheese and crusty garlic spiked croutons. They mixed this with a robust vinaigrette made tangy by adding a green chili salsa. All this pleasure was promised and now the lucky delivery man intended to experience it all.

Paco also had orders that day for Mrs. Dorinda Bliss. Pretty and affable, she loved to tell the story of her New York roots and how she visited Santa Barbara many times as a young girl and dreamed of a grand "casa" in Montecito that would be a cultural center for the community. The day came when her husband agreed so the charismatic Mrs. Bliss hired architect Carleton Winslow, who had designed buildings for the 1915 Exposition in San Francisco. Casa Dorinda, was an impressive mansion, with its ornate ironwork, sturdy walls and graceful tower rising above the third floor, with more than 80 rooms surrounding a central patio. Diehls supplied the provisions for momentous events entertaining illustrious guests including King Albert and Queen Elizabeth of Belgium, and President Herbert Hoover. World famous violinists Jascha Heifetz and Mischa Elman played from the stage of Mrs. Bliss' Music Room shortly after sold out performances in Carnegie Hall. Many other notables of the music world enchanted the fortunate invited to Dorinda's parties.

This delivery was for an upcoming performance by Jan Paderewski, possibly the most famous and popular pianist of all times. The great artist had a large ranch and winery in Northern California plus a private train car that he retired to when he performed but not when he came to Casa Dorinda. Paderewski stayed as long as he wanted. He thought the air was so perfect and the water so pure it helped his painful rheumatic condition. This trip he planned to spend time at The Montecito Club a private spa in the hills said to be the source of the local Indian's ancient sacred spring. Deliveries to The Club were always a daunting specter for Paco who could only drive the truck to a lower plateau where he was met with tiny donkeys, several with carts, that carried the supplies and guests up a precarious pathway to the large two story stone and wood hotel. His body was throbbing and he could feel his heartbeat in the giant knot on his forehead so the delivery today promised to be beastly.

Paco spent the arduous trip concentrating on the spectacular panoramic ocean and island views overlooking many of the grandest estates that he served. He had a clear view of his home, The Quien Sabe Ranch, and Il Brolino close by. To the Southeast he saw the hills of Cima Del Mundo rising verdant and colored with wild flowers. Below there was El Mirador with it's awesome Italian garden. To the north he found the reflecting pools of Il Fluerides, Val Verde next door and Piranhurst Mountain ascending above. He passed majestic Sycamore and oak trees that lined the Hot Springs Creek and Canyon.

Once at the top the caretaker and the cook joined by members greeted him and helped unload. Paco was a favorite at the Club since he had so many stories to tell. He described the events with glorious menus and dishes that the famous Chefs and cooks created. They always gave him full privileges that included the baths, a tasty lunch and hoped he would stay on for a good long chat.

The Club provided in a rustic relaxed ambiance for its members. The large structure contained a number of suites, each consisting of a bedroom and bathroom with a hot tub. The hot tubs were of various sizes; one tub, measuring about 10 by 12 feet, was furnished with several outlets enabling the occupants to select water from various springs with different water temperature and mineral content. In the main lodge, Paco would first sit in the kitchen, bringing the news from town to the staff. Next he would soak in a tub until the meal was served in a long dining room that had a lounge with a huge walk-in fireplace where everyone gathered and enjoyed mellow conversation. On this day they were shocked to see their dear Paco was injured and they set about making a plan for his cure with the Club's magical waters.

Their owners furnished each of the suites so the interiors varied from opulent in the case of the Louis 14th influenced quarters of Julia Sturdwell down to plain and stark. This day Paco was taken to the Blanding family's room where he was warmed by a cozy fireplace and a big brass bed covered in quilts. Nice white linens were there with a very big shirred beaver throw. All the colors were natural except for the bright patchwork of many patterns.

Nanette Blanding was a spinster woman in her fifties with a severe hairdo and a knot so tight it gave her a vaguely oriental appearance. Adding to that would be her Chinese silk pajamas that did cling to her thin athletic body as she rolled up her sleeves to prepare the bath water for Paco. "OK", she said , "take them off, all off", and he cooperated starting with the goggles and aviator cap that had left welts in his swollen areas. He felt very weak now with pain, exhaustion and had not eaten for many hours. Paco thought he was going to pass out as little spots danced before him. Miss Blanding finished the disrobing with deft hands and escorted him to the tub. She began slowly immersing him in the silky tepid water that smelled of scrambled eggs and toast. The feeling was so comforting on all the senses. So soothing on all the areas that hurt so much. Using a giant sea sponge the lady softly drizzled the healing waters onto the swollen and bruised areas of his face.

Nan knew how to do this very well and took great pleasure in giving this indulgence to others. She knew the stories of the ancient Indian healing methods and for Paco she brought out the white sage wands and lit the tips, blowing out the fire and allowing the smoke to whisper out as she slowly waved them around and over the wounded areas. Strangely, Paco slipped into a kind of trance like state with his entire body becoming weightless. All the soreness and misery appeared to float away and he lay in this delicious limbo for some time.

Miss Blanding slowly allowed the tepid water to flow out and new stronger, hotter natural spring water filled the tub. Then she took out a pair of mitts that had a soft bristly side to scrub the body clean and energize her patient with rosemary oil and floating bags of chamomile tea. There Paco lay submerged in a kind of ecstasy until the water cooled. With gifted hands now the lady began to massage his shoulders and neck moving her fingers gently around to his damaged head and face. The waters were changed again now to a cool crisp clear bath and he was pulled to standing as Miss Blanding rubbed him briskly with a big Turkish towel. She wrapped him in a flannel cover and guided him to the bed where piled with quilts he fell into a deep peaceful sleep. Unnoticed by Paco, Nan tenderly swabbed his bruised and skinned areas with a mystic potion she created from wild plants gathered in the surrounding hills. She lit a rose scented candle on his bed stand and tip toed out to let him repair.

The entire ritual took several hours and Paco arose on his own feeling like a new person. He dressed and went over to the mirror. There before him was the old

Paco complete with a mass of bouncy brown curls. The swelling was almost

gone. The bruising was pale and changed to a soft golden color in some of the

worst places. Even the red of his eye and the scraped nose were barely in

evidence. This was a miracle! He was stunned and grateful. He walked to the

kitchen and found a happy group serving up bowls of lentil soup. Dining

together the chatter was energized and the soup, laced with fresh dill, had big

hunks of potato with chopped carrots and peas. He could detect ginger and

paprika but there was also a hint of curry or some exotic note that Paco did not

recognize. He liked to play a little game with his Mother and anyone else who

would take the hook. It was called, "What's in it?" and the one who came

closest won. Now everyone was playing and as usual the winner was the cook.

Shapely individual fresh baked brioche was passed in a big basket. Newly

churned butter and just made apricot jam came too. Paco filled up with all this

goodness and drank plenty of clove spiced iced tea with orange slices. His

resurrection was nothing short of miraculous!

Everyone moved to the area before the giant fireplace and the talk began about

the American Garden Club visit and then the accident where they wanted to

hear the details first hand. Paco was rapidly reminded of the terrible ache in his heart for the pitiful Lillian and it urged him to think of the time and his

formidable little trip back to Diehls where he could make some calls to see if

there was any news of her rescue.

Paco was midway down the mountain when a small bit of memory from the

terrible night at The Palace came to him. He heard the voice over and over. "If

they find out about him they're gonna kill him"? What does that mean? Was it

about him or Victore? And who brought him home anyway? Then his

flashback expanded. The voice, he remembered, said "Oakley". The voice was

talking to someone named "Oakley". That was his name. That was his Father's

name. Now he could not wait to get home and ask his Mother about this.

Chapter Five: A Woman gains freedom and a Father is revealed

On a cold and rainy day, a rarity in Santa Barbara, Penelope Elise Lavigne, these

days know as Miss Penny, a party planner of renown adored by the Hill Barons

and beyond, was walking along State Street admiring her reflection in the store

windows. As she passed the darker ones she noticed how charming the tilt of

her moss green Robin Hood hat with the rusty brown and black pheasant

feather was against her soft chignon. Her hair was a deep auburn, always worn

pulled back and contrasted well with her careful choice of wardrobe colors.

Today it was a grey-green topcoat over a delicate pink chiffon blouse that barely showed her elaborate lace camisole underneath. Her skirt was kilt-like worn short with tan boots that came to the knee. Hurrying along she sheltered herself with a big black umbrella that was a souvenir from the grand cruise ship, Majestic, where she lived and worked for 3 years before coming to California.

No one knew that Penny left her home, the Loire Valley vineyards, in the middle of the night fleeing from a vicious husband who beat her bloody for the last time on the day he found a diary that exposed her soul. The times were rapidly evolving new ideals of womanhood. A progressive morality was in the process of being negotiated, an era in which women were beginning to expand every potential. All this challenged the conventions and standards around them. A modern Independent behavior caused powerful critics to denounce these women as a threat to society. The "flapper" became the symbol of hedonism and indifference to traditional mores. Even worse, the perception that all this new thinking led to an unrestrained sexuality which conservatives believed to be characteristic of any girl with a bob and short skirt, caused enormous suffering in families everywhere.

As a young girl in France, Penny yearned to experience the world the way characters in books of the day described. She followed through with a marriage that was demanded of her. Purely an alliance between families to enhance an iron grip the vineyard owners had on the region, there was violence between the couple from the start. Penny read "The Sheik" over and over and tried to fanaticize while the physical torture was raging.

The book, essentially the depiction of a strong, self-sufficient woman being tamed and subdued by a man who rapes her repeatedly spoke to Penny's heart and in a strange way bound her to stay just as Diana, the character from the novel finally falls in love with her rapist. All this was written with explicit detail in her Diary. Whether the work was placed near the kitchen table on purpose or by accident, even Penny did not know but it caused a violent explosion in the mind of her unsophisticated husband. He took a bridle from a hook near the door and waited for her to come in from the garden. Striped with burning pain she plotted her escape and after a series of connections devised by the miraculous hand of destiny the young woman succeeded. She vowed to recreate herself in the new style of an independent, self-sufficient female, free to openly and unashamedly enjoy all worldly pleasures just as well as the men.

It was this spirit that motivated Miss Penny to head for M.C. Graveport & Sons, known later as The Book Den. The target of her attention was the celebrated Mr. Oren Jefferson Star who was appearing in person to sign copies of his brand new novel, "Paradise Underbrush", a sequel to his very popular "When the Bough Breaks". There was so much published prattle about him in the gossip columns, the literary reviews and pure word of mouth that a movie virtuoso or a sports champion would need to compete for equal treatment.

Even in the rain there was a line of umbrellas waiting to enter the open doors. Crowding in Penny could see Oren seated at a large library table toward the back of the shop. Surrounding all was a remarkable two story finely crafted series of bookshelves and a severe but decorative mahogany balustrade. Six long pendulum lights finished with excellent deco inspired milk glass globes trimmed in black lit the space and on the tables there were double-armed brass fixtures with dark green glass shades. Several massive skylights timidly dripped rain that was strategically accommodated by buckets on the floor. Books filled every opening and there were circular iron staircases at intervals that allowed for upstairs access. The air was moist and heavily scented by a mélange of Shalimar perfume with a handsome combination of leather, ink and paper even a hint of

tobacco.

Oren Star, it was whispered, was suspected to use the pen name of "Temple

Baily", a well-known authoress thought to propagate the new free spirited

feminine psyche. In these books along with his own, very modern notions of

wedlock where husband and wife are companions is described. He dares to say

that the goal of marriage is their mutual happiness and personal fulfillment. His

female characters think nothing of kissing a young man on the first date. They

are not averse to petting, but petting always stops short of completion. To the

ladies it is the power of this passion withheld that makes for a delicious state of

denial. An unabashed sensual teasing without responsibility appealed to the

women so deeply. Penny loved certain chapters, even specific paragraphs, of

Star's work she had marked to relish over and over again, so when he began to

read from his newest piece her eyes became glassy and her heart beat faster.

"Mesmerized by the moment, Delma lost all restraint. She slowly took off all her

clothing and lay flat on the palm and flower strewn sand sheltered by a giant tree

dripping with jasmine overhead. Her breathless body pulsed against his as they

lay full length hopelessly locked in a desperate embrace. Delma's sharp fingernails penetrated the flesh over his breast. She buried her knees into his hips, and bit his earlobe gently. Bernard's eager panting brushed Delma's face. He was trembling as he muttered the words 'look at me'. Delma raised her eyelids slowly and said, 'Kiss me now'."

The writer's rich baritone voice only served to boost the ladies enjoyment and the line formed with eager fingers holding a receipt that would allow them to have a precious moment while their edition of "Paradise Underbrush" was personally autographed.

Penny ambled around near the end of the line often browsing through the stacks waiting to hopefully be the last one and planning what she might say to Oren. Could she just look into his sweet palest blue eyes and listen to his deep mellow words, soaking him up and filling her heart? Penny knew he would be just like the men in his novels who loved their women with a passionate respect. She loved his husbands who treated their wives as a partner, not as a subordinate. Even self sufficient Miss Penny fully expected and wanted to be a wife and mother, devoted to her own home and family. I want it all, she thought, sadly bound by the dark past that still imprisoned her. She left her jacket and satchel at a table and taking off her hat she removed the hairpins to let her glorious dark red hair fall loosely around her shoulders. Walking over to one of the spiral staircases she climbed up and found a tiny desk along the balustrade that almost overlooked Star as he continued to sign the books and woo the ladies with his words. Watching out of the corner of her eye to monitor the end of the line she plucked a book from the shelf behind and began to read. It was a botanical encyclopedia with fine drawings that occupied her for some time.

Finally the last of the ladies disappeared toward the rear exit and Miss Penny stood to conquer. She moved to the spiral staircase that ended almost at the feet of Oren Starr who, adjusting his glasses preparing to pack up and leave, chanced to look up just in time to see a little flash of pink slip and a ravishing red head descend from above in some alluring knee high boots.

Penny smiled at Star, twirling a little receipt in her fingers then placing it on the table. Moving close to him she slowly removed his glasses and flirtatiously undid his bow tie. Oren's wide light cerulean eyes filled with surprise and enchantment. The willing writer raised both arms and guided her to the bookcase behind. Pinned there she felt his body so close to hers that his heat actually warmed her breasts. "So you liked my book?" Oren whispered. Miss

Penny nodded, moistening her lips as if to speak but simply leaning her head

back against the books. She offered her slightly parted mouth to him and he

began to accept when she abruptly spun out of his grasp, heading for her jacket.

Slipping it on she wrapped up her hair and donned the felt hat checking that the

feather was pointed straight. Then grabbing her satchel and umbrella swiftly

headed out the front door disappearing down State Street with a rapid gait.

Miss Penny's naturally flawless ivory skin was hot with bright red patches on the

cheeks. She was ecstatic as she turned into Diehls to find Salvador at the Soda

Fountain and ordered her favorite, a "Turkey Trot Sundae" with four kinds of

nuts over thick dark chocolate, marshmallow whip and rich vanilla ice cream.

Paco was at his desk in the back of the store sorting through orders but really

occupied with the astounding events that occurred when he arrived home at the

Quien Sabe to talk to his Mother about what had transpired the night before.

At first she was unable to break away at his urging. The Wrights were hosting a

remarkable performance by Paderewski, the world-renowned pianist, and this

was drawing everyone's attention to the grand piano set in the most perfectly designed great room, famous for it's balanced acoustics. Paco could hear the

exquisite strains of his music floating into the kitchen and as he began helping

Madonna prepare trays of hors d'oeuvres he asked, "Who brought me home last

night?" His Mother stopped short, looked at him with wet eyes and said, "It

was your father". "But you said he died?" Paco was anxious now. "What is the

truth? Why did you lie to me? Someone said that if they found out about me

they would kill me? What does that mean?"

The famous Maestro's piano was raging as Madonna held Paco tightly and told

him an incredulous story. She revealed how the Families in Italy carried a blood

feud for many generations. When their families came to Montecito to work for

the Hill Barons they thought they would be free from this madness. But sadly,

the peace came to an end when, shortly after Madonna Fazinatos and Pacomino

Oakley were married, it was discovered that the groom's Mother was a

Basinorios, the warring faction of the family who had vowed vengeance.

In Santa Barbara all that seemed remote to the young couple who had just

announced they were with child. Horrified, Oakley, while walking home one

night, was abducted by several who pledged his death and brought him to San

Francisco to stand at his enemies contrived mock trial that would have concluded with a death sentence but for one absurdity that established a strange limbo.

The old Don, Signore Telchide Fazinatos, officiating at this rigged performance, recognized the young man and knew his family well, so well in fact, unbeknown to most, he had shared many intimate moments with Oakley's Mother, Innocenza, and some whispered he even ordered his father's untimely death. She had married a handsome local man, a fisherman by trade whom, to her deep displeasure, spent days at sea. Paco's grandparent's union was made against the Italian family's wishes, so when Mathew Oakley was mysteriously found dead, floating in the bay, it was assumed that some hand of historic hatred was at work. Innocenza was widowed and months later, a time that no one seemed to carefully count, she gave birth to a son that she named Pacomino after a an illustrious ancestor who had been a military hero. Not knowing it at the time, since she was secretly just seeking some monetary support, she saved her beautiful son's life while denying her grandson a father. Innocenza, in utmost secrecy, told Don Fazinatos that this boy was really his own.

So now, sitting in the kitchen with his Mother, Paco learned the real reason that

his Father never returned home. Now he knew why Oakley was separated

forever with his beautiful Madonna and never saw his wonderful son, who was

given his name, save for a few fleeting moments. Madonna tenderly described

how he did come one last time to explain the terrible turn that fate had taken.

For their salvation, Pacomino Oakley swore on the bodies of his wife and little

son to disown them. A captive of this foul legacy he was established as a Captain

in the "Aroncioni" a kind of Western syndicate, commanded by the old Don,

Signore Fazinatos, which had grown rich and extended especially with the help

of Prohibition.

The rapturous melody from Paderewski's spectacular "Fantaisie Polonaise" now

floated into the kitchen where Mother and Son sat arm in arm, frozen with

bewilderment. Then Madonna, so gravely heartbroken, began rocking Paco who

she knew was deeply wounded inside.

Chapter Six: The Gypsy Camp

Paco packed the truck like a robot still dazed by the truth of his Father's life and the enormous complexity it brought to him. He needed time for this to penetrate. He had two more deliveries and then he fully intended to accept the Hoffman's little daughter's invitation to the notorious Gypsy Camp soiree. With mind buzzing, he drove through the elaborate iron gates to Miraflores, meaning "look at the flowers", an elegant mansion designed by premiere architect Reginal Johnson who was just completing the fabulous Biltmore Hotel.

The estate was created from the remains of the Montecito Country Club that was, early in the decade, destroyed by a scandalous fire and murder that was never solved. A superlative example of Spanish domestic architecture it featured a regal carved stone entrance centered at the end of a dramatic straight-line approach that Paco was now passing continuing around to the rear. He loved the gardens, especially the roses. From the rear terrace he could see the sunken pool and formal cultivated elements. The terraced beds were skillfully arranged to display colorful patterns with carefully selected flowers of many descriptions.

The two story house enclosed three sides of a large rear terrace flanked by a romantic loggia, a space that Paco and Salvador knew well since they served often as bartenders for the many parties that John Percival Jefferson and his wife Mary held there. A large beautifully wood paneled living room also hosted the renowned musicians of the moment. The Butler ceremoniously stooped to unlock a trap door that revealed steps down to the splendid wine cellar that originally served the Country Club.

Paco was directed to put the beverages on the shelves below. He inhaled deeply a perfume of famous vintage wines peacefully aging and the rich heady aroma of the fine cigars stored in handsome wooden silver trimmed humidors. Lifting heavy crates he was red-faced remembering a salacious moment stolen away with a cigarette girl, the two forced to remain hidden for more than an hour as the guests above endured an endless recital by an unknown coloratura soprano and a tenor with such a sharp piercing voice it burned their ears even below ground. Up and off now to one final stop.

The grand 70-acre Arcady was one of Montecito's most magnificent estates. It was distinctive including the tower that created a regal image and included a number of buildings throughout extensive grounds with gentle hills giving the overall appearance of a small village. It was the residence of Mr George O. Knapp. Above all it commanded an inspiring eminence with a spacious view.

Behind the estate, customarily viewed from a spectacular vantage point complete with columns and sculpture, soar sudden mountains angling down to the coast, their slopes etched in vertical patterns by a thousand watercourses and outcroppings.

Below and in front of the mansion lies the graceful curve of the shoreline, and the waters of the Pacific that on clear days appear as blue as lapis lázuli. In the distance, Santa Rosa Island stretches its great length like a sleeping giant. All this magnificence soothed the soul of the artist-delivery man who always took the time to drink in the beauty and notice the myriad of wild birds and small animals that scurried across his path as he drove up to the kitchens.

He had three drop off locations on the property. First, the main house, originally built by the fabled Ralph Radcliffe-Whitehead & Jane Byrd McCall Whitehead, a couple who contributed greatly to the Arts and Crafts movement that started in England by William Morris. Here, in Montecito the architectural style of the mansion resembled a Mediterranean villa, designed by an architect named Samuel Ilsley. When Jane's husband died her dream of creating a center for as she put it, "a simpler, a truer, a more vital art expression", that involved living and studio spaces for painters, poets, composers, sculptors and potters, ended and the great estate was sold to the Knapps.

The second delivery point was a large series of buildings that provided for the staff, the stables and a large outdoor kitchen for California style Barbeques. But the best of the three, in Paco's mind, was the delivery to Joannah Hartfield Prang, a masterful ceramicist who lived in the charming hillside guesthouse that perfectly reflected the concept of "The Simple Home", a wooden Craftsman's dream.

The house was her studio-salon, a place to create and exhibit her work as well as a home to receive guests and that is how she treated the Diehls delivery man who she knew, in her psychic way, would be a great artist. He sat by her in the tall main room with a balcony from which hung oriental rugs and Indian saris. The walls, too, were adorned with textiles, rugs and tapestries. Her robust well-formed pottery was casually arrayed on chairs and more formally on a massive round oak table in the center of the space.

Several large armoires with handsome Craftsman style carving provided storage and could be opened for her exhibits to show off many more pieces. The two sat together in straight back seventeenth century chairs. Exotic details like the oriental brass lamps and a giant brazier emitting sandalwood incense intrigued Paco. Moody muted shades of turquoise and rust with indigo blue and deep ochre created a dark impression. The sun made dazzling elongated patterns on oriental rugs and before the stone fireplace that always seemed to be glowing there was a fleecy brown bearskin.

Joannah in her enchanted guesthouse was the last remnant of Whitehead's fantasy and she was allowed to stay rent-free as a part of the Knapp purchase agreement. So the aging artist and the young man discussed all manner of things, sipping chai tea with vanilla cream and munching on chocolate macaroons. They loved to pull out books of art or architecture almost always referencing work from the Arts & Crafts Movement. One such volume was a catalog of the textiles and wallpapers of Morris and his studio mates. This was mesmerizing for Paco who memorized the color palettes to use in his own paintings.

On this day Joannah had a client and so the delivery was brief, as she demanded a kiss before leaving. Paco was on the road back to Diehls now for a swift clean up, a shave and smooth application of a little Murray's Pomade to keep the curls under control. He changed into his soft sweater with his dark brown leather jacket. Hopping onto The Indian he was off to the dream-like Casa Santa Cruz and the excitement of The Gypsy Camp.

Cruising the driveway to the mansion he passed the site of the camp that was crawling with early preparations, the scent of lamb & rosemary roasting in the air. Deciding to check in at the main house he parked the Indian behind a hedge and knocked on the front door. Time passed and just before he planned to walk down to the camp the door opened to see a very merry little face with a big broad grin that exposed two missing front teeth. She had the purest skin and eyes and even though a bit thin, maybe fragile, he could see there was a hearty spirit alive and well. She flew forward hugging him and grabbing his hand pulled him inside.

Paco had never been inside before. Intrigued he caught sight of a hand painted coffered ceiling in the entry with gold embellishments and painted bouquets of flowers in each square. The Butler's station and office was off of the most

impressive dark red tile floor, laid in a herringbone pattern that was glassy with

polish. He peeked up a flight of stairs to see a portion of a brilliant stained glass

window. Stopping at a large door, the girl opened it to show him a fully stocked

bar, walls painted like a circus tent with clowns, horses and balloons. "Do you

want a soda? I can make you one. I'm not allowed to have any Coca Cola but I

can make one for you?"

This little one was so adorable with very bright brown eyes, maybe five tiny

freckles on her nose and her braids in loops, tied up high on the head with many

colors of very thin ribbons matching the trim on her peasant blouse and very full

short ruffled skirt. She wore white stockings to the knee and patent leather

Mary Janes that clattered from the taps on the toes. Paco shook his head and

she led him on skipping and bouncing all the way to an enormous living room,

wood paneled in antiqued ash that included many shelves for books and

collectibles. There was a bank of French doors that opened out to a sizable brick

veranda. He could see large terra cotta pots filled with blooming hydrangeas or

lavender, some glazed with a pale turquoise. "I can read you a story", she said,

shuffling through a stack of books on her child size desk. "Or, I know, let's go!"

She grabbed his hand again and pulled him to the adjoining room that was jaw dropping in size and style. They entered a huge space, again flanked by French doors out to a veranda, but the spectacular feature here was the lustrous parquet floor that provided a perfect ballroom. The little Hoffman ran to the phonograph at the end of the room and with a few noisy false starts put the needle in place and ran to Paco's side for the music to begin. Puzzled he waited seconds with her until a big orchestra played the hit song from "No, No, Nanette", a tap dancer's dream. Automatically she danced her way along, her braids bouncing, ruffles flouncing and tap shoes flashing. Paco pretended to partner up but he really was just playing the game watching her move. She was really very, very good!

He twirled her and stood aside with arms motioning to her for a solo. Now he was stunned, his huge eyes wide with amazement. Her dancing shifted to a new level of dazzling artistry; so much expressive style and tapping that matched the music perfectly. Breathing heavily and now with burning red cheeks the child stood and in turn motioned for his solo.

Feeling silly but committed he did his best. Just at that moment the Hoffmans

walked in and a concerned Mother escorted the little star out as she complained

loudly, begging to stay. Bernard, a true gentleman, in soft tones explained the

critical nature of his daughter's diabetic condition that did not allow for over

excitement. He and Paco walked together out onto the veranda and through

the wild verdant natural gardens passing a splendid Spanish star fountain on the

way down to the Camp.

Around the blazing fire there was a row of massive tree stumps that

accommodated any who wanted warmth and a very wide pounded earth

pathway where the dancers and strolling musicians performed. Surrounding

this was a series of rustic log benches dotted with Spanish shawls and garlands of

various greens. Behind the benches ran a chain of lighted torches and a lawn.

At one end stood the elaborate Gypsy wagon painted with fantastic imagery that

was now a bit faded. Flowers and cupids playing inside a giant golden horseshoe,

magical writing around deep red roses entwined a fortuneteller's hand of fate,

and fancy scrolls in lattice designs with playing cards covered the entire outside.

There were carved embellishments as well as a polychrome spool rail gallery that trimmed the roof. A curved wooden ladder led to a cottage style front door with the top section open. All this was perched high on four enormous spoke wheels so with the shuttered windows, tonight open, it was difficult to actually see inside, but the candle light flickered granting a shadowy peek at drapes of rich red velvet and golden brocade.

Scattered on the other side of the lawn were hand hewn picnic tables. One was jumbo size and served as the buffet, now laden with giant platters of carved lamb, crocks of salsa and big bowls of El Paseo salad, soon to be accompanied by stacks of freshly made steamed tortillas. There was a long bar, tonight attended by Salvador and his little brothers, Juan Carlos and Rodriego, who continually served rows of drinks, the alcohol supposedly provided secretly by the guests. All the dancers and musicians were slowly filtering into this dramatic arena. A certain tension arose; a mysterious wave appeared to bewitch the entire campsite promising a night of revelry and seduction.

Women were wearing strong colors, almost electric. Often the necklines started high with sleeves reaching the elbow then finished in a single ruffle. Some blouses plunged open with a generous décolletage supported by straps, combined with delicate lace and short jackets. Most of the dresses had rows of ruffles and were topped by little fringed shawls. Polka dots were everywhere in all sizes, and closely arranged to show off the feminine form with sensuality and daring.

The magnificent Esperanza passed by in a tightly fitted black skirt dramatically flared at the bottom with a separate bodice ruffled in bright yellow linen and eyelet overlays that properly glorified her impressive bosom. She was arm in arm towering over her man of the evening, famous baritone Fortuno Bona Nova who was meticulous as a classical Flamenco dancer with high-wasted black trousers and starched white shirt under a short waistcoat and a red cummerbund. A soft black fedora made him complete.

Mama Genet and Fayola floated across the lawn in striking Gypsy costumes jingling from layers of jewelry dripping with gold coins. Their heads were tightly covered with scarves and they wore ornate dangling earrings. Heading for the wagon, aided by several bystanders to maneuver the little wooden ladder, they disappeared inside. Now many distinguished and familiar faces began to grace the assembly. Mr & Mrs John Wright, Paco's own Hill Barons of the Quien

Sabe Ranch and Mrs Ellen Bothin of Piranhurst, who everyone called Nellie, arrived together thematically attired.

A congregation of artists began to rendezvous on one specific table including some who were prominent but most known to be fearsome partygoers with flasks already flashing around. There were plein air painters Charlie Borasco and Shadow Woosley, a well known double threat, esteemed printmakers Brian Felco and wife Selma, oil painter Clad McCaskey, the much collected Mathew Farmington and in the center Joannah Hartfield Prang, striking in a dark green velvet ensemble with a tall comb that bore her exquisite black lace mantilla.

The musicians began the traditional gypsy dance music of Spain, in whose undulating vocals, supple arm movements, and stamping footwork displayed powerful Moorish and Arabic influences. Sometimes they danced to the accompaniment of singing and clapping only but this troupe came with many guitars and castanets, several fiddlers and an old man with a concertina. Tambourines with streamers were passed around so any could join in. Everyone at the Gypsy Camp anticipated individual performances distinguished by a passionate inventiveness. They played with the rhythms, each dance bearing it's own striking intensity of expression.

On the pathway around the fire in a regal procession, slowly striding for ultimate dramatic effect came the stars of the El Paseo Revue, the brilliant Maestro Jose Fernandez and his gorgeous partner Carola Alvena, Nina Sandoval a gifted mime, comedy dancers Carmela and Gabriel Cansino, sensual siblings Lupe and Rudy Valesco, Camille De Montez with a voice of gold and the fiery dancer from the Gypsies of Granada, Carmen Samaniego. This signaled the beginning of a potentially premiere event.

The evening was getting seriously exciting as Paco wandered through the crowd smiling and stopping to chat with many that he knew both from work and growing up attending school. He sat and ate with Diehls owners, his bosses, Tahj & Paula Duchamp. Dancing briefly with the great Diva Gana Walska, who had summoned him with a little wag of her finger, he traded partners with Edwin Ballingford, owner of Il Brolino. Taking the very wealthy man's magnificent young wife into his arms that began to quiver with nervousness, they danced the tango arousing a startling heat. Leaving her with a bow and a kiss of the hand as the music ended, he climbed into the sumptuous Gypsy Wagon where Mama Genet and Fayola, hilarity reigning, read his future in a polished crystal ball.

Moving next to the far side of the festivity, Paco spent a long while talking to Oren Star at Lora Knight's table, with the group from Cima Del Mundo including Corliss, his old friend from High School, who was locked in intense conversation with the dapper looking Rennie. Seeing them brought back the horrendous image of the bodies twisted and crushed in the Hispano Suissa. It was amazing they were still alive. His face was flushed as he thought of Lillian and a little lump formed in his throat.

Miss Penny sauntered over and Oren, still using a cane since his miracle survival in the crash, quickly stood in greeting taking her hand with twinkling eyes. Paco moved on noticing William and Dorinda Bliss cheerfully socializing with the Hoffmans and an impressive group of architects including the imposing George Washington Smith and wife were talking to Mary Craig, now gaining prominence since the death of her famous partner and husband. Carlton Winslow was trading opinionated references to the current construction and difficulties for The Biltmore Hotel with Bertram Goodhue who was scowling bitterly.

Paco connected with Chef Victore, his prowling buddy, and the two talked a little, catching up on Forbidden Palace matters, and then found a bench where they lounged back sipping some potent daiquiris Sal had slipped to them under the bar.

The show was underway and weaving it's magic spell over the Camp. At a bench not far away they could see a remarkable collection of guests surrounding a handsome young man, tonight commanding with his perfect mustache, dressed in black and straight brimmed equestrian hat. Paco recognized him from deliveries to Val Verde, his prime property now, with the help of Bertram Goodhue, under intense renovation. The man was the notorious Wright Ludington, heir to several fortunes. Gathered around him was a dazzling array of beautiful people. Paco recognized Ludington's lady, Countess Louise, and his close associate Lockwood de Forest Jr. There was a bevy of platinum blond starlets with Merna Kennedy from Chaplin's new movie, "The Circus", drawing international attention. He also spied a little huddle of Chefs that he knew all too well, namely Piranhurst's Fredo, Il Brolino's Velly, Val Verde's Printise Yonkopolis and surprisingly the Chauffeur from Cima del Mundo, Gunnar, looking extremely fit for falling fifty feet ending smashed under the massive automobile. Printise ambled over to Paco and Victore with a boozy gait and lit up a hand rolled cigarette inviting them to join in. Opening his case that appeared to be gold-plated with little rubies creating a monogram, he began deriding the other Chefs with grand fay gestures, especially concentrating on Fredo who picked up on the comments and loped over looking bizarre in a huge red cape with black mask and brimmed hat, a get-up that could be mistaken for a giant sized Zorro. An outright fight ensued until Wright Ludington himself stepped in to move them on and suddenly sat down next to Paco saying all in one long whiskey scented breath, "Who are you, what is your name, where have you been and where are you going?" Paco, playing the game replied, "I am Paco Oakley, I have been delivering your groceries and I am going to study art in Florence Italy", folding his arms over his chest for emphasis. Ludington sat bolt upright, reaching into his vest pocket he pulled out a calling card and said, "Make an appointment so we can talk". And with that he was gone, the last of his eccentric retinue following behind.

Turning the card over in his fingers he read the name and numbers. Thinking it smelled of providence, he safely stored it in his inside jacket pocket. Looking up now Corliss, her ruffled dress of many small white polka dots and lacy trim, dashed past him. He could clearly see she was sobbing, tears flowing and shawl dragging through the garden, seeming to be headed nowhere? Still amazed that she appeared to be unhurt in the crash, he arose automatically, this time pledging to himself, he would faithfully protect her.

Catching up he cradled her in his arms, flipping the shawl over his shoulder. He guided her toward the house and when they came upon the star fountain, bubbling away, he arranged the weeping girl on a long tiled stone seat. Sitting beside her she began to pour out all that had just happened. "Paco, you know that Rennie is a Count? Did you know his real name is Viscount Renford Combs Fitzroy? From Oxford, that's England? His parents have come for him and he leaves on Tuesday." She grabbed his collar and gently shook it. Then raping on his chest with her fists she cried helplessly, "But I love him. I will love him forever". A sort of passionate little tantrum, enhanced by a few daiquiris, followed. He dried her tears with the Spanish Shawl and tenderly petted her lovely red-gold curls then lifted her chin up to look closely into her eyes. "You are so beautiful", he said with such intelligence it made her stop and focus. "You will have such a fine life even right here at home." Raising her to her feet he said, "come now I'll take you home". Finding the Indian behind a hedge near the mansion's entrance, Paco tied Corliss to him with the shawl, taking off, a big fringe trimmed knot secured tightly over his stomach. After a short ride, she was home and he helped her to the door. "We must always be friends and never forget Lillian", he said earnestly kissing her forehead as her eyes welled up again. "Where could she be?" Corliss wept, "She must be dead by now. So sad, so horribly sad", she exhaled deeply feeling hopeless. "She lives, I think," Paco whispered, as he opened the door and pushed her gingerly inside. He left quickly turning around only once to see her bewildered expression as she gave him a little kiss in the air and closed the door.

Planning to make some phone calls from Diehls he safely parked the Indian in it's shed and unlocked the back door walking directly into his office. The store was empty and dark all except the small lamps glowing on the back bar of Salvador's big soda fountain. It was almost ten when he called Paget at the fire station. They talked about Lillian and reviewed the many puzzling leads that now seem to have evaporated, lost like the beautiful woman herself and so painful to contemplate. Moving to the end of his desk, he began working on a

pastel drawing of five gracefully composed fuzzy peaches, some with a pale

crimson blush. He paused and picking up the phone made a call speaking slowly

in a low voice.

Some time passed and the distinctive hum of her car stopping at the back door

aroused Paco. Standing to meet her while removing his sweater he swiftly pulled

her into him with eagerness, needing so much to delve into the pleasure she

opened to him. He was compelled now; wanting so intensely to feel some

satisfaction and hide from all the worldly pain that was closing in. Unbuttoning

her silky white blouse and smiling wickedly she danced, twirling straight past

him, heading for the giant marble soda fountain. Paco, laughing out loud,

picked up two of the perfect peaches and followed her closely behind. They

were now naked to the waist only wearing shades of tan belted jodhpurs and

knee high boots, showing their beautifully formed bodies to one another with

deep pleasure. He began to peel and slice the peaches as she searched out the

ingredients needed to turn this outrageously sexy game into extreme bliss. He

fed her a slice of sweet ripe peach and then ate one himself. They kissed deeply

as he lifted her to the top of the counter and laying her out like a banquet he found Salvador's rich vanilla ice cream. Placing a giant scoop into a silver sundae dish he unbuckled her belt and pulled the zipper down far enough to see her rounded form. There he started to dot her body with little spoonfuls of ice cream in a line that ended on the lips. Giving her the last bite he slowly licked up each dollop finishing at the zipper's end. Moving to her breasts he gently circled each one in painterly swirls of smooth creamy caramel syrup using his finger as a brush then, thoroughly enjoying himself, he delicately sucked the sticky sauce away, twirling her nipples with his tongue.

She sat up and urged him to join her on the fountain top. As he lay down she slipped her leg over him and then settled, positioning herself right over him. Now it was his turn. She undid the buckle and unzipped a little way down so that she could see the lovely trail of dark curly hair disappearing below. She found Sal's chocolate sauce, spiked with Italian Caffè Al Bicerin, some essence of roses and began writing "PACO" with little hearts on his well-muscled body in a narrow ribbon of syrup that she skillfully dripped from a spoon. Leaning over for a large ice-cold canister of whipping cream she made fluffy daubs that looked like pom-poms starting low and ending at the hollow in his top breastbone. Then feeding him a giant helping she took one for herself, kissing him ferociously, pressing all the cream between them. Heated now they proceeded

taking turns licking up every bit, playfully teasing with little nips and tiny bites

in tender places. Pulling off each other's boots they were sitting on the counter

with legs entwined facing each other. She found the cherries and tempting him

she rolled the glossy dripping berry over his lips then traced little circles on his

chest with her breasts. Now Paco was fully intoxicated by this erotic woman.

He was so grateful. Now thoughts of his father and the beautiful Lillian were

safely stored a million miles away on another planet.

Chapter Seven: The Gambling Ship

Tonight, lolling three miles off the coast of Santa Barbara, was the fabulous

gambling ship Portafortuna. The impressive vessel was originally a British war

ship and after World War I it was retired, auctioned off, then acquired by the

White star line and refitted as a first class cruise ship. The finely appointed

ocean liner was brought to the Pacific where after some years operating at a loss

it was considered to small to compete with the new major super liners.

Oakley's syndicate, Aroncioni, well-known link to a branch of the Cosa Nostra in Italy, purchased the large ship and it was converted into a luxury casino at a cost of $300,000. Her interior was modernized and her boilers were converted to burn oil rather than coal. Oil was more expensive than coal, but it reduced the refueling time from days to hours, and allowed the engine room personnel to be reduced from 350 to 60 people. Named for an Italian monastery on a small Sicilian island, it could accommodate over 2,000 gamblers and was said to generate thousands, a small portion of which was donated to the grateful Church and Convent of the Nuns Collegine, the Sacred Family of Marfata. Over 200 feet long, it carried a crew of 150, including housekeeping staff, waiters and waitresses, gourmet chefs, a full orchestra, with a squad of gunmen. When it arrived near Santa Barbara another layer of service people and performers came aboard on weekends and for special events. It's first class dining room served French Cuisine exclusively. Most important during Prohibition was the extensive fully stocked bar and wine collection. Games available included roulette, blackjack, poker and craps. It had 200 slot machines on board, and a bingo parlor that seated 300 players. The ballroom, a mirror image of the famed Monte Carlo Casino's Bal de Rouge & Noir, commanded a large oval space in the center of the top deck. Doubling as a theatre its brilliance was breathtaking with a black and gold color scheme and jardinières of flawless artificial long stemmed red roses. A classical paneling of white Ionic half columns, interspersed with sections in white cloudlike drapery, surrounded a black and white checkerboard dance floor. Splendid saucer like Deco light fixtures with chrome details and giant globes etched in the style of Lalique highlighted the staff. Men dressed in tuxedos each with a red rose boutonniere, ladies were in fetching brief French maid costumes. Well-appointed staterooms were available for overnight guests and some said ladies of the Forbidden Palace offered their services upon request.

The Captain of this hedonistic enterprise, always dressed in white formal dinner jacket with a handsome assortment of medals, origin unknown, was the very very good-looking Oakley, Paco's father, transformed now from his pastoral boyhood image to one of the sharpest, most powerful casino Lords alive. Even at this he bore a strange nobility. Years of secretly suffering the loss of his one great love and the joy of seeing his little son grow to manhood had tempered him, giving him a compassionate heart. So at the same time he ruled his unlawful domain with an iron hand, he never failed to right the wrongs that had merit. That is why, a night some weeks past, he was on a mission to rescue the kidnapped white woman from the Forbidden Palace's opium den. There he also came face to face with a severely wounded Paco who he immediately recognized, from the photographs he had secretly ordered, and experienced the agony of taking him bleeding to his Mother. Seeing her again shattered his soul and only served to ignite his deep yearning.

Now the wealthy of the region were slowly taking water taxis back to the shore after a night of gambling, shows, and restaurants. Captain Oakley was seated behind his large carved walnut desk mounded with ledgers and papers that occupied the main part of his cabin. There was a small bunk inset into one wall with drawn velvet drapes. Other small doors and cabinetry completed the fine paneling and there was a distinctive black and gold carpeting that bore the image of a bee in the latticed rope design. A sideboard held crystal decanters with bottles of premier liquors and wine. He held his head in his hands hovering over the remnants of his very late night dinner. So much flooding his mind. Earlier that evening the Fong twins, Little Pete's descendants, made a sinister visit inferring they knew he had something that belonged to them. A rap on the door brought him to respond. His right hand man, Carmino, brought the news that a brawl of monumental proportions had broken out in the ballroom and it sounded like members of the Ludington retinue were largely at fault.

Oakley knew Wright Ludington fairly well since he was a blue ribbon patron, always spending freely. They also shared an ardent interest in the collection of art competing often at important auctions. So it was that the Captain and crew disengaged the scuffling mass of guests, pulling Chef Printise Yonkopolus aside for serious detainment and guiding everyone out to the deck.

Seated at a distance with a quiet aristocratic demeanor was Wright, watching the entire episode with amusement. The Captain joined him and once seated, he pulled out two Havanas, offering him one then asking about a Corot painting, suspected to have been recently acquired by Ludington. He talked about a recent trip to Paris and finding the Rousseaus exciting.

Oakley's interest in fine art was legitimate, not only because he carried the Italian gene that seemed to guarantee an affinity for the arts but also he honestly developed an eye for master works during the years that he quietly served the old Don who had saved his life thinking he was his son. Paco's grandfather a fact that was always hidden. This powerful man, the head of a gigantic syndicate, carefully guided the Captain's career, commanding him to represent his interests

in many areas, the most important being a spectacular art collection maintained

in his San Francisco mansion.

Oakley and Ludington talked about upcoming auctions and how the market for

Greek and Roman Sculpture was wide open since the death of Stavros

Archimedes who's entire collection was up for purchase. They reminisced about

the time they both lost out on a Hyacinthe Rigaud painting of Cardinal Henri

Oswald. Surprisingly, at one moment Wright leaned into Oakley and said,

"What do you know of the young woman who disappeared? Lillian Hoover, I

believe it was? Some say she was out at the Forbidden Palace recently, a place

you may know something about?" Ludington was gently grilling the Captain

whose eyes looked away. They sat, a little frosty, for seconds and as Oakley stood

to leave, Wright confided quietly, "I would be pleased to take her off your hands,

that is if you actually have her."

The next morning, primly alighting on deck was the very chic Penny Lavigne,

her French accent flowing. She had come to meet with the Captain and discuss

the spectacular weekend event that would coincide nicely with the long awaited opening of the Biltmore Hotel. Oakley knew this would attract a congregation of high rollers and he intended to get his share of the action so with the help of Miss Penny, "Naughty Nights in Paris", now in preliminary stages, promised an all French festival complete with a twelve foot Eiffel Tower in the ballroom and vivacious French maids handing out complimentary champagne.

Penny had persuaded Oakley's engagement of Il Brolino's marvelous Chef Velly, whose facility with haute cuisine was legendary, to create the menus and instruct the excellent kitchen staff on the Portafortuna. She was ushered into the Captain's cabin and decorously arranged herself so as to show a fair amount of her silky white stockings that clung to a pair of sassy long legs. She had a little crush on Oakley but try as she may nothing stirred his interest, a fact that honestly puzzled the precocious party planner. His handsome face just seriously analyzed her schedules with menus and the price tag for each item. This took a very long time and Penny excused herself to the ladies room several times while Oakley studied everything intently. During her last trip in the corridor, on the way back, she passed a partially open door as Carmeno carried out a tray. She had a fleeting glimpse of a fair woman just sitting very still, trance-like, in a chair next to a vase of red roses.

On this same day, back at Diehls, Paco was also in a meeting. The Executive

Chef of the Biltmore, Phillbert Omeyer, headed a table with Tahj & Paula, the

market's owners, Quincy MacClenny, produce manager, and Mac Massini the

butcher. Salvador joined in as Paco was seated. The plan was to coordinate the

ordering and delivery of many specialty products that the Hotel's monumental

grand opening demanded. Jolly and roly-poly, Chef Bertie, as he was commonly

called, was giddy now with excitement over the astonishing event to come. He

had been Chef to the late King Leopold of Belgians, spending years in Hungary

and France so his accent was somewhere between St. Petersburg and Budapest,

very thick when animated. Paco picked up what he could of a long list of stars

who were supposed to appear including names like Miss Norma Shearer, Mary

Pickford and Douglas Fairbanks, Ronald Colman, Lupe Velez and Ramon

Navarro, Janet Gaynor and Ruby Keeler along with Jean Arthur, Buddy Rogers,

and surely Charlie Chaplin, even Cecil B. De Mille. Deeply interested now,

Paula asked if Rudolph Valentino would be coming whereupon Chef Bertie

grinned and nodded vigorously with big fat rosy cheeks jiggling. He further

described the decor that would enhance the lavish Spanish Colonial Revival

architecture and gardens designed by architect Reginal Johnson and landscape architect Ralph Stevens, reported to cost $1,500,000. Paco thought the man

said, "There will be giant bouquets of bird of Paradise and tropical pink ginger

with a dozen live parrots placed throughout on pedestals". Did he mean the

birds were live or some other kind of flower? Everyone was confused as the old

Chef, gazing up to the heavens with rapture, continued. "And now we must plan

for the food. We will have four dinning rooms, each with it's own theme,

orchestra and menu all this during three days of separate events and we must

expect to serve between two and three thousand guests," panting now,

anticipating the tremendous challenge ahead, Bertie began to weep taking out a

giant handkerchief. Wiping his eyes for sympathy he passed out page after page

of ingredients needed to produce the many menus he designed, luckily written

in excellent English so the little team set about assigning the duties and soothing

the old man with confidence and encouragement.

Later that day it was Miss Penny and Chef Velly who hurried into the market

and asking for Paco they set about making an enormous order for the

Portafortuna's Parisian extravaganza. The party planner's understanding was

that they would actually deliver everything in a water taxi. This prospect excited

Paco and Sal who were over eager to get a look at the notorious operation.

The team at Diehls worked for days to receive and repackage then deliver all the goods to The Biltmore and it was also time to convey the huge order to the ship. The two men packed the truck and arrived at the Biltmore kitchen receiving dock, unloading and taking the paper work inside to see Chef Bertie, his blousy toque falling straight back almost to his shoulders. Combining with the little curls peeking out of the headband it appeared he had a voluminous head of white hair. His big weepy eyes were bloodshot today and intense behind small round gold-rimmed glasses. He was pouring over a multitude of documents on his long counter of a desk that was meticulously organized. Bertie was intently curious to know if some of his most esoteric ingredients had arrived. "You received from mon ami Albéric Guironnet? Chocolaterie du Vivarais in Tain l'Hermitage? And the Pernigotti chocolate- hazelnut Gianduiotto? My Felchlin Cru Sauvage Couverture con lemon et jus pamplemousse?" Then nodding yes, he was now assured that his chocolate sauce would have ultimate complexity, unlike any other, as it poured over fresh peaches with a hazelnut ice cream and combined with his silky cake batters to bake lovely turbans with buttery velvet centers. "I see you have the Hungarian herbs; the vanilla, poppy seeds, cinnamon, coriander, rosemary, anise and the marvelous Floracopeia's

Juniper Oil!" Gleeful, now really childlike, he was fondling the precious items he knew would make his dishes delicious above all others. Whispering, he mouthed a "Thank you mon cher" when he came to an unmarked crate with the bottles of Meyer's Dark Rum, Mumms Extra Dry Champagne, Courvoisier Napoleon Cognac and the treasured Chartreuse made only by the Carthusian Monks in Voiron, all carefully nestled in excelsior. An exotic bundle of pine nuts from Greece and all the way from the old Chef's favorite Souk in Istanbul, numerous extra large bags of pistachios, chestnuts, almonds, hazelnuts and walnuts with a lengthy personal note of greeting enclosed. Now he was satisfied that his Tomato Bisque would be extra savory with an extraordinary blend of rich paprika. The Crabmeat Mousse and sauces for the pastry purses would have an uncommon blend of fresh herbs and spices only this worldwide culinary shopping spree could provide. Paco knew that was why Master Phillbert Omeyer was great. He seriously admired how well the eminent Chef understood what each dish needed and, even more interesting, how he knew exactly where to get the elements to ensure a sublime product. Many other cases and bags of ingredients passed by the connoisseur's watchful eye, each checked in for quality and freshness. Finally with only a few items missing that they promised to find, the delivery was done.

It was very late in the day when Paco and Sal together packed the truck again this time with most of the Portafortuna order and headed for the wharf. They arranged for a water taxi and paced around until one large skiff docked and they loaded everything. Then, connected with the large ship in a special loading area, the two began battling the motion of the waters surge to bring everything aboard. Inside, greeting them excitedly, eyes spinning wildly, came Chef Velly who was aggressively creating his Parisian fantasy buffet. Paco always had a great fondness for Velly who never failed to offer him tea or sweets when he delivered to the great French Chef's kitchen at Il Brolino. The bouquet of his savory stocks and rich demi-glace, always infused with remarkable French vintage wines, would be considered the best of the best. Now Velly motioned to them to follow with the large cartons of Chanson de L'amour Bonbon, tins of Petite Biscuit de Reims , real crystallized violet flowers, a magnificent array of truffles, candied fruits from Poppies of Nemours, Moroccan stuffed dates, Foucher's chocolate covered cherries, cans of Turkish Delights and boxes of Niniche of Quiberon multicolored lollypops, all specifically ordered to fill a series of tiered crystal trees that crowned his dessert table in the big Ballroom now almost completely decorated. Paco and Sal placed the sweets under the table as Velly directed. Walking around with the Chef they were able to get an idea of the dazzling elements that would provide the entertainment for crowds of gamblers and merely fun seekers who would begin boarding soon. "I would love to see this party Velly is there any way?" He smiled broadly bringing two tickets out of his white jacket pocket. "This will get you in mon fils mais danger danger, comprend?" Double kissing the amazing Chef with gratitude, Paco and Sal carefully snooped around on the way out. Wound up now like two springs with anticipation, they rode the taxi to shore without a word and counted the minutes until they would be able to experience all that the nefarious Portafortuna had to offer.

The charm of the Santa Barbara Biltmore was experienced in a far more understated and rustic manner than it's magnificent sister in Los Angeles. Decorated in key areas with frescos and murals; carved marble fountains with marvelous Spanish and Portuguese tiles; massive wood-beamed ceilings; oak paneled walls inset with Moorish screens; exceedingly handsome wrought iron fixtures and giant chandeliers some with fine amber glass hurricanes that provided a golden glow; Vintage casements that adorned the stairwells and doorways; excellent marquetry and mill work; heavily embroidered tapestries and draperies, the ambience conveyed the magic of an early California rancho with luxurious romantic embellishments.

Starting with the "Entrada Court", the lobby that also served afternoon tea. Just to the left was "El Cantina", the spacious bar with a fireplace that would warm any heart. Enhanced by huge palm trees with exotic flowers in big blue and white patterned vases imported from Valencia, there was a long bar with stools and scenic tapestry on the walls. Off the bar to the right was "Parrilla Pacifica", or The Pacific Grill that was a huge outdoor terrace with open braziers, attended by cooks in vaquero attire, barbequing many specialties all surrounding a grand fountain brought in from an Andalusian plaza in the center. Countless hand painted hanging pots filled with red geraniums swung from a giant hand hewn Ramada that shaded everything and included canvas awnings that could be pulled for rain. All the chairs were wood crafted in Mexico with tall ladder-backs and spool details that were painted in bright colors.

"La Aguja Cobriza" or The Copper Marlin, was created as the ultimate seafood restaurant. Just off of the terrace, it had a spectacular bank of large arched windows with a perfect view of the bay at sunset and a massive carved wood ceiling. Highly polished tile floors were covered with choice Persian carpets. Aqua pots filled with orchid laden tree ferns stood against the walls that displayed five large seascapes painted in oil, framed in antiqued wood with softly glowing picture lights. At the far end, mounted as the signature image and detailed on menus and linens, was a mammoth copper leafed sailfish above a black marble fireplace.

"El Loggia D'Oro", or The Golden Ballroom, unlike interiors elsewhere, was themed to be extra luxurious and dramatic. Spectacular with crystal chandeliers it was available for grand galas and nightly a dining room for elite guests and haute cuisine. To thwart Prohibition it featured hidden liquor compartments and to feed the Society Columns there were panels along the ceiling press photographers to take pictures of the events below.

On this night, the specter was sweeping as Paco and Sal pulled into the portico

on the Indian. They were starting here and then moving on to the much more

interesting venue three miles out to sea. The entrance was clogged with

luxurious autos and mobs of elegantly dressed guests filled with gaiety and

expectation for the wonder that was to come. Walking past the lobby and into

the bar the young men maneuvered through the throng including brushes with

some of the familiar Hill Barons, the powerful Captains of industry and their

radiant retinues, glittering starlets and authentic big personalities. Peeking

through the doors of the Golden Ballroom they detected Mary Pickford and

Douglas Fairbanks dining on some of Chef Bertie's best dishes. They saw Buddy

Rogers at one of the bandstands and thought they caught a glimpse of Marlena

Dietrich or maybe Jean Arthur? They knew many were famous but not

appreciated much since their identities were a mystery. On the way out they did

see Charlie Chaplin and a big group from the Flying A Studios swept by. Paco

and Sal, standing out in front under the portico pretending to look for Rudolph

Valentino, were just bidding their time until it was late enough to visit the

Portafortuna.

The waters were dark and choppy when the two boarded the gambling vessel. They had an awkward arrival since the motion of the ship distorted their balance and once inside the big crowd lurched and swayed. Arriving on the upper decks the scene began to level off. They presented their tickets at the entrance to the Grand Ballroom where "Naughty Nights in Paris" was clearly underway.

Passing through the casino and the poker parlor the two climbed the stairs to the ballroom now a throbbing centerpiece of the event. A large swing band played as the revelers danced "The Foxtrot" then turned hot with "The Charleston" and "The Black Bottom". All this action revolved around the big silver painted model of the Eiffel Tower that supported many little mirrored shelves filled with cups of champagne. Four provocative French maids passed out the refills with big magnums. At the far end of the room, centered between large columns that supported a white tulle draped pavilion, was the revered Chef Velly's masterpiece, a sixteen-foot long buffet that gleamed like a celestial city from afar. Paco drank his way across the huge room purposely grazing the lovely bare back of Il Brolino's young Mistress who turned and blew him a kiss.

The two began to study the great spread. Servers in tuxedos with red aprons aided the guests to select from four grand silver domed thermadors, the first serving Torte Canard, a pate and mushroom duxelles densely packed with cognac spiked duck confit encased within thin pastry and sauced with verjus-soaked cherries. The next displayed rows of crusty topped scallop shells St Jacques style filled with oysters, crab, shrimp, and lobster. The third served Carre de cochon with a puree of celery chataigne et truffles that Paco discovered was a thick slice of tender succulent ham seated on a whipped potato like cloud of goodness that perfectly expressed Velly's genius for seasonings. The fourth served a famous classic Parisian dish and the Chef's specialite called "Noisette d'agneau en eroute", a lamb pie, foie gras in the middle and an exquisite orange-chervil sauce of sublime complexity. At the end of the table was a big, shiny metallic, double tiered cheeseboard, designed by Velly for the large elaborate garden parties at Il Brolino. Tonight it was filled with ten sorts of fromage – St Marcellin, Echourgnac, Tomme de Savoie, double Crottin, Boulette d'Avesnes, Manchego, Chabichou, Camembert, Selles-sur-Cher and la caillé de brebis . In addition, as condiments there were jars of honey from Provence, gelée de piments, the famous black cherry jam of Toulouse and a separate plate of pâte de coings the legendary quince paste known as fruit cheese. This generous help-yourself fifth course was just a portal to the piece de resistance, the desert table, glittering now with all manner of Chef Velly's imported candy and cookie favorites. The crystal trees, supporting little plates holding beautiful stacks of truffles and bonbons, were made even more fanciful studded with hundreds of fruit colored lollypops that delighted the guests who walked away sucking and giggling like children.

Paco and Sal danced with anyone who would and sauntered back and forth near an especially pretty French maid and presented their empty cups over and over until they caught the eye of one of the burly bouncers frowning at the crowd in ill fitting evening dress. Soon over to the far left Paco saw Captain Oakley, a figure that struck an unconscious note of recollection even in his bleary condition, who was not amused by their behavior. Motioning to another bouncer the three approached the young men and strong-armed them to the exit marching on to the lower level and to the debarking area. They were being briskly thrown out. Paco was complaining loudly that, he had a ticket and he was twenty-one. Shouting, "this is unfair", while kicking and strongly resisting until the very large hands of the Captain grabbed him by the shoulders and shaking roughly he exploded.

Oakly said, "You are not ever to come here again. If you do you will suffer serious consequences. Do you hear me? I have put you on the list for expulsion and you must obey this order. If you don't there are very dangerous people who will make you pay." Oakley could not help taking a close look at his handsome son, so striking with his mother's coloring and some of his features.

Paco, cussing and hazy, with some sixth sense knew who was holding him tightly. "I know who you are", he blasted out the words, "I hate you, my Mother and I hate you". The words acted like a spring and the huge man flung the young one from him to the handling of the bouncers who quickly sat him next to Sal and the Water Taxi left for shore.

The brisk trip across the sea to the Biltmore dock served to sober the two and leaving Sal at the Grand Opening Party that was still raging, Paco hopped on The Indian, sick at heart, and headed for East Beach, a place he always returned to when he was down and out. He hid the bike and took off all his clothes except for the briefs. Still heated and confused by the confrontation with his

Father, he dove into the cold water swimming out far enough to be challenged by a return to shore. At the height of his effort, summoning all his strength the thought came to him. He reasoned in an instant, "why don't I just let go? I am tainted with a criminal for a Father? I failed Lillian. I'll never be an artist. I can't tell my Mother about the ship. It will crush her" All these issues passed in and then out of his mind as he did let go then exerting everything he found new courage and won his way to the sand.

The evening was warm and balmy as he turned around and around, getting dizzy, slowly drying off. He was just ambling along the water line playing with the surf, missing the edge of the waves as they rolled in. Off in the distance something caught his eye further up the beach. He could vaguely make out the image of a person sailing through the air like a bird and whirling wildly. Moving closer he could see it was a girl, entranced by some unknown music, devising a passionate dance. Approaching quietly he watched her intently and when she seemed to come to the end he clapped and called out "bravo". Startled now the person spun around to leave and then turned back as if in recognition. Coming even closer now she walked straight up to him and said. "Hello Paco, it's me, Huguette."

Chapter Eight: Charlie Chaplin and The Montecito Inn

When Charlie Chapin moved with a big collection of friends to Montecito some distant bell rang out signaling a kind of carnal shift in the firmament. Consequently, the dialog of the day was an unending speculation on who was listening to the ring and what they where doing at that moment. The headquarters for the group was a charming Mediterranean styled hotel, The Montecito Inn, that Chaplin had created as a first class hideout and pleasure palace. Charlie was experiencing one of the worst years of his life. His hair went from dark to snow white in a matter of months.

The source of his pain was threefold. First his beloved Mother, who was for many years confined with mental illness, was dying and this broke his heart. He and his brother Sydney tried to care for her and always knew she loved them deeply. The brothers had been cruelly separated from her at an early age, an experience that would haunt Chaplin throughout his life. In fact this trauma explained many of his motivations while creating the plots of his films, words of his songs and so much of his tumultuous personal life.

The second painful conflict in Chaplin's horrendous year was his extraordinarily bitter divorce that ended in record-breaking $825,000 settlement, on top of almost one million dollars in legal costs. This second wife, Lita Grey, was working for Charlie at his Hollywood studio when she was 12 years old. At the age of 15 she was pregnant by him and at 16 they married. Now after only three years they divorced.

At this same time he was tirelessly battling a Federal tax dispute and navigating a heated affair with actress Marion Davies, the lover of William Randolph Hurst, one of the world's most powerful men.

To complete the suffering genius's struggle there was his turbulent production of a film called, "The Circus". Numerous problems and delays had occurred, including a studio fire, badly processed film that ruined the first three months of shooting and the theft of the final reels that were only recently returned. All this and his owing back taxes culminated in film's release being stalled. It was this agonizing uncertainty that drove the debauchery and excess that played out nightly at the Inn.

Chef Victore called Paco at Diehls to place a huge order acting as the new head of the Montecito Inn's kitchen. He was now liberated from his punishing position working under Chef Pulga at El Mirador. Knowing full well how to produce a complete continental style menu and all the regional Spanish favorites, he was happily in the center of a hurricane that maintained a constant parade of actors, musicians, artists and legendary personalities from all over the world.

"Now please deliver everything as soon as you can. If you only have part of it bring that on. There will be so many parties Paco. You must come tonight. Just find the kitchen door and you know I will be there." Chef Victore added. "The woman are unbelievable and most of them are wearing very little. Oh and please bring some rum. We can make daiquiris."

Paco was instantly amused and accordingly made plans for the evening even though in his heart he knew that he and Victore were a dangerous combination. Looking up now toward the storefront he could see a beautiful young woman entering who he recognized from her photos in the newspaper. It was Merna Kennedy, the star of Charlie Chaplin's new film "The Circus". Paco remembered the article said she was a dancer with muscular legs and that helped her gain the role of the circus bareback rider. Now he was curious to actually see those legs so he walked purposefully over to Salvador now brilliantly presenting his menu to five stunning starlets and Miss Kennedy at the soda fountain. Paco stood by appearing to be waiting to confirm some information on an order but really he was visually dinning on the exceeding loveliness of the showgirls.

Also excited by the new arrivals, up at the entrance in front of the long glorious produce stand now filled to the brim with finely stacked citrus and perfect specimen vegetables, Quincy and Patrice began a daily routine, a little remnant from their Vaudeville act.

Quincy started, "What did you do with the peaches? And what about the pears? You are so dizzy! You are the dizziest Dame I ever met!"

Then Patrice, "I'm not dizzy, not dizzy at all. You know, I've come to the conclusion I'm very, very bright."

Quincy returned. "Oh, so you made up your mind you are very bright? Tell me, how bright are you?"

Patrice, "Well, you know those crossword puzzles? I make them up."

Quincy, "That should be interesting. O.K. I want to see it. Make one up. Let's have it."

Patrice. "O.K. What starts with W and I don't know how many letters? What is it?"

Quincy, "It starts with W and you don't know how many letters? What is it?"

You made that up? You couldn't have made that up. Somebody must be

helping you. (His eyes rolling) Don't tell me the answer let me think of it. Does

it jump? Does it swim? Does it run? I don't know I give it up."

Patrice, "Well, men shave with it. That's a little hint."

Quincy, "Men shave with it. It starts with W and you don't know how many

letters? Well the only thing I can think of that men shave with is a razor."

Patrice, "Yes! You got it! That's it, that's very good."

Quincy, "You made that up? I'd brag about that if I were you", (making a "She's

crazy" sign with his finger).

Patrice, "Yeah, (with a big self satisfied sigh), I have brains. I have brains I

haven't even used yet."

Quincy, "Well leave them alone. Don't bother with them. If you had another

brain you'd have one. You have brains? You know all the answers and you're not

dizzy? Listen to me little lady. You are plenty dizzy! You look to me like you're

always up in an aero plane. Have you ever gone in one?"

Patrice, "No, no, no I would never go."

Quincy, "Afraid to go in an aero plane? There's nothing to be afraid about. You

see, the first thing they do when you step into an aero plane is strap a parachute on your shoulder and if anything happens up in the air all you do is you jump

out and the parachute opens nicely, and then you land on the ground."

Patrice, "Well but supposing the parachute doesn't open nicely?"

Quincy, "Then you just write a letter to the factory and they send you another

one."

This was a popular routine by George Burns and Gracie Allen that always

merged into "Do You Believe Me - I Do", a song and dance performance

peppered with little interchanges. Quincy and Patrice perfected this enough to

go on tour with the Orpheum Circuit Road Show, riding a train that pulled into

small towns from New York to California. When it ended in Santa Barbara

they disembarked and sat on the beach, arm in arm, with a pile of suitcases, as

the sound of the giant engine faded away.

Midway in the song, dancing together all along, Quincy said with an adoring

smile, "You know I think you're very nice", and Patrice, twirling lightly,

returned, "Yes, and I'm smart too." The act continued. Quincy snapped, "Oh yes, if you're so smart name three nuts", and Patrice answered, "Well walnuts and chestnuts and...forget me nuts."

Then during more dancing, perfectly in sink, they sang more humorous chitchat that caused the little Diehls market audience to be soundly amused. The bevy of showgirls, provocatively perched on soda fountain stools, were giggling and producing vigorous scattered applause at key moments.

Quincy, "What did you take up at school?"

Patrice, "Anything that wasn't nailed down."

Quincy, "Your too smart for one girl"

Patrice, "I'm more than one."

Quincy, "You're more than one?"

Patrice, "My mother has a picture of me when I was two."

Quincy, "Do you like to love?" Patrice, "No."

Quincy, "Like to kiss?" Patrice, "No."

Quincy, "Well what do you like?"

Patrice, "Lamb chops."

Quincy, "Lamb chops? Could you eat two big lamb chops alone?"

Patrice, "Oh no not alone, with potatoes I could."

The act finished with a fancy juggling of oranges. While all this progressed Paco was able to see first hand the noted well muscled legs of Merna Kennedy as he walked over to one of the tables that always accommodated Oren Star, who had just ordered his usual late morning black coffee with an orange-currant scone. He inspected every page in the New York and London Times, reading aloud to whoever was nearby, not really caring if anyone was interested.

Today the entire market stopped to listen as Starr read the endlessly fascinating account of the opening of a fabulous tomb in Egypt's Valley of the Kings. Finding Tutankhamen changed the world as it influenced all manner of fashion, architecture and design. It had been years since Howard Carter, upon making a small opening in the wall that separated him from the first storage room, first walked into the antechamber uttering the famous four words, "I see wonderful things". A huge dispute with the Egyptian government had kept him away and the entire process halted until now.

Paco passed around the rotogravure section that pictured unbelievable images of golden statues, stunning alabaster urns with inset turquoise, onyx and lapis decorations, clothing articles and most exciting, many exquisite pieces of jewelry. Now the showgirls huddled over the page with the necklace and bracelets picking out the ones they wanted, knowing full well that copies, like everything else from the tomb, would be available very soon.

Esperanza sat on her throne of a cashier's stand soaking up all the chatter from the Chaplin troupe with only a mild interest in Oren's reading. She was mostly inspecting her dark red lacquered fingernails and adjusting her blouse to the most alluring position. A shiny braid that wound around her head held three creamy gardenias that scented her entire area.

Walking in from the rear and taking a seat at the table closest to her was the beloved baritone, Fortuno Bona Nova. Small framed but impressive in his distinguished highborn Spanish attire, he caused interest wherever he went. There could not be anyone more interested in him now than Esperanza who had recently announced they were engaged. As their eyes met emitting an almost visible electricity, Esperanza's perfectly shaped eyebrows arched seductively. Fortuno responded with a sly smile and a swipe of his mustachio, drawing her attention to his dazzling white teeth and moist lips.

So much passion was passing through these two that it captured the attention of everyone. This grand romance was something of a miracle for Esperanza who grew up abnormally tall and seriously overweight, often the brunt of much bullying. Only recently when her elder sister became a beauty consultant for a door-to-door cosmetics company did the big woman bloom. The two traveled to Los Angeles for a special training session where it was discovered that Espe had the perfect face to demonstrate the amazing effect of rouge and mascara with artful shaping of the brows and painting of the lips. On top of this she contracted a very harsh case of the flu that left her pounds lighter and once up and healthy this serendipitous combination made her astoundingly beautiful overnight. Still mystified by the effects her new born appearance had on men, she was understandably fearful inside that Fortuno, a celebrated idol to many, would love her and leave her if she gave in to his desires so when he proposed she fainted.

Just as everyone fell into a blissful state, experiencing the couple's love and sensuality second hand, there came through the back entrance a well dressed woman in an absurdly ornamented hat that included two stuffed birds and a bouquet of silk violets, with three children in tow. She headed directly to Fortuno and to Esperanza's horror, kneeled to kiss his feet and whimper, "Tu amor, tu amor, tu amor. Soon the two little girls in matching yellow pinafores and the boy in a sailor suit joined her. They were begging, "Papa, Papa, via en su casa, por favor, por favor".

Esperanza's huge luminous eyes were frozen as black tears began to seep down her bright pink cheeks. Salvador, sensing the gravity of the situation, bolted from behind the soda fountain and stood between Espe and the cruel event now unfolding. The baritone, all the while glued to some unknown point on the ceiling, finally stood with a flourish and walked out, with what would later be known as his wife and three children following behind.

Sal and Espe grew up all most next door to each other on the lower East side of the city so he knew her inside and out. He walked over and gently took an arm, escorting her to the ladies Room where she stayed for most of the afternoon. Everyone else moved on with downcast eyes sensing the heaviness of spirit that had just settled like a dark cloud. Paco went back to his order desk and then packed the truck for his final delivery of the day to The Montecito Inn. As he started to leave Salvadore emerged, a distraught Esperanza on his arm, her face looking like a messy artist's palette with all the fine makeup smeared, marred with lines of dried mascara. Paco just opened the delivery truck door and the two were seated next to him as he drove them home.

Sal and Paco shook their heads watching the big woman hurry to her door. Parking only one house away, they stopped and walked to the big front porch that was filled with aging furniture, toys and some laundry drying on an old hat rack at the end. This was Casa Rodrigez where Salvador, his wife, five children, little brothers, the entire family, four generations in all, lived a rich and spirited life in high style with very modest means. Almost every dinner was chicken with beans and rice and vanilla flan or rice pudding as desert but the tastes were so outrageously delicious and the volatile personalities bouncing off each other

with such good humor made life a banquet. Paco wanted to stay but this

evening he needed to make his delivery to Chef Victore and stay on for an inside

look at Chaplin mania, a subject that had the entire town mesmerized.

Before he left Sal brought out two cold cervezas and they sat together on the

porch sinking into an old sofa with serapes covering nearly half a century of

wear.

"So Paco, what was that all about when we were kicked off the ship?" Sal asked.

"You knew him? And you hate him? Who is he?"

Paco admitted, "He is my Father but I don't know him. He disappeared when I

was born. I didn't know he was Captain of The Portafortuna. I'm sorry Sal. It

was such a nightmare. I'm just worried he will cause trouble. He knows where

we live. They say, because of him we are marked for death. He is a gangster. An

important part of the Syndicate, you know what I mean? This changes

everything for me. I'm always looking over my shoulder to see if I'm being watched. I can never have a woman like you have. And", picking up a little toy motorcycle that looked like a tiny Indian, "No children for me".

Now, as two little sons raced by sparring with toy weapons and the splendid Beatrice, Sal's always pregnant wife, came menacing by, waving a wooden spoon and reeling off threatening curses in Spanish, he turned to Paco and in all confidence said, "you could be lucky?" And then dissolved into a deep peel of laughter that lifted their spirits.

"What happened to you? Sal asked, "The Biltmore party was wild and I saw Louise Hay. We were this close", demonstrating by touching noses. "I just walked right up to her and bowed in her face. She smiled. It was wonderful. You should have come. There was a big jazz band that played until two. Where did you go anyway?"

Paco was gazing at some distant landscape, "I just went off to the beach and the strangest thing happened. Sal, you know the Clark girl? Huguette? Well I went to the beach to cool off and down the shore a girl came dancing up and grabbed my hand. We walked for a long way and then climbed the steps up to

the Cemetery. She sat on the bench near the edge of the cliff and I just talked to

her. We walked way down to the big wall covered with vines and I helped her

over the top to her own property. It was Huguette Clark, you know,

Bellesguardo".

Sal was scurrying around now chasing one little guy who was attempting to

escape with out his clothing and as Paco left he said, "Yeah Buddy, it's the

women who make it all better, chica-chica brother."

It was nearly six when Paco pulled into the parking rotunda and around to the

kitchen entrance of The Montecito Inn. Inside he found Chef Victore

butterflying shrimp with two helpers who were chopping tomatoes, tomatillos,

onions, cilantro and peppers for salsa. He pointed to a giant basket of avocados

and said, "por favor?" Paco took off his fine tailored Diehls delivery jacket and

rolled up his sleeves, grabbing an apron, and began cutting up the dark leathery

skinned fruit making perfect quarter moon slices and drenching them with

lemon juice to preserve their buttery green color.

"You are here on the very best night me amigo", Victore said. "Chaplin is having

auditions for his movie. He wants Circus people so if you open that door and

peek out you will not believe your eyes! It's fantastico, magico! Clowns and

magicians and beautiful women! It's incredible and they are all hungry and very

thirsty". He was filling platter after platter as the waiters came through for

refills.

True and more as Paco pushed the swinging door to see this sight for himself.

The spacious lobby that opened out to a big patio restaurant and garden was

filled with a mind-bending array of spectacularly costumed performers. In many

cases they had their equally well-dressed animal co-stars. Just in front of him

was a magnificent Clown in a billowy white satin suit, a big ruff around his neck.

He was dancing with three huge white poodles that were at that moment

standing on their back legs and twirling around, all in matching high peeked

hats embellished with silver sequins and diamonds. A stately blond woman

with pigtails that were wired to stand out, topped with a daisy decorated straw

hat, dressed in a revealing little gingham pinafore was comforting her small curly

lamb.

The beautiful Merna Kennedy, with those fabulous legs, was far across the room posing on the back of a braided well decorated dapple-grey pony complete with three ostrich plumes on his head. She was a delicious sight as the flash bulbs exploded. Her frilly short tutu displaying silky stockings and pink satin toe shoes that tied far up her legs. Her little horse bucked at the photographer's lights and she jumped off with surprising grace. The housekeeping staff, standing on the sidelines, was kept very busy with brooms and dustpans, continually cleaning up the mess.

Further on appeared the giant Russian with his famous feline act setting up a tight rope with the help of his chunky little harem girl helper. The cats were waiting; two or three together in cage-like suitcases, for their release that promised nice little dried liver treats after each trick. Paco could see their ears twitch with annoyance as a row of five tap dancers in bathing suits made a huge racket singing, "By the Sea, By the Sea, by the beautiful sea". And on they went weaving through the crowd.

Passing the audition area with this mind bending collection of performers, Paco

teamed with Chef Victore to carry a savory assortment of appetizers and fruit

daiquiris to the pool area where a stunning group of nearly naked women were

playfully batting around hundreds of pink balloons, now bouncing off the

turquoise water that was sudsy and piled high with masses of bubbles. The sight

of the drinks compelled a number of the soaked and soapy starlets to leave the

pool and circle around Paco and Victore, dripping with excitement. The girls

took the drinks, next their trays and then their clothes, with wet kisses, hugging

them closely and pulling them willingly into the bubbly soup.

"With wet kisses, hugging them closely they pulled

them willingly into the bubbly soup"

Paco was thick headed and still dazed by the excesses of the night before. As he

parked The Indian and removed his leather jacket he felt the card that Wright

Ludington had given him at the Gypsy Camp. He propped it up against the

lamp base at his desk and eyed it throughout the day. Around three he made the

call. A pompous voice answered asking, "Who may I say is calling?" A little

unnerved Paco explained that he had been directed to call by Mr. Ludington.

"Oh my God, what does he want with you? " Sounds of disgust and then some

muffled shouting, "Just let me do it". Soon the voice was back, "Allow me to see

if the Master is in". More scuffling and quickly a deep voice that was actually

Wright Ludington inquired, "Who is this please?" After some explanation,

Paco had a 5:30 appointment to bring his portfolio and meet with this man he

knew had one of the region's finest art collections. He was so excited that he

could think of nothing else for the rest of the day. Even the memory of floating

in Charlie Chaplin's pool filled with pink balloons and playgirls evaporated.

Chapter Nine: Val Verde & The medallion d'Oro Competition

Arriving at the appointed time Paco found his way to the entrance of

Ludington's estate, Val Verde, with its spectacular landscape now expanded.

Manicured hedges artfully formed the passages and gardens that were now in the

process of displaying his exceptional collection of Greek and Roman sculpture.

Normally he took a service entrance route but today he selected the main

entrance. Featured at the entry, off of the motor court, was one spectacular

reflecting pool with a graceful statue of Aphrodite floating on a pedestal at the

far end.

Climbing the steps with a roll of drawings, including nine of a single orange, he

rang the bell. A flash of fabric streaked by French doors and then returned.

Soon an apparent specter of Isis, her eyes decorated with heavy kohl liner and

audacious crimson lips, inspected him slowly from head to toe. He heard the

loud clacking of high heels disappear down the deep red tiled floor. Time passed,

the footsteps approaching. Doors swung wide to reveal a huge woman dressed in

a deep blue glittering evening gown with big shoulders, a matching headdress

that was held in place by a golden cobra and a black and gold striped scarf that

flared out with Pharaonic style. She was smoking, wielding a very long cigarette

holder, and as she beckoned him in he noticed the perfectly groomed sandy

blond mustache that revealed his true sex.

"Come this way Paco, Mr. Ludington is in the galleria unpacking. We are

completely crazed with exhaustion and tonight, oh my God, it's bloody awful,

we are having the King Tut Party!" Chef/Butler Printise Yonkopolis threw his

arms skyward and then with dainty balletic steps led the way through an entry

and large living room cluttered with giant crates and multi-sized packages.

"Watch your step, my Darling boy. The Master has gone potty. Everything is in an ugly tangle, a shamble. Renovations, renovations everywhere!"

Paco knew Printise very well because as the Chef at Val Verde he ordered either by phone or in person all the extravagant food selections from Diehls and he delivered at least once a week. Unusually fair with classic Roman features he was quick to tell anyone that his Mother, British, fell in love with his Father, a Greek Sicilian, on an archeological dig at the ancient site of Delos. She spent just long enough in the hot dusty ruins to create him and divorcing quickly went back to her family properties near Oxford. There, his Mother, still intensely in love with classical Greece, raised him as a golden child of Olympus. The toddler, dressed in tiny togas and sandals with wings, was called Apollo until he left for schooling.

Printise departed college early, partly because of his heavy drug use and notably due to his compulsion to neglect his studies for work in warm kitchens. He had done this since a child, content next to his great love, the family Cook Martha, possibly in order to escape his bizarre circumstances. Attending Magdalen College, planning for a career in literature, his room was in the famous Old

Parsonage just steps away from Oscar Wilde's student quarters. Printise found

the kitchen and attached himself to the wondrous Chef de Cuisine, the

legendary Eugene Plazermine, who had been fired from all the greatest

restaurants in France due to alcoholism. The old drunk Chef loved the boy and

taught him well until the terrible day when he burned the kitchen down

including himself. Simultaneous with this tragedy his Mother married an

Ancient Antiquities Professor who hated the young man on sight. Rising one

morning and packing lightly, Printise left for Sicily where he was taken in by his

dead Father's big extended family. There he languished for some years, refining

his art, always watching, learning and cooking in one of the many warm kitchens

he craved for solace.

With all the nurturing of Sicilian society, sun and good eating, Printise became

the personification of his childhood name. He was as beautiful as Apollo should

be. Very tall and muscular with a crown of golden curls and azure eyes, he was a

remarkable sight. Soon it occurred to his ever-enterprising Yonkopolis cousins,

who ran a rustic restaurant under the arbors and olive trees, to take advantage of

what nature had brought them.

The majestic young man found himself again dressed in a toga portraying the Sun God. This time it was for a brutally cut up production of several Greek tragedies. Created to entertain tourists on the steps of the great Temple of Segesta and often in the well-preserved ancient theatre on Delos, Printise became a local celebrity. These events, done on order by British tour agencies, included a lunch that Printise and a few relatives prepared and served with dramatic effect. This added income was a boon for the family. Now they clearly adored their newfound relative and gave him every accommodation but all he seemed to want was to cook.

The plays were actually concocted by an aging Yonkopolis Grandfather, a mathematics teacher for years. The gentle ladies and men, taking the grand tour of ancient and exotic lands, where highly amused and often drawn back by the sexual antics and bloody accounts drawn from an unending supply of Greek and Roman mythology. One of the most entertaining presentations combined snippets of Euripedes' "Heracules" and a completely fabricated version of the myth of Cassandra. This quirky adaptation told that her beauty caused Apollo to grant the gift of prophecy. For this she spent a night at his temple, where the sacred snakes licked her ears clean. That, they asserted, was why she was able to

hear the future.

It was during one such event that destiny brought Printise and Ludington

irrevocably together. Sitting in the theatre audience, feasting on a sumptuous

basket of just picked vegetables drenched in thick green rosemary scented olive

oil, a mound of herbed goat cheese and the most glorious tomatoes ever tasted,

was Wright and his architect Bertrand. They were smirking over the dialog but

swooning with joy over the food. In the hot sun drinking wine like water they

were soon intoxicated with the vision of Printise. His magnificent body, tanned

and glistening with sweat, was enough to garner an invitation to join them at

their hotel. That was all it took for the eager Apollo to pack his bags and waving

goodbye to his grief stricken Greek family, he simply showed up at Ludington's

door unannounced and declared, "I'm coming with you."

So on the evening of Paco's visit to Val Verde, almost two years later, the true

nature in the child of Olympus appeared fulfilled. He was deeply in love with

Ludington and passionate about his kitchen that he treated as personal territory.

Even impersonating Isis he was a very attractive figure with the most hilarious palaver, rich in expletives, polished by an elegant British accent, continually delivering bountiful eccentric wit.

Paco presented himself with a bundle of drawings to Ludington who was wrestling a large framed painting that he pulled gently from the crate. Awesome with powerful imagery the piece was done by the Parisian artist Georges Rouault. The heavy black thickly painted line work followed the contours of a body in motion with glowing colors filling in the volumes suggesting leaded glass. Sitting back the two men eyed the impressive piece with excitement. This began the education of Paco and launched his dream to study in Florence at the Academia. Wright brought out canvas after canvas of the new purchases he had just made from young artists like Picasso, Matisse and Braque. There were large portfolios of drawings selected from obscure British artists and leaning against the wall at the end was the splendid oil, "Lady in Pink" by the great teacher William Merritt Chase that was inherited from his Mother, an avid collector of the impressionists. The piece was almost six feet tall and a brilliant display of the artist's sublime painterly strokes that made the lady, his wife, come magically alive from a distance.

Paco spread out his work on the dark tile floor as Ludington paced back and forth over it, fingers brushing his lips in thought. "You have it", he concluded. "You have possibilities, but your work just begins. You must create a portfolio that will convince the Board of Entry you can be committed to the challenge."

Wright went to a closet nearby and returned holding a fine black leather portfolio. He collected Paco's pieces, placed them inside and handed it over saying, "Here is the vessel, fill it with your inspiration and intelligence. If you prove to me you have the talent, I will pay your way. Now go and help Chef Printise in the kitchen. You are invited to the evening's festivities. I imagine you will make a handsome Egyptian."

Paco was a little dazed by this good fortune and setting his perfect portfolio against the wall near the entry he found his way to the kitchen almost floating on air. There was Printise along with a number of cooks and staff borrowed from Java Sir's kitchen at Il Fureidis, an adjoining property. Everyone was working with all the elements that made up the grand buffet of an ancient Pharaoh. Roasted onions, sweet fig, apple and nut forcemeat for stuffing duck, beef marinated in scented spices then grilled in chunks with whole leeks, coconuts ground for creamy milk puddings that were scattered with pomegranate seeds, mounds of grapes, olives, dates, various baked and fried breads being taken from the ovens and stacked in woven baskets supposedly from Thebes. To complete the menu there was a very large crock filled with honeyed beer, accented in the ancient tradition by adding citrus and touches of lavender.

The sight of it was astonishing. There was Chef Printise, the kohl from his make up now creating grey rings around his eyes like a raccoon, shouting orders in a high fey voice. "Make it silky Darling", he said to one cook slowly stirring the thickening coconut cream. "No, not that way, like this". He demonstrated his fine chopping method and with an impassioned demand. "It must be thoroughly squidgy my Darlings". Then motioning to Paco he said, "Join us if you will and carry the dishes to the atrium as they are finished. There's a fine lad, and get yourself a caftan with a turban from the Indian gents. They can make you into a little King Tut!"

So it was a stunning night to remember for the aspiring artist, sitting cross-legged at a long feast table set up in the outside courtyard that was designed as a noble's house from Pompeii. The food was eaten with hands, only picked up with the thin flat bread. His guests were sophisticated and properly profound. In the gathering he knew Gana Walska who trumped everyone with her spectacular Cleopatra costume, once worn in her disastrously reviewed musical production of Julius Caesar. Bertram Goodhue and Lockwood de Forest, both in matching togas looking like Romans were sketching on napkins. Oren Star was in his customary chambray shirt with jodhpurs and Miss Penny, his companion for the evening, was delectable in her shimmering deep green harem costume. Joannah Prang ignored the line in the invitation that specified, "ancient Egyptian attire required" and came dressed in her preferred Gothic style. Many others who were familiar from Diehls did arrive as proper members of Tutankhamen's court making the spectacle appear strangely authentic. Paco listened intently to the fascinating conversations, getting very drunk on the Theban beer. Late that evening came an elaborate hookah with sweet apple flavored tobacco and then the finisher, they passed the tiny pipes filled with opium laced hashish.

Paco was dizzy and feeling he may soon be sick so, escaping down into the gardens, he wandered for a long way in the cool air. Following a rocky stream through the property, the path went down and then up to a large rectangular

pool. He tasted the water that was fresh. Then, disrobing, he walked in and lay

down floating in a dreamlike state. The stars were out on this clear night as he

contemplated the immensity of a deep indigo sky.

Out of the corner of his eye he noticed a movement high up in what he

determined was a tower with a balcony. There he could see a woman. As he

strained and stood up moving closer to get a better slant she turned her head,

looking directly at him. Paco was standing stunned at the foot of the tall

structure straining to clarify the face of this figure high above. She was so angelic

and fair, so familiar to him, breathtaking with her alabaster skin gleaming in the moonlight, he knew it was Lillian and he loved her deeply, hopelessly. Finding

the door he climbed the winding staircase and moved across a circular sitting

room. He could see her silhouette through fluttering curtains to the balcony

ahead. Pulling the drapery aside he gently called her name and as she turned he

bent down on one knee. He held her hand and told her he was ashamed to have

left her in the Sevilla Club. He kissed her fingers and begged for her forgiveness,

then standing he held her in his arms for long moments, promising never to let

her be hurt again. Finally their eyes met but he could see by her empty gaze,

glistening grey focused on some point miles away, she never heard a word he

said. Slumping to the ground he laid unconscious for hours.

Waking just at dawn Paco found himself on a small living room sofa, his legs

draped over the end. Rushing to leave before anyone woke he found his clothes

and grabbing his new portfolio raced to the Indian and sped home. He was

trying to put the pieces together. 'Was it really Lillian? Is that what opium does

to your mind? Was I actually holding her? I remember her body next to mine.

That is unforgettable even if only a delusion.' He was concentrating hard trying

to separate his fantasy from reality but gave up, thinking instead of the

opportunities Ludington had described. As he found his bed on the sleeping porch and layback with Ranger nuzzling his neck it came clear that there were voices in his Mother's room. Low whispers but definitely sounds of a conversation. He could make out the low voice of a man and then Madonna answering. Before he could stand to move closer the door opened and Captain Oakley, his father walked out the door with his Mother following. He could see them through the window as they embraced. Paco was touched by the apparent great love they shared but forgiveness was far from his heart and he faked sleep as his Mother returned, not able to face the strangeness of it all.

Arriving that morning for work late there was a line of customers waiting for him to open. Like a theatre performance all the characters filtered in and began the show. Quincy and Patrice started to move the vegetable stand out in front as Salvador made the coffee, whipped his cream and heated the luscious hot fudge in case anyone ordered a "Mocha Frappe". Libby, the cook, began the magnificent pepper spiked, corned beef and potato hash, then whipped up her famous pancake batter that produced Flap Jacks lighter than air. Esperanza, having survived her horrendous disappointment over the loss of Bona Nova, was feeling much better. Ever since her sister recruited her as a partner in the new door-to-door make-up business, she flourished. They had taken the entire

County of Santa Barbara exclusively and it would not be long before she intended to leave Diehls to make a small fortune. Mac Massini, the butcher, was in his enormous refrigerator while his assistant, Sal's little brother Martine, made the sausages, seasoned with a secret Sicilian spice combination that had the whole town addicted. All the regulars took their places at the small tables or the big soda fountain.

A convivial chatter arose, just an ordinary morning at the finest culinary establishment in the region. Opening a large grey envelope with a seriously important return address that Paco knew would bring great interest, he found a stack of forms with a hand written note attached that read.

Dear Sir,

Kindly circulate this invitation to any Chefs of quality you may consider fit for this challenge.

We will conduct the American competition at the Santa Barbara Biltmore; therefore your facility to supply products will be necessary. Please find applications enclosed herewith.

Sincere acknowledgement of your noble establishment,

Master Chef, Director General, Medallion d'Or Foundation of America,

M. Gus Wasser, The Biltmore, New York, NY

The forms were actually applications that stated the following:

Application for Team USA:

The Medallion d'Or World Cuisine Contest is the most rigorous international culinary competition, held every two years in Paris, France. Twenty-four countries are selected to compete, and each country's team is comprised of one chef and one assistant.

Each team is provided five and a half hours to create two elaborate platter presentations, one centered around seafood and one on meat, each accompanied by three original garnishes. The platters are presented before twenty-four judges, each of whom is among the most esteemed chefs in his/her own country. Honored this year as the Co-Chairmen of the Board are Master Chef Auguste Escoffier, Savoy Hotel, London and Master Chef Fernand Point, La Pyramide, Vienne, France. The judges evaluate the overall harmony of flavors in the dish, the presentation of the platter, the techniques employed and the efficiency in which the teams work.

The intensity of the spectator's enthusiasm is unique. Thousands of fans attend the event and are seated in sections in front of their competitors' booth, waving flags, singing national chants, and providing general encouragement. The noise level of the arena elevates as the candidates race to complete their presentations to the judges. Hundreds of international photo and film journalists canvas the location, broadcasting the competition live around the world.

The day following the competition there is a ceremony to honor the top three teams by installing a plaque engraved with their names and countries on the wall of distinction.

Competition for Team USA will be held June 10 ~ 14 at The Santa Barbara Biltmore.

Paco read on to see that the form requested all information about the education and work description of the applicant. His mind ran on thinking of the Chefs who might qualify. Certainly Chef Velly would and Fredo too. Chef Pulga and Chef Victore of course could compete. Bertie, the great Chef Omeyer, had to be invited, might even win. He would take one to Chef Java Sir, but he probably would not be interested. Mama Genet should be added to the list just because she made the best dishes he ever tasted. Cannot forget about Chef Printise, he thought, wondering which gender he would choose for the competition. There must be more he thought as he went through his orders and added another half dozen names, making almost twenty in all.

Oren Star, seated comfortably at his usual table across from Diehls big marble Soda Fountain, began reading aloud, as was his want, a newspaper story that headlined, "Portafortuna ordered beyond 30 mi. limit." Continuing he quoted, "Although gambling is not a Federal crime, in the interest of Public Safety and propriety, Governor Frederick Hastings Storm has issued a public statement declaring his intentions to shut down any gambling ships found inside the newly set 30 mi. limit for California waters. In an effort to enforce this ruling, local and state authorities were recently repelled when a committee tried to board the Portfortuna but the crew forced them away with the use of well aimed fire hoses. The Governor specifically denounced the ship and it's Captain, Pacomio Basinorios Oakley, who was considered blatantly unwilling to cooperate with the Government demands. Storm said he intended to call the Navy and Coast Guard if necessary and there is an arrest order issued for Captain Oakley."

Paco heard these words plainly and his face began to flush. He put his fingertips to his temples and began to rub in a circular motion, his eyes closed. Now his father was a wanted fugitive. His heart was breaking for his Mother who would take this news very hard indeed. Just as he was sinking into a deep black mood, Chef Printise, followed by a breathless Miss Penny, swooped in to announce their newest culinary undertaking.

"Wake up Darling!" Printise crooned, "we are having a fabulous party and we need you. Ahhh, the little Darling has a little hangover? Someone said you almost drowned in the Persian water garden last night? Must learn to party with a bit more panache my Darling. We carried you in to sleep it off on the sofa. Really," clicking his tongue with disdain, "Quel dommage Darling. You are such a bebe."

Miss Penny hugged his shoulders and pulled him to standing. "We are having another spectacular event on the Portafortuna and your services are essential. Salvador too. I've had a meeting with Captain Oakley. We can pay you even more than before and guess what the theme will be? Just like last night at Val Verde we will have an Egyptian extravaganza. It will be called, 'Naughty Arabian Nights!' Oh I can just see it, up in the ballroom, little striped tents with all of Chef Printise's best dishes and leave it to me the entertainment will be mad. I can get the performers from El Paseo to dress in Persian Palace costumes. All they need to do is change a few songs and find some Egyptian instruments. We can get caftans and turbans for the crew. It will be another sell out."

"What do you say Darling?" Printise urged, sounding extra sugary. Paco was astonished. "They must not have read today's paper", he said to himself. 'What do I do now?' He felt cornered. 'Should I admit the Captain is my father? They would surely put two & two together once they read the name?' his mind was racing. 'And what about the threat to shut down the ship? Where they crazy?' Paco pointed at Owen still sitting with the paper and said, "Go and have a look at the article about the Portafortuna and then come back."

The two headed for the paper where they both finished reading at the same time and then dropped it on the table. Racing back to Paco with a distressingly cavalier disregard for the possible dire consequences, Penny demanded again with her pretty French accent, "Are you in or are you out? They would never attempt to attack a ship in the middle of an event filled with a thousand or more guests. Everyone who is anyone will be on-board? That would just be insane. This is an issue that will take months, maybe years to play out." She emphasized this opinion with her hands, palms up, motioning up and down then dropping them to her sides with a final flourish she implored, "You have to do it!"

Next Chef Printise started in. "And, my dear boy, just how well do you know this Captain Oakley who appears to have your very same name? Is this a mysterious relative of yours? Someone you've been stuffing under the carpet? Someone you wish would go away? He can't hurt you Darling. We would not let him. What is he anyway some old uncle? A cousin? What is the connection Paco?" With his head down, eyes focused on the tip of his boot, he whispered, "He's my Father".

Now he was filled with an intense anger that turned into a strange tender courage. Silently he made a commitment to confront the Captain in person and secure his promise to leave his Mother alone. Looking steadily into Miss Penny's brilliant golden brown eyes, he agreed to supply the event with anything they needed. Later as he rode the Indian home to confront his Mother he took dangerous chances racing toward dips in the road and skidding around a hairpin turn that was referred to by the locals as "suicide corner". The pain in his heart had moved on down to his stomach. He felt sickened by this mission to prepare Madonna for such an ominous future. Paco even pushed Ranger aside as he danced around the driveway in circles of welcome. Entering the kitchen where he knew he would find his Mother gracefully preparing the evening meal, he inhaled the nostalgic aromas of her celebrated cooking that was both classic Italian from her ancestors with touches of California style that turned the traditional into her signature cuisine.

He stood by the door just watching as she rolled out long strands of dough from mashed potato, butter, cream and a trace of mace with just enough flour to hold it together. He knew this recipe by heart and loved to help cut the small pieces and roll them on the trines of a fork making a large pile of gnocchi that would be tossed into the highly salted boiling water. They were removed as soon as they floated to the top. Paco crossed the kitchen and kissing his Mother softly on her warm rosy cheek he quietly took over and completed the job. With a giant slotted spoon he added the little pillows to a silky sorrel leek sauce that was waiting on the stove. Tonight the dinner began with this rich starter and after grating a generous coating of Madonna's favored Parmigiano-Reggiano from Montova with it's nutty salty top notes, he carried the large platter into the main dinning room serving the patron's family and guests with his impeccable manners, eyes crinkling at the corners while sharing his devastating smile that curiously connected with everyone heart to heart.

There was a fish course and the meat was fiery skillet fried veal chops with tomatoes, peppers and garlic. A lightly braised lettuce, fennel and olive dish followed. Finally, Paco brought out a doily lined silver platter mounded with Madonna's prized Cannoli and a sterling saucier filled with hazelnut spiked melted chocolate. He proceeded to clear and help clean the kitchen. All the while he felt the knot in his stomach. Wanting but dreading the right time to report the devastating developments, he practiced saying the words that now made Captain Oakley a dangerous criminal. Finally as he polished the big copper skillet, he just said it out loud. "They are going to send out the Coast Guard to stop the Portafortuna. There is an arrest warrant out for Captain Oakley. He is considered an outlaw. They will be coming to talk to us. We need to expect trouble."

Madonna's big eyes filled as she found the closest chair and began to weep. Paco

sat on the floor at her feet and mumbled over and over, "it's going to be alright,

it's going to be alright, it's going to be alright." But in his heart he could not

imagine any way it ever could be. Unprotected they would now be discovered

and could be associated with the Captain in crime or worse yet they would be

vulnerable now to the forces from the old country who pledged to have them

killed. For his Mother it was the final blow and meant she could never be with

her one great love. Deeply wounded now she began to speak.

"You don't know him Paco, and now you never will. He is kind and loving, an

artist just like you. He would never hurt a soul, never." Now this was

unacceptable for the young man who saw first hand what his Father was like and

it was far from kind, more like brutal. The only time they spoke he was violent.

"No, Mother", Paco said ferociously, "I'm hurt and you are hurt by him. I was

on the Portafortuna. I know what a gangster he really is. You would hate him if

you saw this. He makes a fortune from the gullible drunk people who engage in

all forms of debauchery. The ship is a floating den of depravity." Paco was now

even surprised at himself for such a fanatical outburst and he finished with a dark oath, "He is our enemy and I want him dead", whereupon Madonna

whaled even louder.

Chapter Ten: A Garden Studio and the Portafortuna Disaster

Exhausted by emotion Paco stood and charged out heading down to the estate's

rambling gardens with Ranger innocently excited to be on an evening walk. He

came across Oneda, the Japanese head gardener, who possessed some secret

power to convert everything in his sight, apparently transforming all to a higher

level of order. His black eyes were softened with a grey caste and appeared

limitless when his gaze locked onto another's. Now he had Paco in his sight. The anger vanished with a sudden burst of wind taking away the hatred too. As if stepping out of a nightmare he ambled gently with the old man discussing the different exotic plants and admiring the luminous creamy cactus flowers that only emerged at night.

Soon the crickets were playing. The underbrush squeaked and rustled when Ranger nosed too close. They came upon a dark green shed and Paco asked if it was in use explaining he needed a place to paint, a studio where he could work on his portfolio. Oneda nodded approval and they opened the door to see a long open space with one side all windows and the other side windowless. How perfect! He found stacks of smooth shingles that he would prepare with gesso and paint with his oils. There was even a row of windows on the ceiling that created a long narrow skylight so even at dusk there was enough illumination to work. Almost invisible, the Japanese gentleman stood aside resting on his tall staff and watched Paco brush off all the pieces of wood. Using old nails and the heel of a long forgotten boot he constructed a shelf that would act as an easel along the windowless wall. Time passed and darkness forced the two men out to walk silently through the moonlit paths to the house where the big collie bounded ahead to have his fill of water from an old algae clad tub that was continually filled by a tiny drip of the Fawcett above. Oneda held Paco's hands firmly as if blessing them and then bowing slightly left him with his spirit mystically revived.

Feeling helpless knowing his poor Mother lay inconsolable in her room, he made a quick call and stepped into the shower where he washed away the sins of his Father with some milky lavender soap, feeling his body slip by his big hands with a sensual rub down. He was soothing himself with the caresses he needed to mend. He dried and splashed Vetiver on his handsome chest. Tingling now, wonderful curls naturally arose and for once he left them alone to encircle his head like a Renaissance sculpture. The night was warm and he walked from the house in a pair of shorts, a shirt that he left unbuttoned, and hopped on the Indian barefooted. He rode only a short way down the road to the beginning of a very tall hedgerow and jumping off hid the bike in some low-layered foliage. He slipped through the bush to arrive on the green velvet lawns of Il Brolino, possibly the greatest estate of them all. The proud manor house loomed in the distance its brilliant architecture perfectly expressing Tuscan simplicity.

Paco raced toward the pool house passing an ancient marble well acting as a centerpiece for the partier style gardens that unfolded in tiered sections. One level was all roses while others were ornamented with perfectly shaped topiaries. He could see a giant sea horse and a dolphin. Moving on he arrived at the pool, glowing pale turquoise, disturbed only by small rivulets that came from a hand of the beautiful woman he knew so well now floating bare in the moonlight at the far end. Paco tossed his clothes on a chaise and joined her. She was dazzling in the rippling water her delicate rosy nipples rising up as he stroked her body. Then, drawing her into him, they were entwined and kissing deeply. The lovers languished in the shallow waters feasting on each other's silky wet skin. Slowly, savoring each moment, they were moving closer and closer to ecstasy.

The next morning Paco and Sal set about preparing the boxes of provisions for the party. The orders were placed for many of the exotic ingredients. They planned to make the deliveries to the ship in several trips. All along Paco scanned the news for warnings of an impending attack on the Portafortuna. One article caught his eye. There had been a sensational robbery of San Francisco's de Young Museum. The theft included a number of paintings by Manet that were on special exhibit and the two magnificent El Grecos, worth a fortune and considered the jewels of the institution's permanent collection. Some images of the pieces were pictured and the mystified guards were shown embarrassed and possibly implicated in the break-in. Something about this story rang a remote bell in Paco's mind. Was Ludington talking about the Manet exhibit? Was he saying I should study the style of this artist?

He began to concentrate on the work he needed to produce the portfolio for submission to the Accademia dell'Arte in Florence. He knew they would want to see his drawings of hands in many positions and drapery. He needed a live model and fabric to work with. Maybe the bronze skinned Rosalita with her big curvy body that always fascinated him. Her hands were so pleasing, he thought, as he remembered how nimble and esthetic they were when she performed her housekeeping duties. Just seeing her take down the laundry from the line, rhythmically folding each piece was a treat to him.

Now he was on fire with ideas and it carried him up and out of his fears to a new place where he felt happiness never experienced before. He could not wait to get home to his studio deep in the Quien Sabe gardens. There he brought all his materials and beautiful sable brushes that he cared for like babies, washing them in pure castile soap after each use, giving them perfect points with his mouth. They were standing in a chipped crystal vase to dry next to several white porcelain plates he used for palettes. Little mounds of each color circled a center where the delicate blending process took place. The paints were mixed to the right consistency with damar varnish, big crystals kept in a jar of thinner producing a powerful odor. Paco thought of the way Chef Velly created his magnificent sauces. He used this same careful regard for each nuance of color, using a trace of this and a touch of that, creating the hues and tints needed to forge an exquisite complexity. He experimented with the thin transparent layers of paint brushing one on top of another to make a new color of wondrous depth and quality. The overlays had an uncanny glow created by the millions of oil molecules, each transporting a tiny fleck of color that caught the light creating a singular eminence. Paco knew this was how the world's greatest Masters created the art of illusion and he ached to know their secrets.

It was the day of the huge event on the Portafortuna. All the orders were filled and delivered to the ship. Paco had been to Val Verde the night before showing Ludington some of his new work. They talked about the process of oil painting and how it varied so completely from watercolor. Generally, Ludington, who studied fine art and was a painter himself, approved the pieces. The discussion went on at length covering many areas of the basic process and color mixing.

Chef Printise appeared at the doorway off and on, growing more and more weary of all the attention now on Paco. Ludington's back was turned to the crazy antics that began to flow from Printise in the form of outrageous body language and hand signals. Paco was having a hard time pretending not to notice. This loony Chef, with white blond hair festooned out from a gold headband, big blue eyes heavy with make up, flaunted his gestures that mimicked Ludington's long-winded lecture. When all this failed to get some attention Printise just barged in and blurted out his request to have Paco and Salvador come to assist him cooking for the Portafortuna extravaganza and that is how early in the evening a fast skiff brought all four men to the boarding deck of the giant ship.

Paco was wearing a caftan over his clothes and a turban with a scarf across his face as he passed by the same two bouncers he recognized from the time they bodily threw him out. Sal also had a caftan and Printise wore a classic white Chef's jacket with his King Tut headdress. Completing the party, Ludington appeared as a proper British archeologist, sophisticated in khaki jodhpurs, boots, a fine tailored tan jacket with epaulets and an Ascott tie. He carried a pith helmet that had nearly blown off during the trip over a rather choppy channel. Chef Printise with Paco and Sal headed for the kitchen but Ludington mounted the grand staircase, climbing past the lower decks already crowded with players at the gaming tables for Black Jack and Craps. Poker tables filled one entire deck including a popular venue that offered sporting wagers with an elaborate mechanical horseracing track. He continued on to the top deck and the ballroom that now was turned into a fantasy Kasbah. Romantic striped Berber tents filled with fineries and mysteries were erected around the perimeter of the dance floor. The giant room was beginning to swell with excitement. Java Sir's entire caftan clad staff, tonight directed by the grand old Chef's noted assistant, Handeep Perupuran, called Handy, was gracefully attending to the guests, filling drink orders and beginning the food service that started with palm leaf lined baskets of candied fruits, stuffed dates and nuts. An odd assortment of musicians bearing a resemblance to the El Paseo Mariachi band began to play a sultry "Bolero" which seemed oddly appropriate. Ludington could see Miss Penny fluttering around in her steamy harem costume, layered with golden bangles, issuing demands softened by her song-like voice, sweetly drenched with honeyed French tones.

From behind a screen at the far end of the room, Captain Oakley, looking impressive in his deceptively authentic uniform that even sported a row of medals and bars of unknown origin. He walked directly to Ludington taking him aside and the two entered a small unused tent that was furnished with only an oriental carpet and large tasseled pillows for lounging. There was a low octagonal brass candlelit table in the center that the gentlemen now sat around cross-legged in native style. Rapidly they were served with a fine bottle of Macallan Whiskey and a silver bowl with ice. Two cut crystal tumblers were prepared and the men began to drink and talk about intense issues that were curiously common to both. First, surprising a nosey fly on the wall, was the subject of Paco. The Captain appeared ardently concerned about his wellbeing so Ludington took a long time describing the pathway to the art academy in Florence that the young artist now traveled and how really gifted he was considered. This pleased Oakley who lit a cigar and drew his head back, blowing a wispy train of smoke that drew attention to his remarkable profile.

"Anytime I can provide funds for him, anonymously of course, you have only to indicate a bank account and the money will be there", asserted the Captain.

"Sadly, it is all I can do to be a Father for him." Now Ludington nodded with some sympathy seeming to understand the complex set of circumstances that made his parenting impossible. " And how is Lillian? I am still not clear about your interest in her."

Ludington looked away with a distant view and said, "It isn't what you might think. No, not a love interest at all. As you possibly know, Printise and I have been together for some years now. No, I care for Lillian because she is the daughter of my Nanny Francis who was like a Mother to me. When I left for schooling she was given a pension and soon married an upstanding bank teller, Armand Hoover. They had Lillian who I have know throughout the years. Francis called when she was found missing and that is how I came to connect with you. Her family is enormously grateful for your rescue and her safe return to me. She is a very beautiful woman who now is deeply traumatized by her torture. She does not speak and lives a half-life, seldom even acknowledging her surroundings. We are committed to keep her whereabouts secret thinking it possible that her captors, the Tong syndicate undoubtedly, would want to steal her back." The Captain was nodding thoughtfully. "She occupies the tower suite in one of my guesthouses that we keep guarded and there is a young woman companion, the daughter of the steward from Il Fureidis, who comes each day. We are hoping that with time she will mend."

The Captain and Ludington shared even more and sipping the silky liquor became jovial. After a time the subject turned to art and collecting, something that engaged them intensely. The recent theft of many great pieces from the de Young in San Francisco came up. They speculated that it must be an inside job since the marketing of such spectacular paintings would be impossible. "So it was done for a private collector. If you run across any Manets that may need a home call me", said Ludington with a big smile. "I'll do it", promised Oakley. And with that he rose, shaking hands, then quickly leaving the tent he walked straight into Miss Penny who was delighted to hold onto him if only for a moment.

"Chef Printise and I will come by your cabin to collect our money whenever you like", she said, her lovely arms expressing the delicate issue of payment with a jingling of bangles. "I have a complete accounting all ready for you", she said, making it sound like something exceedingly pleasurable. Checking his watch he agreed to meet them at nine and so it was set. "Ta ta, see you then", Penny

danced in pretty circles for him as he walked away.

By now the huge ballroom was becoming crowded with guests. Most of the men

were in tuxedos but the women appeared clearly delighted to dress in theme.

"Naughty Arabian Nights" produced a profusion of exotic costumes seemingly

interpreted loosely since there were Chinese maidens in silk pajamas, Cleopatras

and Arabian dancing girls right along side elegantly coifed ladies in Grecian

togas. It was the spirit of the event that gained brilliance as Chef Printise

proudly presented his dishes, each carried by the Persian staff and placed on a

long palm leaf covered buffet table with grace. There was gaiety, ample

drinking, some dancing and plenty of gambling in the tents that offered all

forms of gaming.

Shortly after nine, as the night wore on and the food service was completing,

Paco took off the caftan and set his plan to confront the Captain in action. He

searched around the decks for him and then after some careful inquiries found

the corridor to his cabin. Paco calmed his fast beating heart and knocked on the

door. At first it was unresponsive but then opened wide and rough hands grabbed his shoulders pulling him into the lighted room as another black-garbed

man slammed the door behind him. Dazed by the treatment and brilliance of

the quarters he stood astonished as one from behind pulled his wrists to his back

and tied them harshly together. He could focus now on the others around him.

Captain Oakley was seated at his desk tied to the arms of his chair a binding

over his mouth that prevented his speech. His eyes told immediately how

fearful he was when he recognized his son as the new captive. Chef Printise, his

big muscular body now wrapped tightly with layers of red silk rope that covered

him from chest to knees, was crying softly into a blindfold that had become

blotched with big circles of mascara tinted tears over each eye and his mouth was

stuffed with a kerchief.

Looking around, Paco detected possibly five or six small men dressed in black

wearing strangely ornamented facemasks that only revealed an awesome

viciousness radiating from their eyes. Then, failing to see it before now because

of it's shocking specter, seated on a chair in the middle of the room, was the

bound, gagged and blindfolded Miss Penny, her sultry harem dress pulled aside

showing her fine shapely legs. Her bodice was ripped, the gold coins hanging in

strips, shamefully revealing one of her breasts. He saw a gun pointed directly at her head held by the leader who Paco inwardly identified from news photos of the Tong. In a sinister Chinese accent the man whispered, pinning his evil eyes on the young man. "What is your name?" Further threatening, "If you wish to see her undamaged you must answer swiftly".

Just as Paco began to speak there was the sound of sirens blaring with a loud speaker warning that caused the Tong leader to force him to the wall and there he was gaged with a binding over his mouth. Coming from somewhere outside, blaring from a Coast Guard loud speaker came a continuous demand for the passengers of the Portafortuna to carefully evacuate the ship. Alarms began to go off throughout the corridors and the thousands of guests on all three gaming decks began to panic. Those that could boarded many lifeboats that were filling up fast. A small fleet of water taxis that always hovered around the loading platform took on as many as possible and one large cargo ship was standing by to receive the fleeing guests. A multitude of searchlights were scanning the gambling ship now and the warnings continued over the speaker to evacuate with caution. This was coming from a large Government vessel moving in closer and closer to the Portafortuna.

Through the bedlam the Tongs forced the Captain, Printise, Paco and Miss Penny down to a tiny utility deck that connected to a fishing boat, bouncing on the water below, with a chain ladder. Each prisoner was handled by a gunman and the warning that Penny would be dead if they disobeyed commands kept them cooperating. The climb down was perilous but each one finally hit the deck hard. As the ship pulled away one of the Chinese lobbed a firebomb into the corridor behind the deck creating a brilliant orange explosion. Now Paco could see an awesome catastrophe from a vantage point that revealed the massive proportions of a tragedy unfolding. He was forced to sit while the captors chained him along with the others to a bench. It was clear now that they were leaving the channel, gaining power and heading for the open sea. As they continued on the vision of the Portafortuna now glowing red with flames was continually appearing smaller in the distance. Paco could not really see the condition of Miss Penny since she was still held tightly by one of the gunmen but he heard her whimpers along with Printise who was having a hard time breathing. The Captain, his ankles shackled to the bench, remained strangely composed even though in serious pain from the handcuffs that now made his hands white with lack of blood flow. Paco's mind was speeding through the many potential damages they may incur and all the ones who would think they drowned. What about his poor Madonna? Would anyone look for them? Where were they going anyway? Out to sea in this tiny boat?

Paco remembered a small detail but something important. When they were forced out of the Captain's cabin one man, maybe a crewmember was left behind. The leader struck him hard on the head and then stuffed an envelope into his jacket pocket. What was that? Were they being kidnapped for a ransom? And who would care to pay the demand? Maybe Ludington would do it to save Printise? No one I know of would care that much for me, he thought, and probably not for Penny either. The Captain seemed to be a worthless criminal to Paco. So why were they valuable? Thinking through all this he felt sick and dazed as he looked up to see the black outline of an enormous sail, a shape so huge he could not imagine anything that big at sea. It was also silent and surprisingly close. He recognized it now as monstrous Chinese junk and they were about to be forced aboard.

The morning after the great Portafortuna catastrophe was just a continuation of a horrible ordeal. Families seeking information about missing relatives and friends had the phone lines hopelessly jammed. An ugly debacle had erupted at the wharf. Small boats, still lined up to unload the last of the passengers and crew from the ship, were jammed with angry confrontations flaring. The Portafortuna was still afloat but damaged by the fire and without power was headed toward open waters followed by an odd assortment of small vessels attempting to salvage valuables. Only a portion of the lower deck was seriously harmed and parts of the engine were crippled. Now the eerie remnants of "Naughty Arabian Nights" rocked helplessly, along with the giant casino areas, chips and cards scattered, as the ship left the channel and entered the rugged Pacific Ocean. The last small ship carried some of the crew on a mission to find the most important papers and the contents of the ships safe from the Captain's quarters. There they found Carmino, Captain Oakley's first mate, unconscious with a bleeding gash to his head. They brought him with the valuables to the little boat waiting below and made their way to shore. Only hours later Madonna who sat desperate for news of Paco opened her screen door to find a strange gaunt man with a bandaged head covered by his hat that now appeared too small for his head. Carmino's large black eyes looked soft and weepy. He asked to come in explaining there was an important message that she must hear.

Once inside he sat down across from her and started in his heavy Italian accent, "First dear lady I must say that I believe your son and husband are both alive."

She exhaled with a little sigh. "We were in Captain Oakley's Cabin with the woman who planned our event and her Chef when the Fong Twins broke in and held us at gunpoint. They tied everyone up threatening to kill the lady. Suddenly your son entered the doorway where he was cuffed and gagged as well. We heard the sirens and a demand to evacuate the ship. That made the Chinese force everyone to leave, all but me who they hit in the head". He motioned to the wounded area with his hand holding it away not daring to even touch this still throbbing source of acute pain. "They left this note in my pocket."

He produced a wrinkled and stained paper that Madonna seized and read out loud. "The Captain and his associates are captives and the demand is for $100,000 to be paid in currency at a meeting that will be arranged in San Francisco. Contact our representative there immediately." She looked up bewildered. "Where is Paco now? How can we pay this? Is he hurt? Did they beat him too?"

Carmino, looking even more yellow and waxy by the minute, said he believed he was the only one injured, skipping over the dirty details of the abuse to Miss Penny. He was using all his strength now to bring this message, pleading with her not to worry about the money and the negotiations for release. He absolutely pronounced, as if relaying a verbal pledge from a higher authority, that the Captain's Syndicate was handling all this. "They will return lady, you can be assured. We are very powerful and the Fong twins, who have your loved ones, know we can kill them off anytime we need to." Standing to leave with Madonna, huge beautiful eyes glassy, following him to the door, he turned with a fierce warning. "Please lady do not tell anyone about this. If you do the boy and his father may die." And then summoning the last of his energy he delivered a similar message to Ludington at Val Verde.

Down town at Diehls it was Salvador who, surviving it all, stood describing the disaster from his soda fountain now crowded around like a pulpit with many craving news. Oren Starr was there, breathless from racing to see if the paper had arrived. It was late coming but finally came. He grabbed a copy and saw that the entire issue was filled with pictures and stories. One headline read, "Six dead, hundreds injured and missing." The Governor was being pressed for answers as to why this horrendous event was clearly caused by the Coast Guard's unreasonable demand for immediate evacuation. Another story told of the overwhelmed St. Francis Hospital that had never cared for an emergency of this size since the earthquake and that some patients were taken to facilities in Los Angeles. Further eye-witness reports detailed the moments when a small party of Government agents with a photographer appeared in the casino and began, axes in hand, chopping down the big roulette wheel and several crap tables, then smashed all the liquor in a the big bar, all with flash bulbs blazing, then left.

Oren walked over to Sal and grabbing his hands begged him to remember if he saw Penny and if she was able to get into a boat. He was hanging onto any little shed of information that might help his search for her. With a disappointing negative shake of his head Sal described how he did see her earlier in the evening during the banquet and the last he remembered she and Chef Printice were going to the Captain's office to get the money for all the services. "She promised to pass out our pay but then I never saw her again." Oren now knew where he might begin his inquiries. He was off to call Ludington who must also be searching for Printise.

Meanwhile, sitting at the Cima Del Mundo kitchen table piled with recipes and cook books, Mama Genet and Fayola, crisp as always in their starched pink and brown uniforms, argued gently over the exact composition of the dishes they intended to present for the Medallion d'Oro Culinary competition coming up at the Biltmore in only two weeks. The Fish platter was settled since Mama's version of "Truite Pontchatrain" was her signature dish of perfectly crusted trout with crabmeat sautéed in brown butter and secret spices. This would be served with four mandatory side dishes including her beloved Pommes de Terre Soufflés, the large puffed balls of deep fried whipped potatoes, crunchy outside and an inside that literally melted in the mouth, a verdant creamed spinach, a savory cooked slaw with just the right balance of piquant flavors and her delicious little cakes made from grits and cheese formed into shell shapes using madeleine tins. Mama and Fayola felt confident they would win with this but the meat platter was worrisome. The women knew that their competition would be highly skilled with fowl also the beef and lamb entrées would be hard to beat.

They poured over the options like Antoine's "Poulet Rochambeau" a deep chocolate brown roux laden breast of hen stuffed with sliver's of Virginia ham or the choice center cuts of lamb chops grilled and finally brushed with thick mint jelly but these may be to common for the event. They thought of the popular tips de filet of beef en brochette with the Marchand Sauce or maybe just a steak with a Demi-Bordelaise? All this sounded too ordinary to be a winner. With the two cook's noses buried in recipes, Latrice ambled by, carrying six cans of sweetened condensed milk, surly on her way to the thick wall of supplies that lined her room, and said, "Why don't ch'all make the Chateaubriand with them skinny fried potatoes and the three sauces, Marchand, Bernaise and Bordelaise, then do some caramel carrots and the duchess peas with a braised celery in remoulade?

And in another corner of Montecito, ferociously fussing over lists and meticulously hand printed outlines with charming little drawings of his two platter entries planned for the competition, stood Chef Wilfredo Henriques of Piranhust, known as Fredo, index finger tweaking his ample nose, eyes unfocused in deep thought. His latest version of the fish course featured a fancy carved and dressed marinated herring in the center, an Austrian classic, surrounded by lovely round towers of sour apple compote, white bean soufflé, pickled baby vegetables and a floret of hard boiled egg segments decorated with tiny violets. 'It does look gorgeous' he thought, first romancing the idea, then having a huge argument with himself, 'you are such an imbecile, the eggs look like a farmer's breakfast. You are never, never going to win with that one'. Then talking back to himself in his native language an elegant German, 'that is a perfect compliment to the herring! What else would you put there?' Then countering himself with, 'this is just not working. This is trash, manure, you need to start all over'. And the mental wrangling went on for hours hitting a crescendo over the Sautéed Calves Livers wrapped in very thin streaky bacon accompanied by truffled champignons as opposed to the venison with rowan berries and chestnut pears for the meat selection. Finally slapping himself briskly on the cheeks he ran to the sink and removing his tall toc put his entire head under the cold water.

During that week other contenders for the coveted honor to compete in Paris among the greatest Chefs in America were working out their dishes. Chef Pulga, Lolita Armour's darling little dragon in his fine El Mirador kitchen, paced pompously back and forth in front of a captive staff dictating his ideas that were copied down word for word, an exercise that caused great confusion later when the notes were read back. Half Spanish, half English as was the Chef's habit, when written out made no sense at all. Infuriated by this painful reality Pulga ran toward the closest cook and stomped hard on his foot causing a fast brutal scuffle that ended with both men running outside disappearing into the enormous estate gardens. It would take Chef Victore, now heading the line at the Montecito Inn, who graciously agreed to assist Pulga at the Biltmore, to sort out the plans and recipes for each platter.

The highly acclaimed Phillbert Omeyer, loveable Chef Bertie, now years past retirement age, hired to open the Santa Barbara Biltmore, would be a favorite going into the event. Spies, when sent from several competitors' kitchens, were appalled to discover no menus at all. Their mission was unsuccessful simply because the old Chef just planned to get up and search the markets early the day he intended to cook, then prepare what came to him naturally, and that is exactly why he was so great.

Also imagining his platters for the competition was Chef De Vielmond, called Velly, who stood working with a large slab of beef, beautifully butchering the meat with his favorite skinning knife and occasionally bringing out the saw or massive cleaver to expertly cut the desired sections apart. This was a skill he mastered as a boy in the kitchens of his Father's legendary Parisian restaurant, "L'Essence". He had been forced to leave France when his older brother, who took over after his Father died, found out that there was a secret romance raging under his nose. Velly and the bodacious Elodie where found together in a pantry and a horrendous battle royal broke out between the brothers. They fought, seemingly to the death, with their butcher's knives leaving scars that would last a lifetime. The hatred was so deep it transcended the indiscretions of a lover and evidently exposed the deeper wound. All through his life Velly was the gifted one, the one who amazed with his culinary capabilities and the one who was most beloved by the Father.

Loosing the deadly conflict, bleeding from several wounds about his head, face and chest, Velly was hidden for some time by friends and then secreted out of the country to America where he began his distinguished career in the kitchen of Master Chef de cuisine, Maurice La Mer, who was sent to open the New York version of Maxims' de Paris. When some years later members of the famed Russian Imperial Ballet fled to America from the Bolshevik Revolution and set up The Russian Tea Room, it was Velly, now Master Chef De Vielmond, who was selected to head the line. He became a sensation for his sublime dishes and a kind of bon vivant with a wild nightlife in the company of dancers and artists who taught him many things especially the art of drinking massive quantities of vodka. A short time later spent from excess he was hired by the millionaire tycoon Edwin Ballingford and brought him out to California to his newly

acquired Montecito estate, Il Brolino. There, with all the pleasure of creating

his best work yet, he healed. His fine tanned olive skin began to glow. A new

happiness enhanced Velly's noble face. He was charismatic now, his fascinating

darkest brown eyes danced with excitement over any subject that might delight

him at the moment. For Paco his spirit was irresistible and living at the Quien

Sabe Ranch just up the road, he spent as much time as he could watching him

work, taking in the rapture of cooking as art.

This morning, sitting on a stool at the end of the kitchen in a floating negligée

was Charmaine the devastatingly beautiful twenty six year old blond wife of the

aging Ballingford, Baron of Il Brolino. Little whimpers and sobs punctuated her

reactions to Velly's chopping as she tried again to make a call to Diehls and

connect with Paco who now was on the formal list of missing from the

Portafortuna disaster along with Miss Penny, Printise and many others.

"He's not there Velly", she swooned, "Could he be in Los Angeles? Maybe in a

hospital down there with bandages over his face", she fanaticized, "maybe he

can't speak? No one would know who he is? Do you think Salvador will go down and check?" Velly looked at her bewildered and bit his lip with head down, the large scar that marred the left side of his face turning red. Pulling out his largest cleaver and making a ferocious chop at the carcass, he was sick with worry but carried on, insides now fully exposed. Flouncing out dissatisfied with his response she announced in a stubborn tone, "If the Master comes home, tell him I went to Los Angeles to visit my Mother. I'm calling the chauffeur and going to find Paco myself." Storming out the front door and looking up Charmaine saw her husband's car pulling in and fearing trouble cancelled her plans but secretly carried her yearning to verify Paco's wellbeing deep in her heart.

Chapter Eleven: The Mio Cuore and Paco discovers his Family

The giant Chinese junk, decks swaying from a challenging voyage against the current from Santa Barbara to it's destination in San Francisco Harbor, accommodated the captives in quarters on a lower deck, guarded twenty-four hours a day. The Tong had created tiny wooden cubicles to imprison those who were taken for the white slave trade, enemies awaiting punishment or, as in this case, valuable prisoners held for ransom. Each space had only a woven pallet on the floor and a fowl smelling whole in one corner that was a toilet. When they first arrived the guards removed their clothes, dowsed them with an odd smelling vinegary water solution then roughly drying them off dressed them in kimonos and locked them in the cells finally un-cuffed. Penny was afforded special treatment being tended by two homely women who provided some privacy from a large black silk sheet ornamented with an intricately stitched blood red dragon. She actually appeared unhurt and even defiant supported by an inner strength rightfully earned suffering the heinous abuse from her still legal husband.

The dark quarters were misty with smoke from numerous sticks of incense that the attendants continually replenished. This together with the shock and pain of his ordeal made Printise vomit often down the whole in his cage. He was clearly the worst for wear suffering chills and sweats secretly caused by withdrawals from probably a number of drugs that normally kept him going. The Captain was treated strangely different with a brusque but begrudging display of respect. He and Printise were far too hefty for the space and almost filled the little cell. Paco, in good condition, except for the raw wrists bruised and skinned by the cuffs, like the others, cooperated lest the captors follow out their threat to punish Penny. He appeared sullen, almost outwardly angry, a myriad of worries and questions passing through his mind as he sat cramped on the pallet.

The cages were set up in rows on both sides of the long space and some held other captives. Paco could see Printise across and down a bit but his Father and Penny were on the same side with him. They could talk but when they did it caused the guards to rise up with menacing gestures. After a time one of the women prepared noodles and tea on a tiny charcoal burner, slowly serving each prisoner in small paper cups, no utensils. After rocking and little sleeping for what seemed like hours the door opened and two intense Chinese men walked to the cage where Captain Oakley was kept. They were identical in every detail including their arrogant expressions. The Fong twins were viciously good-looking with fine aristocratic Asian features talking through aesthetically defined lips that were both sensual and sinister. They came to notify Oakley that the ransom had been paid and when the ship docked there would be a party waiting to take them, as it was described, to his most glorious Father, the Honored Don Signore Telchide Fazinatos. The change in treatment was astounding and all four of them stood up with surprise and elation. 'They would be freed', thought Paco, but he was dumbfounded with the additional

news that he had a Grandfather?

Their clothing had been carefully washed and folded in neat little packages tied

with black silk twine. Even Miss Penny's harem dress was repaired and the

bangles sewn back in place. As they alighted from the gangplank onto the dock

there was a Chauffeur in classic navy blue livery standing in front of an

enormous tan and black Pierce-Arrow Touring car. Behind that was a similar

dark green sedan with four burly men in caps and long overcoats hovering

nearby possibly hiding their firearms? They all acknowledged the Captain

immediately with esteem more than courtesy, the Chauffeur even sporting a

snappy salute. They boarded the luxurious auto putting Paco, Penny and

Printise in the back and Oakley taking the front seat next to the driver. The

engine was so loud they could barely converse. All the questions would need to

wait for the time when they reached some destination unknown to the back seat

passengers.

They drove through the city from the docks, over the newly constructed Bay

Bridge, and then into the wooded countryside, heading north. After a time they pulled off the main road and traveled for many miles finally coming to large lacy

iron gates with a red brick guard station topped by an elaborate roof in the

center. Several armed men stepped out of the foliage on either side and came up

to the cars for inspection. Upon recognizing Captain Oakley they also saluted

and to Paco's amazement one said, "Welcome home Boss".

They were driving on the estate grounds now and Miss Penny along with

Printise could only roll their eyes and stare intermittently at Paco with disbelief.

The most surprised of all was Paco himself as he passed some of the most

magnificent landscape imaginable. There were verdant wooded enclaves, an

Italianate columned gazebo, oriental water gardens with a pagoda peeking above

the foliage, at one point a small Ferris Wheel and possibly a merry-go-round,

formal gardens on one side of the road and across the way, shining in the

distance, the mirror like surface of a lake, an ornamental barge, decks outlined in

fancy iron balustrades, floating in the center. The approach to the old Don's

manor house was jaw dropping. The light, fading now as evening approached,

made the stately avenue of tall pointed blue-green Cyprus trees cast a remarkable

row of shadows on the manicured lawns. Closer to the entrance a large stone

surfaced driveway began, the perimeter planted in hedges enhanced by large terra cotta pots bearing small orange trees laden with fruit. This ended in a circle that had a carved stone fountain now bubbling with a nice water display. The building itself occupied an immense horizontal frontage with a two story segment in the center then continuing in a balanced design with single story segments and two story tower-like structures on either end. The architectural styling was definitely Italian Palazzo inspired, stately and stern with a soft ochre surface and many glossy black louvered shutters on the many carefully aligned windows.

Pulling up to the main portal the Captain alighted first and opened the door for Printise then helped Miss Penny out. Paco, leaving from the far side, followed the other three into the doors now opened by a butler with other domestics standing there visually happy to see Oakley alive. The floor of the entry hall was a striking harlequin patterned black and beige marble with a grand staircase in the Renaissance style, starting at the far right and turning to cross the space along the back wall then turning again to the second story on the left. The ceiling was domed with a remarkable painted sky element and polychromed architectural supports topped with a beautifully carved and gilded geometric icon from which suspended the Venetian glass fixture, really a fantasy art piece.

The walls were covered with oil paintings of the finest quality by European Masters in handsome gilded frames. This attracted Paco immediately. The entire impression so far was that someone with a brilliant knowledge of art and architecture had created a masterpiece.

Captain Oakley directed the staff to help Miss Penny and the weakened Printise to their rooms that appeared to be upstairs in the wing to the right and then with utter seriousness he motioned for Paco to follow him down the corridor to the left saying, "Come, we have things to discuss". The young man was so dazed and perplexed by all that had unfolded he obeyed without question. They walked along a wide hallway with gallery walls displaying portraiture that Paco would later learn portrayed many of his Italian ancestors. Opening one of the doors they entered the library, a dark wood paneled room with shelves of finely bound volumes and glowing glass show cases containing weapons and small sculptures even antique jewelry including curios from several centuries. Again there were paintings but here they were by modern artists. Paco recognized a Matisse and large de Chirico, even a bold black and yellow Leger picturing machinery with figures in an industrial landscape. He marveled at how it tricked the eye using a dramatic delineated vanishing point. The floor was parquet in a unique dimensional lattice pattern with several fine Persian carpets. The

Captain walked around his ornate desk embellished with ormolu on curved

cabriole legs. He motioned for Paco to take a seat across from him.

Standing, head down seemingly in shame, he began. "When your Mother and I

married we were so deeply in love we ran away one weekend and secretly found a

Justice for the ceremony then returned to our homes thinking we just needed a

little time to become independent and begin our life together. Not long after

this you were conceived and our plight became urgent. At this very moment my

Mother, your Grandmother died and when this news reached Don Fazinatos,

who thought he was my Father, I was abducted. He brought me here thinking

he would at last have his son to partner with, an idea that my Mother strongly

resisted through the years. He intended to teach me the business of the family,

the operations of the syndicate that was at that time in a desperate battle with

rival factions for ownership of territory and assets."

Oakley sat down now and continued, his intelligent blue eyes meeting Pacos

bewildered brown ones with a tender sensitivity. "Once I saw the sinister power

and wealth of this organization it was apparent that I could not bring my beautiful Madonna or you into this life. At that time there were dark

transactions and blatant criminal activities operating within the vast American

association even including factions of 'The Black Hand'. I never told the Don

about my marriage or my son to keep you both safe. I have thought about you

and prayed you were well every day of my life." He shook his head in despair

eyes now watery. "I wanted so much to see you grow and secretly I attended

some of your Birthday picnics in the park. As time went on I served the Don,

traveling back and forth to ports throughout Europe and Italy establishing a

network of import and export activities that multiplied our holdings and wealth

beyond imagination. There are continual competitors to deal with like the Fong

Twins and old enemies who are always dangerous adversaries but now our

operations are ethical without any involvement in the drug trade. Ethical, that is

excluding some gambling and the issue of Prohibition", he added with disdain.

The Captain finished with a plea, "All I can do is tell you how much it grieves

me to be apart from you and your Mother and to simply ask for your

forgiveness. I know it must be so painful for you too. The Don, your

Grandfather knows all about you now. I told him as soon as I knew I could trust

him never to interfere. He is almost 100 years old and very weak. We do not

think he has much time left. It would be an enormous thrill for him to meet you

and see us together as Father and Son. I don't want to force you. Take some time to think this over and just know I will always love you as I love my precious

Madonna. And now you must call her and let her know you are safe." With

that he dialed the phone and waiting for a voice he handed the receiver to Paco

who stammered still in shock, "Mama, Mama I am safe".

After an emotional conversation and passing the phone to the Captain, he said,

"She wishes to talk to you". They were speaking in Italian that Paco only

partially understood so he began to scan the objects in the cases. On several

shelves there were collections of antique rosaries, some with jeweled crosses,

rubies, emeralds and diamonds, but others were decorated with hand painted

miniatures of the Saints or an intricately detailed Madonna with Child. Further

on he found a case with Roman pottery. Each piece had a natural glossy surface

in colors from light orange to a bright red. Some were detailed with dancers or

warriors in a delicate raised relief. Paco was attracted by an antique Italian

prayer book bound in fine black leather delicately embossed with gilded scrolls

and gold edged pages. There was a pressed rose lying to one side and next to it he

saw a small picture of a beautiful dark woman framed in gold on a tiny easel.

The Captain rose finishing his call with, "I'll talk to Ludington right away". He walked over to Paco and gently placing an arm over his shoulder, noticing what had captured his son's attention, he said in his deep voice softly touched by an inherited Sicilian accent, "That is Innocenza, my Mother, your Grandmother. Now let us get you to your room to wash and rest before dinner."

The idea that Oakley knew Ludington weighed heavily on the young man's mind but he said nothing as he followed upstairs past a number of carved doors to one opened by the Captain who beckoned him inside. The room was painted soft grey with glossy white woodwork. Set into the paneling Paco marveled at a series of Venetian landscapes looking to be authentic pieces by Canaletto, considered among the greatest scenic painters ever known. A big bed had an Upholstered headboard in flaxen brocade that matched a long bench at the foot. Bed linens were bright white with a tailored grey embroidered trim. The chamber was masculine and so serene that as the Captain closed the door behind him, Paco dove into the silky sheets and passed out.

Several hours later he awoke to hear a round cheery woman asking him to rise and come to his bath. It was all in Italian so he needed to think it over. Looking up he watched her, crisp in a grey maid's uniform with a white apron and lacy little coronet over her shiny black hair pulled back in a neat bun. She motioned at him and he followed. Walking into the sizable white tiled bathroom that he found warm, moist and fragrant from a huge iron tub filled with suds, he removed his clothes to lower himself into the soothing water. There was a silver handled shaving set laid out for him and he noticed a full suit of clothing on the chaise. Clean, refreshed with his hair carefully slicked back, he emerged from his room dangerously good-looking in a splendid tuxedo and velvet slippers.

Finding his way to the central landing, hearing voices from the corridor ahead Paco found Miss Penny and Printise likewise dressed in stunning formal attire giggling over some shared caprice. They all embraced and ushered by the Butler down on the main floor they entered a long dinning room. Like the entire mansion the style was lavish but at the same time spare. The ceiling was very tall and three lacy Venetian glass chandeliers hung over the long table from an ornamented coffered baldachin. The walls were pale sienna maybe even silk with a row of giant mirrors in plain gold frames on one wall reflecting the breathtaking light fixtures, creating an unforgettable illusion. Arched doors on the other wall hinted at the amazing view of the gardens now too dark to see. At the far end, featured with soft light, was an enormous oil painting of a group, mostly over plumped women, elaborately costumed, one feeding a parrot, in a wild Italian garden dining alfresco. Paco's eyes landed on a beautifully painted pet monkey in a velvet suit playing with a string of pearls. He recognized the style from his recent studies in Art history and the huge canvas looked like it was painted by the Master Peter Paul Rubens. 'How could this be here', he thought, overwhelmed by the quality of the priceless pieces throughout the mansion. He was hopelessly dazzled now, really almost speechless. They were seated toward the far end in upholstered chairs of rust and cream stripe satin awaiting the head of the table who appeared, bowing slightly, taking his proper place. Captain Oakley, regal in his evening dress that was vaguely military in cut but all black, even his silk shirt and tie, was so impressive. His hair, perfectly in style, was slicked back accentuating his classical Roman features only made more handsome by the character lines forged from his years of dangerous engagements.

"I have contacted Mr. Ludington, I believe Printise, you spoke with him as well? He will arrive some time tomorrow to take you back to Montecito so for now please, let us enjoy the evening and in the morning I will give you a tour of the estate. It's called 'Mio Cuore' and was created by Don Fasinatos many years ago when he fled from Italy. As a young man he was an instructor in The Accademia di Belle Arti in Firenze and sat as a Director of the Uffizi. Over time he brought architects and artisans from Florence to do the work. The Don himself with my help has amassed the collections of paintings and sculpture that you will see. He still retains a passionate love for this endeavor that he has passed on to me." Then turning to Paco with a nod he continued, "I believe my son has inherited this obsession for the arts naturally?"

"Instructor at the Academia?" Paco murmured, his fork clattering as it dropped on the plate and his startled eyes now enormous. Miss Penny was bubbling over in French, raving about the sublime style of the mansion and it's contents, whereupon Printise added his superlatives to make a little chorus of overwhelming approval that surpassed highest praise.

Chapter 12: Madonna's Surprise and the Practice Dinner

The dining experience in the great mansion at Mio Cuore began to unfold with

a delicate little puff pastry turban filled with asparagus tips, served in a scant

pool of tart lemon sauce. The wine was a perfectly crisp Orvietto and only

served to assure the guests they were about to be entertained by an elite

epicurean. Next came a seared lobster tail on an avocado fan and spicy orange sauce. The conversation centered around the amazing collections of art that would be on a promised after dinner tour. Paco was urgently curious to know more about the old Don, so long hidden, and his connection to the Academia. He began to question then follow the story as Captain Oakley calmly revealed a man of enormous complexity. A first course of artfully crafted ravioli filled with sea bass and wild fennel in guazzetto jus splashed with Bruno Giacosa sent Chef Printise into orbit, actually rising from his chair to do a quick tango of ecstasy, kissing his fingers all the while. Then finally back in his seat, the Captain described Don Fazinatos' beginnings in Sicily and his brilliance early on as a writer and an artist, talents that would take him to Florence, first to study at the Instituto Superiore di Belle Arti in Florence then to apprentice in the studio of his teacher Telemaco Signorini, an artist credited in Italy with transforming neo-classical painting and the academic portrait into a new poetical interpretation of natural landscape, much like the Barbazon School in France. As a forerunner of the impressionists, he loved to paint outdoors and that is how the Don met Filippo Mazzei. As the Captain described it, Fazinatos was out on the grounds of Mazzei's Villa Mangiacane with his easel set up when suddenly a pack of ferocious mastiffs came toward him with savage intentions. Saved by their Master on horseback, the two began a friendship that would last many years and bring the old Don to America when he was forced to escape.

The fine dining continued throughout the fascinating saga of the Don.

Presented next, the main course, was a marinated lamb chop; sautéed baby

artichokes served Venetian stylewith polenta and bottles of a light fruity

Sangiovese.

Noteworthy was the masterly way Italians rely chiefly on the quality of the

ingredients rather than on elaborate preparation and these dishes were pure

examples of this art. Paco, with big innocent eyes, finally asked the question that

seemed to be hanging in the air. "Why did Don Fazinatos have to escape from

Italy? What did he do?" adding in case he had gone too far, "If that is not too

difficult to explain?" Oakley appeared almost pleased that his son expressed an

interest so he continued with more of the old Don's life story.

"The reason for his rapid departure from Florence was political. He was living

at the Villa Mangiacane and had become part of an anti-fascist movement that

his benefactor now, Fillipo Mazzei, had helped to shape. The estate was historic

for being the home of Machiavelli and the place where he wrote 'The Prince', an infamous piece of literature professing a militant leadership style that demanded love but depended on fear. Later generations continued this serious commitment to philosophical exploration but flourished in a different direction. The passion for governance evolved down to the Mazzei family who produced a movement that was dedicated to curb or end the brutal atrocities committed by the powerful tyrants then griping Florence and most of Italy. The philosophers of the enlightenment and especially Fillipo's legendary great uncle inspired the young men of the new movement. This ancestor spent years in Virginia at Monticello where he was invited to bring the famous winemaking skills his region was known for. There he became involved with the unfolding of The American Revolution and a friend of Thomas Jefferson. Over a hundred years later this connection with Fillipo's great Uncle Mazzei was still active, the Mazzei family still owned several farms near Charlottesville, so when the fascists where about to arrest Don Fazinatos and Fillipo Mazzei a speedy method was devised to send them to America and a safe refuge in Virginia."

Paco thought the story remarkable and the dinner rich. What came next brought the entire experience to a new level of satisfaction. A sublime cheese tray, the giant plateau presenting a collection described below, all set out on big fresh grape leaves. The assortment included; a special blue cheese from sheep's milk produced in Maremma, a little masterpiece Castello de' Pecorari Pecorino seasoned on planks of wood with twigs of Summer Savory, natural Gorgonzola made from a double milking, mature and sharp Montasio from Friuli region served with garlic aubergines in olive oil, traditional Taleggio cheese from Taleggio Valley, Castel Magno from the Alps in the region of Cuneo matured from 4 to 8 months, served with red currant jam, and assorted goat cheeses served with dry tomatoes on quince jam. All this sent Printise off into delirium again along with Penny and Paco who also understood the rarity of this glorious collection providing some of the most esoteric products Italy had to offer.

Iced parfait with raspberries, Limoncello liqueur and espresso followed while Captain Oakley finished the chronicle of the old Don's audacious lifetime. He recounted the strange yet miraculous series of events and connections that allowed Fazinatos to manifest his dreams. Always in the wine business with his friend Fillipo they learned of the natural climate for vineyards and the cheap cost of land in California so ending up in regions north and south of San Francisco they purchased hundreds of acres of land and began the development of imported varietals. Along with the viticulture they discovered pristine spring waters and distilled excellent quality whiskey, ale and gin.

To market the bonanza their operations produced, they began to rely on the American Mafia as a distribution channel. Soon thereafter a twisted series of circumstances generated both tremendous pain and great pleasure. With sadness clouding his handsome features Oakley told of the bomb blast that killed the old Don's wife and three daughters in a hotel in San Francisco as an act of retribution by his enemies. He grazed by the wars that waged over domination of the syndicate and lightened when he spoke of the joys the old man experienced creating his spectacular Mio Cuore, the dazzling estate that had everyone enchanted that evening.

Chef Printise was so fulfilled with the culinary talent he asked to meet the Chef, whereupon the Captain, smiling, pressed a secret buzzer on the floor, whispered a request in the waiter's ear and out rolled four middle aged women wearing black dresses, each one had the little flower printed aprons of a proper Italian Mama. Dark and deeply tanned they now blushed red from the kitchen heat and embarrassment. The dinner guests murmured, "Bravo, bravo", finishing with applause. Just at that moment, the Butler announced the arrival of Carmino and only seconds later the big man walked in toward Oakley, bowing to the others, still showing his head wrapped with a bandage now holding his cap. He greeted the Captain with double kisses obviously glad to see him alive then bowed to the others.

It was Carmino who bravely delivered the messages to Madonna and Ludington and working desperately negotiated the ransom with the Fong Twins. Looking intense now Captain Oakley asked everyone to follow as he led them away through the glorious entry with the stunning harlequin marble floor into the large corridor of portraits and to his office door where he asked Carmino to enter then escorted Paco, Penny and Printise to the double doors ahead revealing, as they opened, an enormous ballroom featuring gallery walls with many great pieces of art. There he left the three to investigate. Returning to Carmino the Captain outlined his plans for retaliation against the Fongs knowing their incredulous act, the very idea they would dare to kidnap Oakley could not go unpunished for fear it would display weakness. He said nothing would satisfy him except the capture of the twins and a doubling of the demand for money. Then as Carmino left with a salute the Captain added, "Also state that the paintings recently taken from the de Young Museum must be returned before any negotiations can start", thinking to himself, 'that will save us the trouble of finding them ourselves'.

The huge room was done in a combination of pale and dark bronze silk drapery on arched doors along the right side opening out onto the terrace and silk lined walls covered with paintings on the left side. There were more magnificent Venetian crystal chandeliers hanging from ornamented coffered ceilings and a parquet dance floor inlaid with an intricate star design. Fine upholstered settees and chairs around small game tables were scattered throughout the room. The paintings held Paco's attention. 'This could be the most spectacular collection of Impressionist work ever brought together', he thought. Displayed as a group this body of work expressed a fresh new style considered by experts to be a result of the development of photography. The artists now had freedom to interpret the world in a subjective way and this moment captivated the young artist, opening a door in his mind never to be closed. His eyes caressed the many

Monets and Renoirs, stopping to memorized his favorites by Degas. There were

more, artists he had never heard of, some wonderful pieces that were unsigned.

While Penny and Printise danced up and down behind him, he floated

immersed in the excitement forged by pure inspiration.

Presently Captain Oakley entered and assuming they were as exhausted by the

day as he was suggested they get a nights rest since he would like to show them

the gardens, the lake, the winery, his dogs and the horses. He finished with,

"There is much much more and Ludington will be here to take you home

tomorrow." With that Printise heaved a sigh and Penny was elated. Paco's

mind was still lingering over the pictures he loved so profoundly. When Oakley

asked, "Did you decide to meet your Grandfather? If you will I need to prepare

him. Maybe sometime after breakfast?" Paco looked vacant then with

acceptance he nodded yes, eyes thoughtful, concentrating on his Father's face

that quickly brightened.

Meanwhile in a barn on a remote part of the estate grounds, guarded night and

day, two metal chairs, each with a whole in the seat and steel restraints, sat the

Fong Twins, fed on a diet of noodles and tea waiting for a $200,000 ransom to be paid. In a little office just off the main space, Carmino sat at his big desk filled with spiked paper holders, the receiver from one of several telephones in his hand. His head was aching from the vicious blow he suffered from the very men who sat chained up and he had some small satisfaction as he watched them through a big window. Their black silk Tang warrior uniforms with the tightfitting red dragon emblazoned helmets had been removed and they now wore the common shirts and pants of the gardeners. They had long pigtails bound up with tiny gold cords but instead of looking anxious or uncomfortable they appeared to be deep in meditation, head bent slightly with eyes closed. This fact irritated Carmino as he made final arrangements for the trade off settlement. He spoke with the Chinese on the other end of the line in Italian reverting often to English, continually needing to ask for "ripetere, ripetere!" All along heavily armed men were coming and going, picking up orders and leaving to load up the barrels or cases of wine and liquor the syndicate's customers requested. Truck after truck continued heading out to deliveries throughout the western states that marked the Don's territory. This was the heartbeat of the "Aroncioni", the operations that inflated by Prohibition brought multi-millions back to Mio Cuore.

Paco had spent the night sleeping fitfully, having a fever dream, waking between haunting segments filled with images and snippets of the many experiences he had recently endured. There was a fire but it was the monstrous Chinese junk burning not the Portafortuna and he became the old Don studying art in Florence, fleeing to America. One sequence began pleasuring him beyond imagination. He was dancing with Charmaine in the ballroom when all the doors on one side with drapery flowing out from the wind opened to a terrace with a pool like Il Brolino, glistening in the moonlight. They moved slowly toward the water and all the while he was removing her clothing. He carried her to a soft grassy knoll. Pulling her arms behind her back he gently kissed and bound her wrists, covering her eyes with silk wrappings. She was smiling; delighted with his sensual game when suddenly he saw her crumple to the ground weeping. Then rapidly removing the bindings he drew back as he saw it was his Mother and he realized he had become the Captain, his Father. Reaching down gathering his wife up in his arms, he comforted her, pledging to love her and care for her always, whereupon he looked closely and saw the woman was Lillian. He woke from this dream without any remembrance at all.

The same little lady woke him in the morning with a jolly attitude, pulling him to standing, massaging him briefly then ushering him into the same blissful bath leaving him to play with the suds like a child. He understood enough of her conversation to know he was wanted in the dinning room for breakfast so he hurried to shave. He found his clothes freshly washed and pressed to perfection, his fine tan boots were polished, his leather jacket arranged on the back of the chaise. Comfortably dressed he walked slowly to the stairway studying each painting he passed carefully. Paco wanted to remember every piece and be able to savor the details in his mind's eye whenever he wished it. As he passed large double doors in the center of the second floor landing he stopped short. The portal opened flashing the interior of a splendid room filled at the far end with a giant canopied bed and propped up in a mound of white pillows Paco could see for a split second a tiny person, the fine points of it's features obscured by a rapid closure of the doors. Oakley whispered, "we will visit Don Fazinatos directly after we breakfast".

Arriving again in the dinning room, now with the row of doors out to the terrace opening on a bright morning, they came to a table under the outdoor canopy set with baskets of fruit. A silver domed serving cart with hot dishes and smoked meats stood waiting. One of the little Italian cooks asked for requests.

The sunlight made the flowers glow and the walkways with tall Cyprus trees cast

stately shadows down to a large pool ornamented by sculpture in the distance.

Paco felt a little dizzy. The landscape was breathtaking. Captain Oakley

suddenly looking severe began to confer with Carmino who stood some distance

away. Chef Printise and Miss penny, now bonded forever by their shared

capture and freedom, could not help but indulge in every inch of the Captain's

paradise, including a bubbly bottle of prosseco spumante.

Penny, waving at Paco from a chair where she had been sipping her coffee and

nipping at the heavenly cornetti alla crema, began with a persuasive tone that he

could tell meant she wanted him for something. "Paco dear, we have a brilliant

idea that our fabulous Chef Printise has just created. He is such a genius."

Printise, beaming in agreement, concentrated his azure blue eyes on Paco,

attempting to be hypnotic. "Yes Darling boy, now, with all gratitude to your

distinguished Father, we are evidently not going to die, at least not before the

culinary competition at the Biltmore next week. Remember, Darling, the

"Medallion de Oro"? I dare say, dear boy, I will be the winner. There's no doubt about that", the Chef's almost white blond curls whipping around with emphasis. "It would be a perfect idea for you to assist me, hmmm Paco? We work together beautifully, you take my direction with such haste and you are gifted, lovely man, with preparation. My Darling Penny says you must do it! And you know what that means? Say you will and we can start planning the platters now, one for fish and the other for meat, each with four side dishes. What do say Darling?"

Paco was lightly amused and nodded clearly distracted, nervous to meet the old Don who, by the fleeting looks of him, presented a frightening appearance. He filled his glass with the Italian champagne at least three times and tasting the smoked pork with a bit of rosemary scented corn porridge he rose to follow the Captain back up the stairway to Fazinatos' chamber. As they entered Oakley put an arm around his shoulder and with a formal introduction presented Paco to a startling figure, body hunched into a ball, with a face so small it could only accommodate two very large red rimmed eyes that oozed with tears and a broad mouth with skin stretched so tightly it appeared to be without lips, just all teeth yellowed with tremendous age. He spoke in elegant English with just the slightest Italian accent like the Captain but the tone was high and often broke for his labored breathing.

"It is one of the great pleasures of my life to meet you Pacomino. Your Father and I have wanted this moment for many years. Come closer to me so I can see you better. Rosalena, bring my opera glasses. I want to see my Grandson." Paco stepped forward and sat on the edge of the giant bed holding his hand out to meet the fragile claw-like fingers offered by the old Don. His skin was discolored, almost black in places, and except for the perfectly pleated and pressed white night shirt of finest linen, he looked ghastly. He peered at Paco with the little gold binoculars and finally pronounced, "You have your Grandmother's smiling eyes, your Father's physique and the hands of an artist like me." The old man was panting intermittently now and with his energy seriously waning he whispered, "you have come to carry our flag", and with that he lost consciousness. Captain Oakley guided Paco out of the room, closing the doors and directing him to find the others and wait for him at the entrance.

Out on the circle drive, Miss Penny and Printise were laughing hysterically as they attempted and failed to mount the horses waiting for a tour of the property. The Chef was limping in a zig zag fashion to demonstrate his bad

back and begging for mercy, "Please, please Darlings bring me the car, or an

impressive supply of serious pain killers, cocaine anyone? Pass me the magnum

of champagne and I'll just wait for you here. Paco Darling you can describe

everything to me a little later, after my nap." He was ever resourceful with the

many ways he could feign ailments to avoid anything rigorous. Penny looked at

Printise knowing he was really just desperately hung over and with some

sympathy she agreed to stay and keep him company. Secretly she wanted to try

connecting with Owen Star who had not been answering his phone. This left

Paco and the Captain to set out together on fine boned horses muscled like

athletes with arched necks and high-carried tails streaming out as they began to

canter then gallop.

Passing through gardens of many forms they came to the merry-go-round and

Ferris wheel. Slowing to a walk the Captain told Paco that the Don created this

for him when he first learned of his existence. Oakley knew it was best for his

son to never know of this place but he imagined it often, seeing him laughing

and playing with his Mother looking on but only in his dreams. Paco was

beginning to understand the depth of emotion and grief his Father had carried for so long. He began taking in this hidden affection and accepting the

attachment that was so painfully missing from his childhood. He was feeling the

love but at the same time he noticed a little unsettled area deep in his heart

quietly pulsing with fear.

The two men proceeded to a perimeter road traveling rapidly by the dazzling

countryside filled with oaks and stands of eucalyptus often opening to fields of

poppies and lupine. After a time they came to the vineyards, precisely covering

soft rounded hills with row upon row of grapes in mid flight to ripening. The

Captain took great pleasure in pointing to the varieties in each area. He

indicated the white wine producing Pinot and French Sauvignon. Next came

the reds, Sangiovese, Trempanillo and Nebbiolo. All these were brought by

Fillipo Mazzei, the Don's partner, from Europe and planted very early on. Each

variety had it's own area on the miles of land dedicated to viniculture. Finally

ahead Paco could see a rocky mountainside with giant green metal doors that

folded upon themselves to cover a broad entrance. There were numerous men

all along the way including guard towers and two in dark coveralls with obvious

firearms in the doorway. As a matter of fact the Captain was armed with a

revolver in his shoulder holster and he had a riffle in the leather sling attached to his saddle. Obviously there was a small army of private soldiers under Oakley's command protecting the entire estate. This was beginning to bother Paco. Exactly who was his Father? Was he the erudite intellectual capable of unending love for his family? Or was he the dangerous criminal who would stop at nothing to rule a dark empire existing totally outside of the law? Paco now knew he was both.

Walking inside the enormous cave like space filled with row after row of barrels and room after room of bottled wine sitting in crates waiting to be delivered, the Captain pointed out a stone stairway leading down to the gated and padlocked entrance of a small space that harbored a collection of wine that Paco had only read about in the Diehls catalogs. Once in a while a customer would order such vintages and the cost was enormous. Oakley unlocked and pulled out a dusty bottle marked with "Napoleon Cognac Grande Champagne", the numbers not clear enough to read, maybe 1811? He poured two glasses, first sniffing then checking the dark mahogany color by holding it to a bare light bulb hanging from the ceiling. He passed one to Paco who did the same and then remarking, "Salute" they took a timid sip. The precious wine was still vital with a nip and slight burn on the lips to start then turning sweet and mellow. It morphed to a tawny caramel, smelling vaguely of French perfume and tobacco. The syrupy liquor passed the taste buds leaving a hint of smoke and oak then on to cause a strange glowing sensation that could be clearly felt as it finally arrived in the belly causing the heart to race. Father and Son shared their rare ability to savor the full experience, whether tasting a glass of wine, or drinking in the complexities of a fine oil painting.

A certain light in the eyes of the older man ignited a place deep in the young man's soul. Paco was forever hooked on his Father's devotion. As a tasty tray of cheeses, prosciutto and warm sfilatino magically arrived, they sat and talked about many things genuinely enjoying each other's company especially when the subject turned to art. The stories about acquiring the Don's fabulous collections fascinated Paco beyond imagination. Time demanded they return to the Villa and now, to Paco's astonishment, two shiny red Indians were waiting outside, the horses having been retired to the stables. One motorcycle was a Scout like Paco's, but brand new, and the other was Oakley's "Big Chief", considered the top of the line, a powerhouse. Taking off, they followed the main road that passed by a stand of trees sheltering the kennels and motioning to pull over they stopped in front of the keepers who smiled and shook the Captain's hand with an honest fondness, appearing to be family, like the entire staff of Mio Cuore.

"We will take Brasco and Bocci for a run" and out bounded two magnificent

blacker than black Cane Corsos, the ancient Italian "guards of the courtyard",

an elegant property watchdog, muscular and athletic. They were the descendants

of the originals brought along with the grape vines by Massei from his ancestral

home called Mangiacane named for these mastiffs who eat trespassers. The

Corsos were moving with ease toward the Captain, massive dignified heads and

proud expressions, greeting him joyfully with streams of saliva flying out in all

directions. They laid down, rolled over at his feet, whereupon Oakley kneeled

and lovingly scratched the huge scary dog's stomachs. The dogs sat on command

and even shook Paco's hand. Then like a couple of bats released from Hell they

raced right along side the bikes all the way to the Villa entrance.

Father and son parked the Indians and walked toward the front doors as Miss

Penny, Chef Printise and the Butler, Zio Badare, walked out waving with

excitement. Turning around Paco could see a large black touring car enter the

circle drive. The Chauffeur opened the doors and Ludington alighted from the

front seat, Owen Star peeked his head out of the back seat and once on the

ground turned to offer his hand to another. A small figure moved forward. She was wearing a veiled hat but her movements to Paco were unmistakable. It was Madonna. He felt a little chill. His Mother had come and he could see the emotion in his Father's eyes as she embraced him saying, "Grazie Madre Maria" over and over again. She moved on to Oakley and falling into his big arms she began to weep and thank him for saving their son. Ludington and Printise as well as Owen and Penny had greeted each other affectionately but the temperature of the moment changed when the Captain held Madonna close murmuring, "Mio amore, mio amore". It was as if the earth stood still for these star-crossed lovers and this was the day of consummation. There was no denying the union any more now; Paco knew that better than anyone.

They were all brought into the Villa through the giant entry hall out to the terrace with marvelous tiered gardens down to a pool in the distance. They were seated and Zio Badare passed out orders to a little staff. Carmino walked in to have a private word with the Captain who found it hard to break away from his seat on the arm of Madonna's chair. After a few serious whispers and nods the two had a very hearty laugh together, Oakley patting Carmino's back with approval and, unbeknown to everyone else, there was a truck leaving the estate's big gates. In the back two large wine barrels punctured by numerous holes for ventilation containing the Fong twins were bouncing around promising a harsh bumpy trip to a secret San Francisco destination.

After drinks and rousing conversation describing the events in softened terms that brought them to Mio Coure, the Captain suggested that they be escorted to their rooms and rest before a late dinner. The group mounted the staircase and while Ludington along with Printise, Oren and Penny followed Zio, carrying luggage, to the right. Oakley held Madonna's hand and led her up to the left by the old Don's portal then past the door to Paco's room on to his own chamber at the end of a long corridor. With this the Son could not help noticing that the Mother never looked back.

Still thinking that over he went to his room, removing all his clothes and headed for the shower as if something had made him feel very dirty. He scrubbed it off dried and began to shave as the little housemaid entered, not giving him any notice, and hung several beautifully ironed white shirts in his closet where he also saw a collection of tan pants along with his handsome tuxedo. When he looked in his drawers he found under garments and sox to last a month. There were cuff links in a polished mahogany box and in a black velvet case marked

Cartier he found the splendid gold watch that was engraved with "To my Son on his thirtieth Birthday" in Italian. Paco, just twenty, understood immediately that this was his Father's watch from the old Don and now passed to him.

All this was just too much to deal with so dressing fast and heading out to explore more of the Villa he came upon Printise snooping around looking for the liquor. Zio appeared from out of nowhere and indicated a mirrored wall on the way to the dinning room that revolved around to present a fully equipped bar with spirits of every description and glassware to serve any concoction. "What will you have my Boy?" said Printise rubbing his hands together like an alchemist. We could make Daiquiris? Or what about an Ojen?" he examined the rare bottle of absinthe laced liqueur from Spain as Paco looked negative and found the Captain's Sangiovase. Chef Printise, as usual, settled on champagne and taking the bottle walked with Paco through the dinning room, pushing open two swinging doors at the far end that he imagined would take them to his favorite place in the world, the kitchen.

Huge, gleaming with stainless steel and a fireplace with oven at one end, the culinary center of Mio Cuore did not disappoint. Two of the cooks were at work and looked up surprised when Prentise and Paco entered with bewildering enthusiasm. "Let's cook Darling," said the Chef as he began to check through the cupboards, the giant pantry and a big refrigerator-freezer. "We have just about everything we might want. We can work on some dishes for the competition. What do you say my brilliant man?" Paco was eyeing the cooks and Zio who stood silent now mystified by their intentions. After some negotiations they began to create a series of elements designed to be good enough for the Medallion d'Oro platters. Tonight they would use the dinner party gathering, actually an interesting assortment of culinary experts, to be the judges. Printise found a fresh swordfish waiting to be butchered and this delighted him thoroughly as the cleaver and boning knife flashed. Paco was put to work on the mint herbs and vinegary green apple sauce the Chef planned to use on smoked eel to be caramelized, as one of the sides for the fish platter. Jerusalem artichokes would be blanched and fried until lightly crunchy then garnished in black truffles that must be shaped into ovals with tiny scalloped edges. Printise was shouting orders in his fluent Italian and then translating for Paco. The kitchen began to vibrate as only it does when a passionate production is underway. The mood elevated. This larger than life, frizzy blond haired wild man, nearly six foot three, inspired everyone, even Zio. He oozed a continual line of chatter that was both masculine with deep toned emphasis for signs of displeasure and high like a Diva, all brushed with a sophisticated British accent. He was funny and outrageous all at the same time ordering everyone to prepare his dishes perfectly.

To accompany the fish platter Printise added two other sides to the eel and artichokes. He had the cooks working on a lemon-ginger cabbage salad topped with grilled scallops and a spectacular sauce for the boiled lobster made with mango, orange, scallions and coriander. Then the Chef turned to the meat platter plan. There was an entire side of beef on hooks in the refrigerator but he also noticed a row of ducks looking to be just in from the hunt. This put him in mind of the most memorable meal of his life, from Maxim's in Paris, and the entre idea he took to his own kitchen, doggedly perfecting a personal version. It was an unusual presentation of Duck a la Greco with plumbs, Grand Marnier Brandy and black olives. Printise made this dish for the Yonkopolis cousin's restaurant and it became his signature entre, most often switching the duck for a nice fat chicken. He spiked the sauce with touches of rosemary and finished with pine nuts. This could be a gamble at the competition because many of the European Chefs would know spectacular recipes for duck and be very skilled producing a winner. Printise reasoned that the American competition may not be so capable and anyway he wanted that duck tonight, nothing else would do.

Two of the cooks began to prepare the ducks while the four side dishes were planned. There were several enormous bunches of beautiful white asparagus standing upright in a tray of water. "This is perfecto", bellowed the Chef, "I will simply steam and garnish with aged Mimolette, or something like that. Check the cheeses will you Paco dear? Then we can simply do a mound of bitter lettuce salad with chives, something sour, and sauté sweet onions in honey, as a balance." Now he was thinking of the drunken Chef Eugene, his mentor from the Old Parsonage who pounded that word, 'balance', into him. "Finally we will make my Greek cousin's family favorite, the Chaniotiko Boureki!" Paco looked his eyebrows lifted with interest. "That my dear boy is baked slices of potatoes with zucchini, myzithra cheese and mint." And then bouncing around in a circle with his arms up like a champion, he pronounced the menu as, "Prepared by a genius!" And with that, flying high from the Chef's undeniable charisma, the kitchen continued to hum with vibrant activity.

The Captain's four exceedingly capable cooks were brilliant, proving the dinner could not have been done without them. They were all less than five feet tall with identical black uniform-like dresses and simple white aprons. There was Nona who appeared to be the head of the line, then Nona Nana the grandmother of someone, next Rosalena, the one who also cared for the old Don, and then Mimi, the youngest who Chef Printise, sensing she was a comedian at heart, continually teased producing a wicked banter. Paco worked intently on the preparations and was even allowed to help with the sauces.

After several hours the entire menu was waiting at various levels to be finished and served with exquisite refinement when the guests arrived. Printise and Paco were both sweating and rosy from heat and fatigue. Gathering their wine of choice the men walked out onto the terrace finding the table they used for breakfast. There they sat as Printise lit a tiny pipe and the cool air refreshed them. Quiet now, Paco was taken over by the view marked with a striking gradation of color proceeding up from the horizon. He could see intense cadmium red-orange, through the cad yellows to a light cerulean and then a darkening ultra marine blue with many subtleties in between. He could find some of the brighter stars twinkling out and his mind rambled through a list of worries with his Mother at the top.

"This must be quite an experience for you, my Darling?" Printise looked at the young man who was softly suffering. "I take it all this is a total surprise? It's going to take some sorting my dear man and it's best not to tackle it all at once." This was sage advise from someone who suffered a similar personal catastrophe and a sudden severing of his rather bizarre Mother's apron strings.

"It's Madonna that sickens me the most", Paco admitted. "She could have prepared me for this. She could have been honest about how much she loves him. It sounds like she was in contact with the Captain all along. What happens next Chef?" He buried his head in his hands.

"Happening next Darling? Just have a look through the doorway to the kitchen." Out walked Oakley with Madonna, holding hands, looking at the sunset, and then seeing Paco they began to approach the table. "It's time to grow up my beautiful man, we all do it sometime." Printise said then stared off into a space where he must have visualized the last time he saw his own Mother.

The Chef commanded the conversation with a description of the evening's dinning experience and how he hoped for a good revue since these will be the dishes for the Medallion d'Oro competition. He explained a bit more about the rules of the tournament that would test the best of American culinary talent. Now fascinated to know more about the menu, Oakley began to work with Printise to select the wines. As they talked Madonna came over to Paco and running her fingers through his curls then kissing both cheeks she whispered, "Now my life can begin. Please see that. Now you have both of us, something you have deserved since a baby." With big luminous eyes she pulled him to standing and begged him to smile. "Come with me amori mio and help make the cannoli, I promised your Father."

Retiring to his room Paco showered for the third time that day, lounging for a long time on the bed contemplating his options, and finally slipping into his evening dress with the velvet slippers. He went to the dresser and put on the extraordinary Cartier watch giving the gold band a little snap. 'Ok', he thought,

'If this is how it will be, let it start my new life too.' When he entered the dinning room, Zio, seated him with a dignified flourish. Captain Oakley was at the head of the table with Madonna on his right side and now Paco on his left. Miss Penny and Oren Star were across from each other, then there was Chef Printise's chair now empty while he performed the last minute preparations in the kitchen. At the other end of the table Ludington sat, his polished looks and attitude evident, chatting with Star. They remarked on the sudden return of art stolen from the de Young Museum. Evidently a truck just pulled up to the front doors and unloaded some shipping crates filled with the missing Manets and the El Grecos. The subject turned to the current financial down turn that was beginning to plague the country. He pointed to the breakdown of international trade, and Institutions who expand under development with over-investment threatening an economic bubble. Star described a recent piece in the Journal that predicted possible malfeasance by bankers and industrialists and the incompetence by government officials that is putting the experts on edge. "A large-scale loss of confidence could lead to a sudden reduction in consumption and investment spending", Ludington speculated while at the other end of the table Penny and Paco were discussing Chef Printise's resume and chances to win the competition.

Zio emerged from the kitchen followed by two servers each rolling out with identical fish platters on little serving carts. Diners were given an artfully arranged plate. In the center tilted one upon the other for best presentation were the pan seared swordfish steaks slightly crusty, cut into triangles rimmed with strips of very thin bacon then barely drizzled with browned butter. The four side dishes were served in little mounds surrounding the fish. There were delicately sautéed Jerusalem artichokes garnished with perfectly scalloped truffles then the smoked eel on Paco's green apple mint sauce. To complete the arrangement lemon-ginger cabbage salad with a giant scallop and three slices of lobster tail glazed with mango-orange dressing and scattered scallions sliced diagonally.

The Captain selected one of his clean crisp white pinots for this course, brought straight from the barrel it was served by Zio from a crystal pitcher. Miss Penny was sharing some of her stories about producing the famous white wines from her original home in the Loire Valley. She described the Vouvray and the Pouilly Fume that were her favorites and explained the reason for their complexity was actually the long practice of aging in chalk caves along with the regions' cheeses. This diverted Oakley only momentarily from watching

Madonna intently, captivated by her now shinning beauty; almost unable to

believe she was sitting next him. Chef Printise came from the kitchen to sit and

experience the taster's reactions. He was wearing a traditional white chef's

jacket that had appeared from some unknown closet in the Villa's big staff

quarters that jutted out in a two-story wing from the kitchen. Delighted by the

hand of applause that greeted him, he winked at Paco and sampled each dish

then kissing a stunned Ludington on the forehead he hurried back to complete

the meat platter that tonight would be the Duck a la Greco, his private hope for

gaining culinary glory.

This time the platters rolled out on the serving carts covered with giant silver

domes that Printise and Zio removed together with great dramatic gestures.

The guests clapped in anticipation knowing that something extraordinary was

about to be experienced. Each platter was filled in the center with a roasted

duck beautifully browned, glistening with the fragrant plumb-orange brandy

basting sauce and a savvy scattering of sautéed pine nuts. It had been precisely

carved then reconstructed using sprigs of fresh rosemary as a cradle. The aroma

was bold and intoxicating. Surrounding the duck were the four small mounds of mandatory side dishes starting with white asparagus bundles carefully tied by green scallion strips and bright orange curls of French Mimolette cheese that Paco found among the Captain's amazing collection. Next a bitter lettuce salad dressed only with champagne vinegar and chives along side the sweet onions in honey that created a kind of marmalade. Finally the Chef chose to exclude the zucchini from his cousin's Greek potato dish, just baking them scalloped in little ring molds each layer brushed with butter, cream and sprinkles of Caprino a tangy goat cheese then laced with a hint of mace.

"Eh Voila mes amis" exclaimed an exhausted but blissful Printise now imagining the ribbon with a golden medallion around his neck as he bowed and waved to a packed audience. He was floating around the table, running on adrenaline, high with excitement and possibly the many sips of champagne that were often interspersed with tiny drags on his little pipe. Urged to be seated by Ludington the feast evolved paired with Oakley's Sangiovase and a tasting of the Nebbiolo that was dark and rich both perfect for the duck.

At the end of the meat course there was a silence, a quiet relishing of the memorable evening and how uncommon it was to have a talent like Printise prepare his showpiece offerings in this intimate setting. The Captain rose and ringing his crystal goblet with a silver spoon, popping a new bottle of Champagne, this time Mumms, he proposed a toast, "To the rarest of moments that I have ever had, to my beautiful wife Madonna and my brave son Paco. You are perfect beyond all imaginings." And after a rousing "here, here", and "Bravissimo", he continued, "Throughout my travels I have experienced the worlds finest cuisine by Master Chefs on three continents and I proclaim this Duck by our brilliant Chef Printise to be the best I have ever tasted!" More boisterous acclaim and then, "We are now privileged to have a dessert made by the angels, namely my Madonna and Paco. A dish I have tasted only in dreams since were very young. Zio please call for the Canolli." And so the magnificent dinner closed with this final superlative from an antique recipe with a secret dusting of sugared chili powder, a little taste of the Quien Sabe.

By now it was late and after a promise to assemble early for the trip home to Montecito, everyone was released to their own pursuits. Paco was feeling faint from too much of just about everything so with embraces all around he disappeared into his room totally worn out, and fell asleep the moment he hit the bed, having first changed into a pair of the newly discovered black silk pajamas with a red satin piping and the letter F surrounded with a gold

embroidered crest.

Chapter 13: The Culinary Contest Begins

Paco was groggy when his little maid who he discovered was called Nella

brought in a tray with steaming coffee, thick cream, a bowl of melon and

raspberries along with a plate of honey drenched frittellas. She made him

understand after several tries that he must bathe and pack and meet the others

downstairs at the entrance. The chauffeur, who had enjoyed himself immensely

chumming with the Captain's large staff in the more than comfortable quarters,

had already pulled Ludington's luxurious touring car around into the circle

drive for the trip back to Montecito.

While Paco bathed he thought about going home. He and Madonna would be back to normal. He worried momentarily about Ranger left alone at the Quien Sabe then thought about Diehls and the huge pile of orders that would be waiting. Shaving and finally giving himself a flirty smile in the mirror, his mood clearly upbeat, he found a nice piece of leather luggage waiting for him to fill on the bed. Thinking seriously about what he wanted to take home then going to the dresser he selected a generous helping of the underwear and sox. Next to the closet, Paco pulled out his own shirt and jodhpurs to wear home then, hesitating for an instant, he put a pair of pants and a shirt in his suitcase leaving the rest along with his perfect tuxedo and velvet slippers. He opened the Cartier case and took a last look at the superb gold watch knowing it represented an image he did not quite fit. Packed and ready he threw his leather jacket over one shoulder grabbed the luggage and skipped down the staircase two steps at a time as if he was eager to escape.

At the bottom he met the Captain looking serious. "Come with me to my office Paco, we must talk about the plans for our family." Following Oakley and entering the imposing room, half museum and half library, he was stunned to see his Mother sitting in a chair. She arose as he entered and the Captain moved to his command post behind the big desk. He started, "Your Mother and I have discussed the idea of your coming to stay at Mio Cuore and of course that is entirely your decision. We know you are determined to enter the Academia in Florence. We are especially proud of your talent and passion for this endeavor. For many other reasons it is not a good idea for you to join my wine business. Maybe one day, when this abominable Prohibition is over, and it will be over, you will have a choice in the matter." With that Madonna moved toward him with her arms outstretched saying, "Mio amore, please understand, I am going to stay here with your Father. I know it will be so hard to be without each other but the safest course is for you to go home to the Quien Sabe and fulfill your dreams there." She was hugging him closely now as he slightly slumped noticeably in shock.

It was a rough journey home. His mind was scrambled. The car was loud and bouncing wildly around the treacherous coast highway that provided spectacular views of a glistening ocean made endlessly fascinating by the sight of birds and marine life that appeared and disappeared like a movie. He was actually sick to his stomach and declined the offers of delicacies Miss Penny brought out from a wicker hamper, many left over from the Chef's great dinner the night before.

When the wine was opened however he accepted all they would pour and then asked for more. As he stepped from the car, hours later, finally in the driveway of the Quien Sabe, Paco's head was aching right along with his heart. He was alone, all the others having been taken home before him. Standing with his suitcase in a kind of stupor, the big bounding form of Ranger came lovingly at him forcing his return to reality. He kneeled down for the full impact of the dog's greeting, grateful for the warm sticky kisses and the long wet nose that poked into private places.

They entered the small dark quarters he and Madonna had called home for years. He went to the kitchen and removing some steaks from the icebox he turned the fire up high and heated the big iron skillet to scorching with Ranger sitting in his corner savoring the scent of meat with anticipation. Crusty on the outside and rare on the inside the beef was unbelievably tender and succulent with a big pat of butter as garnish. Paco was reviving. He started to plot and plan a future that would take him to Italy to see the world and leave his insane family behind. As the dog ate some liberal leftovers, Paco made a phone call. 'Guess who", he whispered, "Can I see you in thirty minutes?" Smiling inside he went to shower, shave and wash away all the confusion and grief. 'Just let it all go', he thought, 'There is so much left', visualizing what he loved, 'my art, and yes', he thought with delicious contemplation, 'there is Charmaine'.

It was late August so the night air was hot and laden with the scent of night blooming Jasmine that hung in great curtains on the hedges all the way to Il Brolino. He had jumped on the Indian shirtless and arrived at the secret entry point he often used. She was there, waiting for him in the shadows. Appearing secretive she explained with a dash of fear in her shining golden eyes that the Master was home but sleeping deeply in his own chamber. She was confounded, not knowing what to do. Paco flashed his irresistible smile licking his perfect lips then with his eyes crinkling he took her hand and led her through the hedge. Swinging an excited Charmaine behind him on the bike, the two rode a short distance to the Quien Sabe.

Ranger was waiting and dancing around them as they entered the tiny living room and in the interest of privacy, Paco reasoned, he headed for his Mother's room, pulled the altogether willing young woman along and shut the door. Charmaine was removing every stich of clothing on her way into the bed that smelled of lemon-scented starch, a result of Madonna's technique for ironing the linens. She sat on top of him teasing with an unashamed flaunting of her delectable full breasts each centered with lovely pink rose buds now standing out nicely. She noticed a bottle marked almond oil on the side table and taking a taste smiled with approval. Now this went onto Paco's chest and then lower, causing him to arch and rise with pleasure. Charmaine knew how to slow him down and magically extend the evening's enjoyment so turning him over she massaged his back and neck with an uncommon skill that exposed her early life growing up in a high-toned brothel. Wild with desire by now, Paco turned and grabbed the woman forcing her to the bed. This started a powerful physical pursuit for fulfillment, slowly building the movements from soft and gentle to a kind of sensual fury, heated to the limit, finding the way to quench an undeniable thirst. Then they were limp and glistening with sweat. Laying back on the moist pillows slowly bringing their fast beating hearts to normal, Paco and Charmaine began to talk about their intimate emotions, private desires and personal stories, something they had never done before.

Paco walked into the back entrance of Diehls early the next morning noticing the fine delivery truck sat with a layer of dust. He surprised Taj and Sal who had been doing his job for almost a week. Overjoyed to see him alive they hugged and pounded his back with pleasure asking for a full account of his ordeal. This caught him a little off guard. He had not prepared the story he wanted known about the kidnap and Mio Cuore. Quickly he said, "I was picked up by a ship and taken to San Francisco. It has taken all this time to get home", hoping that would be answer enough and it was.

The business at Diehls was brisk. Many of the Chefs, arriving just two days away, had ordered crates and baskets of goods they needed for their submissions to the Medallion d'Oro judges. Salvador worked to prepare them all and now wanted to pass this over to Paco fast so he could return to his fans at the big soda fountain. Energized now by the mounting excitement over the competition and momentary flashes of Charmaine in ecstasy, he checked the orders, filled some more and then answering the phone with his free hand he heard the sweet, softly French, sound of Miss Penny.

"Paco, are you all right? I cannot believe what we did? I am exhausted and you must be too. Are you all right Darling? I mean did you spend a lonesome night without Madonna? I was thinking about you and wondering if you will stay here?" He asked her to keep everything quiet for now and she quickly promised, saying all that had been worked out with the Captain before they left the mansion, then continued, "Printise just called me and wants us to go with him this afternoon to see the set up at the Biltmore. He is getting very, very anxious already. You can imagine how serious this is since he rarely leaves his bed before ten in the morning. Can you? We will pick you up at two?" Paco agreed and planned to take the things Printise requested for the competition along.

And so it was that the three of them arrived at the giant oval Biltmore Ballroom called "El Loggia D'Oro" because of the opulent black and gold color scheme. The location was perfect for press photographers who had a special vantage point in the ceiling. There was a team of workmen covering the glossy parquet floors with matting and then a black linoleum-like carpet. Utilities were being installed capable of supporting twelve complete kitchens outfitted to please the world-class needs of competing chefs from around the country. Chef Printise was unusually dignified and business like as he signed in with the event coordinator. They could see the layout of the room emerging. On the floor, lined up on one side of the room, there would be a row of the twelve kitchens all done in stainless steel with partitions between each one for privacy. The front was left open for the audience, seated in an elevated grandstand on the other side, able to have a full view. The alternate half of the floor would be set up for the panel of ten Judges and the serving tables that surrounded the main pedestal to display the platter for brief minutes so the audience could cheer and the photos could be done. There was an electrician working on the spotlights that would make dramatic pools of illumination.

On the stage Paco recognized the Santa Barbara Chamber Orchestra practicing together, sounding wonderful. They were honestly bowled over by the extravagance of the preparations. This would be an event the city would remember for a long time. Miss Penny stole three programs from a cardboard box on a side table. The three walked to the patio and finding a sunny table ordered drinks and began to analyze the list of participants. There were only thirty-seven in all, mostly coming from major cities like New York, Chicago, St. Louis, New Orleans, Boston and several from San Francisco and Los Angeles. Then there were five from Santa Barbara; Chef De Vielmond, Chef Pulga, Chef Madam Genet, Chef Printise Yonkopolis, Chef Wilfredo Henriques and Chef Phillbert Omeyer. The long journey plus the two hundred dollar entry fee did prove to make the list a little shorter than in the past.

Printise nervously murmured observations as he read little snippets of the biographies attached to each picture. He acknowledged knowing Chef Henri Bassetti of the Ambassador, "He's a prick my Darlings", and Chef Gus Wasser from the Biltmore, "Just stay out of the lu when he is in it, that's all I need to say". Printise worked with both men in Los Angeles during a charity event given by Les Gourmands Regal Society. Nodding and rubbing his forehead he admitted they were, "formidable". A noticeable sigh and an anxious glance at the ceiling began to show even more stress during the reading of names like Chef Grevillet, Delmonico's, and Chef La Mer, Maxim's, both from Manhattan and considered legendary. The cocky Chef's confidence began to wither.

Out of the corner of his eye Paco noticed Chef Fredo walk by with several of his staff in tow followed several minutes later by Chef Velly who came alone, striding rapidly, deep in thought. As fate would have it they both arrived at the sign in desk simultaneously causing a dangerous dilemma. Unbeknown to the officious organizer overseeing the process these two were a potential powder keg, capable of a messy blowup if they wanted it, and so she innocently selected Velly to begin. Whereupon, instantly outraged, Fredo grabbed the pen and attempted to sign the entry form. Hot with displeasure the short muscular

Frenchman circled around coming up between the arms of the tall Austrian and recovered the pen attempting to regain the front position. Wild scuffling ensued and the security guards were summoned. Their old habit of spewing out fowl insults began but, upon references to fornication, ended abruptly as the official grabbed the sign in form and threatened to disqualify them on the spot.

The pair now both had a firm grip on the pen but displayed cheeky saccharin smiles faking an over polite attitude. The official eyed the chefs' hands with a vicious glare that worked to dissolve their grip and then, separating, each man bowed to the other, offering first place. Two guards finally arrived as Velly, following the lady's original directions, signed in and with his heavy French accent apologized, "No trouble, pas de problem Policiers, pardonnez-moi, excuse me Madame". Fredo was biting his tongue, waiting for his turn, thinking all the while that he was maltreated and storing up a deep hatred for the woman. A bitterness was spreading in his mind, expanding to indict the entire administration of Medaillion d'Oro, a bad omen that would predict his downfall if he dared to include the judges.

That evening, after calling Rosalita to keep Ranger with her, Paco went to Val

Verde instead of home so he could practice producing the competition platters

with Printise. Unknown until now the famous French culinary event was not

new to the Chef who actually attended several and worked as Commis for Chef

Eugene Plazermine his mentor from the Old Parsonage. They really did travel

to Paris to compete although, Printise admitted still wounded by the experience,

the Chef passed out drunk and after a desperate effort to revive him, was unable

to cook. That left a pitiful Printise on his own, undaunted, to watch and

commit to memory many techniques and tricks that he dreamed of using one

day.

They worked for hours refining every detail of the menus then hunting for an

appropriate platter Printise decided to call Ludington and ask if he had anything

stored away that might work. It was almost midnight but he had been up

reading so passing out powerful flashlights, proceeding up stairs in his cashmere

robe and slippers, he led the three to an enormous attic. There they found the

furnishings left from two of his family's sumptuous homes when they moved

everything to California. One lot was traditional English style from the

Pennsylvania estate and the other Deco from the very modern Manhattan apartment that occupied two top floors of a 5th Avenue building. Ludington had

no idea where to start so the three split up and began searching through the

boxes and crates, uncovering long forgotten tables and sideboards filled with all

manner of china and crystal. Printise came across several large silver trays that

could work but the decoration was so ornate he decided it would detract from

the food. Paco began snooping around paying more attention to the paintings

that stood leaning against each other than a platter. He carefully pulled them

apart enough to get a glimpse of the top portion. Some looked like very fine

work and he wanted to pull them out for a really good look. At the far end of

the room Ludington called out, "Here is something. Printise come and have a

look. It isn't a platter but I think it may be even better."

What he found was a large rectangular mirror that looked to be lightly tinted in

a bronze hue. The frame was simply two small strips one gold and one silver.

Centered on either end were decorative embellishments in gold and silver with

severe clean lines that looked like handles. There were very small adornments

centered on the long sides that repeated the same pattern. "This is a bit modern

and a brilliant example of Art Deco. Do you think this would work?" Chef

Printise looked dazzled by the idea so they decided to carry it to the kitchen to have a better look and measure to see that it conformed to the size requirement. Sitting on the big center worktable, the Chef found a ruler and declared it was perfect. Ludington said that Paco must stay the night and then left the two who carefully cleaned the stunning treasure that would present the dishes to very sophisticated judges with uncommon style.

Diehls was sizzling with excitement the next day as many of the competing Chefs arrived from all over the country to pick up their telephone orders. Everyone was aware that tomorrow would begin the first level trials, selecting the twelve finalists who then will have the opportunity to endure the two days of judging. The first day was for presentation of the Fish Platters and the final day for the Meat Platters culminating in a spectacular awards ceremony. Each platter must be completed in five hours and feature a main ingredient with four side dishes. These elements will be prepared to create ten servings of each selection to accommodate plates for the ten famous Chefs on the panel of Judges.

The rules of the Medallion d'Oro were strictly enforced. The finalists must have a Commis or assistant and a Coach who remains outside the kitchen and can consult, but more important, keep track of time. Teams may be immediately disqualified for tardiness, knife or equipment mishaps and contamination issues. The Chefs must bring their own knives, presentation platters, unique implements and all ingredients, except for the necessities to prepare the preliminary test and basic supplies that will be provided by the Biltmore. All items must be delivered to a Hotel supply center no later than one hour before the contest begins. Presentation of the plates comprises 50% of the contestant's total score, broken down to 10% for texture and cuisson (perfection in doneness), harmony of flavors, sophistication and creativity. The presentation of elaborate platters counts for 30% of the scores with 10% each attributed to complexity, technical knife skills and originality. The final 20% of the score is kitchen organization, broken down to 10% for the Commis performance, 5% for cleanliness and 5% for efficiency in timing.

Now all was in place to begin the event. It was publicized that Auguste Escoffier, considered the greatest Chef alive and recently exalted by the French Government, as a Chevalier of the Legion d'Honneur, now in his eighties, would travel to Santa Barbara to be honored and act as "Juge en Chef". Other culinary luminaries were expected along with glamorous devoted fans that attracted the press from all over. Locals had been following the newspaper stories that served to advertise the historic competition so the tickets were sold out weeks ago. In Paris the Medallion d'Oro caused a sensation every year and drew crowds carrying flags of their countries and banners for favored entrants. They blew horns, beat drums and in general created a hullaballoo. Now, occurring way out west in California, no one really knew how much revelry to expect.

So Chef Printise, Paco as the Commis and Miss Penny who was appointed Coach gathered in the great Val Verde kitchen on the last night to polish their performance. Paco had exceptionally strong knife skills, something that the Chef noticed way back when he helped to create the King Tut Party. It was something he learned from Velly who was a Maestro in this art. All the time hanging around the Il Brolino kitchen, secretly wanting a tiny glimpse of it's bewitching Mistress, Charmaine, had paid off. He spent hours practicing the proper French method to create all the mandatory cuts. Paco knew, the large and small dice, battonet, allumette, julienne, brunoise and the fine form of each.

Printise demonstrated the way this knife work should be done so that the judges and the audience would fully appreciate their talents. Basically he recommended a style of slicing and chopping, guiding the knife away from the fingertips, that would allow them to look away from their work scanning the other action in the kitchen with a calm slightly arrogant expression. This, he promised would earn them points. He warned Paco that they must taste, taste, taste, as often as possible and when they arrange the dishes they must give the appearance of an artist painting a portrait. All this he described and demonstrated with theatrical gestures then going over all the proper food safety issues he finished with a final admonition. "You must treat me as you would a symphony conductor, establishing eye contact continually, in order to convince the Judges we are working as one."

The great Medallion d'Oro culinary extravaganza began with an opening ceremony, accompanied by the Chamber Orchestra, with enough pomp and circumstance to stir any heart. The room was dazzling with the magnificent crystal chandeliers, all the gold and black creating a perfect backdrop for the long line of thirty-seven Chefs, in white jackets and matching traditional toques that stood very tall. Some of the thirty-seven wore striped ribbons with gold or silver medals they had already won in previous years. The audience was brimming with excited onlookers waving pennants or banners and set off a tremendous ovation as the line of Judges paraded out to their table set with pads, pens, crystal goblets and individual silver carafes of water.

When the bent but amazingly agile figure of the world famous Master Chef Auguste Escoffier entered, flanked by two assistants looking like French soldiers carrying flags of the French and American culinary organizations, the crowd went wild, bringing out the noisemakers and shouts of, "Bravo, bravo". The old Chef, at eighty-two, had a splendid face with intelligent bold features and a large white perfectly manicured mustache. He wore a black tam trimmed with some sort of gold medallion pinned to a small black ribbon. A black cape that turned back on one side to show the dark red satin lining covered his suit and there was a dignified array of braid and medals that decorated his chest. To have such a man come so far gave the entire event such credence. The photographer's bulbs flashed from the ceiling like fireworks as he took a seat of honor set at the far end of the Judges table.

Both French and American flags stood at the podium where an announcer spoke in English that was followed by a French translation. After the beginning salutations, a brief reading of the rules introduced the dish that would be prepared by each chef within two hours determining the final twelve. Four large carts rolled out with heaps of wild California trout, caught locally, garnished with greens and little carrot rosettes, sitting on big beds of crushed ice. Additional carts brought potatoes and all manner of vegetables artfully arranged like parade floats. The audience cheered with a standing ovation. All competitors had drawn lots earlier since there were only twelve kitchens. This demanded three separate groups, the first two with twelve chefs and the third with nine. When the high-pitched whistle blew, the test began and when it blew again, they must stop immediately and walk away from the kitchens to begin the service of plates to the judges.

Paco and Miss Penny were standing on the sidelines among a sizable group of those waiting to assist their Chefs. He could see Printise, among the tallest, standing stiff along side others he did not know. Further along there was Velly, so short but looking fierce, almost dangerous, with his dark chiseled face, a scar darting down one side and black eyes always flashing. Paco admired him so much and knew it would be a miracle if he were to win and return to Paris, reclaiming his rightful place as one of the cities' great culinary artists. With that title he could possibly rise above the brother who was determined to have him killed, maybe even retake his family's famous restaurant? If it had not been for Printise who asked him first, Paco would have loved to Commis with Velly. Thinking it over, the great Chef may not have even asked him since he had a very capable kitchen staff who followed him like disciples.

All this was running through Paco's mind as he scanned the lineup and recognized Mama Genet's little round figure, the whites of her eyes and big teeth matching her formal jacket and tall hat. 'What an incredible woman she is, so strong and able to create a taste that equaled the best I ever had and the only woman', he wondered if she had a chance. Fayola and Latrice where standing nearby with anxious faces, probably overwhelmed by the enormity of it all. Chef Omeyer, always called Bertie, was as wide as two people and cherubic as ever, in his own Universe, swaying and gently giggling as if listening to a funny story. Chef Pulga was there and Victore was also waiting. Chef Fredo, looming over everyone, looked gloomy. Sadly he drew a position in the third group. It was well known that this could be a handicap since the Judges pallet would be saturated, no longer able to taste the complexities required of the wining dishes.

Paco picked out all the famous faces that he only knew from their pictures and biographies in the program. He knew Chef Printise was going against tremendous odds but he took a giant breath and strode across the floor with a purposeful gaze along with the other assistants who's Chefs were in the first round. This was considered a prime place to start out. All the Chefs with their Commis and Coach stood at attention in front of their kitchens. They waited for the whistle that would allow the Chefs only to go to the carts and carry away their selections in baskets. This was done rapidly and for the most part with respectful manners. Printise passed almost a dozen or more trout to Paco to begin the butchering process. He rushed back for the potatoes and found three kinds of squash along with big sweet yellow onions, garlic, peppers, scallions and greens including a bundle of chives with lovely lavender flowers. The additional items needed could be brought from the baskets they left in the Hotel's supply center. All the dairy products and basic necessities would be waiting in the kitchens. Penny looked officious checking her watch often, waiting to receive directions.

For this test they must prepare ten small tasting plates that had to be not only magnificent but also show creativity in presentation. Thinking of this first the Chef cut the scallions and ultra thin strips of zucchini and yellow squash into shapes he knew would bloom and curl as they sat in ice water. He worked with Paco to perfectly scale and fillet the fish. Printise made a list of things to be brought from the supply center. He wanted the herbs, spices and two bottles of Ludington's best French Sauterne, alcohol allowed by special consent for culinary purposes during Prohibition. Knowing he was dealing with Masters of Haute Cuisine, he concentrated on refining his style that was normally a little rustic, influenced by Greek and California style.

Chef Printise decided to sauté small rectangles of trout on the skin side in the iron skillets using butter only, knowing this would produce the crunchiest skin. Taking the skin off additional fillets cut to the same rectangular size, he would clad them in very, very thin perfectly identical circles of potato that would mimic fish scales. He and Paco would fashion small fish heads and tails from potato, poaching them separately, then place them on the ends to finish the illusion of a whole fish. These he could delicately sauté and serve golden brown propped to the side of the crunchy piece. Each plate would have one of each and then under this Printise planned a small salad that he intended to express the beauty of a California garden but not detract too much from the fish. So that was the plan and Paco was impressed thinking, 'Maybe the crazy Chef really was a genius?'

Two kitchens down, as the giant room filled with aromas both savory and sweet, the little team of Chef Madam Genet was working like a well-oiled engine. Lora Knight, Mistress of Cima Del Mundo, the raucous bevy of Grand children with friends and Gunnar, the chauffeur, waving a huge flag, sat well positioned in the crowd. Mama immediately knew to duplicate Antoine's legendary Louisiana specialty, "Trout Amandine", and for good luck add her signature side dish, Potatoes soufflé. In her experience the trout selected were small, just enough for an individual serving, prepared whole including head and tail. Stuffed with a combination of sautéed tasso sausage, finely chopped shallots, garlic and aromatic herbs, they were put through her secret method. Washed clean, then dried well, they were massaged lightly with a little lard then dusted with flour. The whole fish was first rapidly pan seared then sautéed briefly in butter, finally stuffed then baked in a very hot oven just to finish. The sauce was made in the same pan after removing the fish to a heated dish and covered to keep warm. Adding more butter she fried the thinly sliced almonds and removed them while adding splashes of finest Montrachet, the great white burgundy from Chardonnay in the Côte de Beaune. Swirling this around scraping off all the brown bits and allowing the remnants of the flour to thicken the sauce she finished with a teeny drop of almond extract, a bit of sugar, final salt with a touch of white and cayenne pepper. This was quickly put through a sieve and then spooned over the fish sprinkling the almonds on top. Preparing this dish for ten Judges set Mama to whistling just like she did back in New Orleans, working in Antoine's stifling hot kitchen, serving a full house. This relaxed Fayola and Latrice too as the plump potatoes soufflé expanded nicely like little golden brown balloons.

At the same time the audience was riveted to the kitchen of Georges La Mer, the Executive Chef of the American branch of Paris' landmark Maxim's in Manhattan. The crowd maintained a continual hum, a kind of buzz, that would waver in volume based on the competitors' actions. Many of the onlookers had binoculars and opera glasses that allowed them to see exactly what technique the Chefs were using. They would pass the word along to others about the selections of herbs and spices as well as the vintages of wine or other exotic elements that might appear.

The hum hit a crescendo when La Mer set up smokers using large covered roasting pans with little grills over some smoldering chips of his favorite oak. He did this for only minutes to give the trout a delicate touch that would layer over the other subtle flavors including lavender and champagne. He stunned everyone when he removed the skin then broke the fish apart into pieces and mixed it with a light creamy mayonnaise making perfect quenelles that were topped with finest caviar dotted by tiny pink and blue flowers. To the plate he added several spears of chartreuse green asparagus and all these components were finally set in a small pool of thick potage parmentier, a very light green potato leek soup. Four matching parsley leafs were floating equidistant from each other to complete the composition. There was a big round of applause when the first plates were finished.

Paco had no idea what was happening outside his kitchen. Miss Penny kept the stress level high with her continual calling out of the time. Printise was turning red and sweaty asking Paco for anything that came to mind and prompting him to affect the style he predicted would win the Judges favor. They created the little faux fish out of the potatoes as planned and then brushed them with butter. The light sauté needed to cook the trout inside yet keep the color consistent cooking the potatoes to perfect doneness was daunting but it worked like magic. There resting on grill pans sat the ten skillfully sculpted fish that even sported a slight smile that just made them all the more irresistible.

The Chef pulled together the salad that was very simple, only frilly leaves of butter lettuce and some strands of radicchio that looked surprisingly like undersea flora and served as a great bed for the trout. The final garnish was made with discreet positioning of the pretty curls of scallion and twisted tendrils of green and yellow squash. As they finished the front row of plates there was a nice response from the audience, someone even shouting, "That's a winner Chef Printise, bravo, bravo." They were coming down to the wire now time wise. Miss Penny began the countdown as the final touches were made. Then the loud shrill whistle blew and holding their hands in the air they walked out of the kitchen exhausted. Both men stood stoic waiting for their moment to serve the panel of Judges now sitting with solemn faces. Chef Printice and Paco, returning to their kitchen, watched the important Chefs who would determine their destiny intently as they made notes, generally giving the appearance of pleasure. What this meant they could only guess and the process would go on through two more rounds. The finalists would be announced at 5:00 pm so they could make further plans for the two grueling days ahead.

All the dishes passed through the critic's palettes. Chef Bertie received a big response from the crowd, certainly expected since he was a Santa Barbara star chef well known for his opening of the Biltmore. Chef Pulga was as always petulant but extremely focused on producing an Escabeche of Trout, his creation that was Spanish inspired with his California style. Chef Victore his Commis made the most beautiful julienne of carrots, peppers in three colors and celery that altogether looked like a confetti of matchsticks. These were lightly blanched so as to preserve the color and then topped the trout after it was baked in a rich red chili sauce. To mimic the shape of the julienned vegetables the potatoes were cut into skinny batons and deep-fried then stacked beside the trout. A delicious creation for sure but it probably lacked the refinement and presentation needed to win.

A wide variety of styles emerged. There was the classic Truite Meuniere on silky puree of potato, Trout Fillets with mint pipian, Trout Choucroute, Troute Genobloise, and so many more, Paco, joining the audience, was astonished. As the final group stood waiting for the blast of the whistle, signaling the Chefs to select their ingredients, a shocking incident took place that drastically changed the tone of the day. Paco could only shake his head, knowing how big a crisis it would be for Chef Fredo, a man of extreme complexity and in some sense an old friend. As Fredo walked to the carts of vegetables now somewhat depleted, picked over by the preceding contestants, the Chef grabbed at the last basket of chanterelle mushrooms, something he had eyed for hours. This was the one element he must have to make the dish he envisioned and win a chance to compete.

Fredo was so tall that he stood out automatically. Added to this was his piercing voice now spewing expletives in German at the offending Chef who dared to take his mushrooms. Disqualified on the spot for his bad temper, he refused to leave the floor, flailing around in desperation, pointing and waving at the judges and especially threatening the woman who first enraged him at the sign in desk. The security guards came running and to finalize his total downfall, Fredo turned his back on the audience and lifted up his jacket in the back. With the whole room aghast, he pulled down his trousers to reveal a bizarre looking pink and white derriere, oddly striped with ugly purple scars, so offensive visually that the crowd began to hiss and boo, some threatening to attack.

This was a painful end for the proud Austrian who was forced to flee followed by his frightened little team. Paco, worried he might be suicidal, found him, head in his arms, seated by the Hotel fountain. His staff was huddled a little distance away fearing another blow up. Kneeling down and placing a hand on the heartbroken Chef he whispered, "You are still the same great culinary artist you have always been. Nothing can change that." The big man raised his head and looking into Paco's sweet eyes with a confirming nod just quietly said, "Thank you, danke sehr, das ist rightig, das ist richtig mein Junge". Then Fredo stood tall and motioning to leave commanded, "Marsch auf!" To Paco's relief, the little group just walked away, it's leader now striding with an imperial attitude, his head high, chest out, inside thanking his lucky stars that his employer, the highly respected Mistress of Piranhurst was on an extended vacation in Europe.

It was nearly five and the big ballroom was filling to capacity. The Judges had resumed their places and the long line of contestants stood waiting for an announcement of the twelve finalists. Paco was again on the side with all the other assistants and he could see Chef Printise standing at attention, his handsome face flushed with anxiety. After a salutation the names were read with bursts of applause after each one; "Chef Peter Wan, Chef Maurice Grevillet, Chef Francoise De Vielmond," 'that's Velly', Paco's heart beat faster, "Chef Manuel Acurio, Chef Raymond Olvera, Chef Phillbert Omeyer," 'I knew it!' thought Paco, "Chef Alejandro Ruiz, Chef Sebastian Molina, Chef Printise Yonkopolis," Paco staggered backwards and caught himself leaning on Chef Victore standing next to him. The announcer read three more names but he was too excited to hear them. As the winners were called they stepped forward from the line. The spectators went wild with drums and noisemakers, bouncing the banners high. Flash bulbs were popping madly from the photographers positioned in the ceiling and sidelines. The orchestra played Tchaikovsky's Military March for Brass. Running to the side where he spotted Ludington clapping wildly, with Oren Star catching Miss Penny, revolving around in circles, Paco was beyond thrilled. 'This is unbelievable' he said over and over to himself.

Chapter 14: The Medallion d'Oro, the Winners and the Mystery

Chef Printise and his team stayed for publicity shots after winning a place among the twelve contenders with a coveted chance to win the Medallion d'Oro. After making arrangements for meeting that night at Val Verde to practice for the first platter competition, Paco rode the Indian fast all the way to the Quien Sabe, high on the promise of tomorrow. Pulling into the driveway he could see Ranger dancing around and he worried about leaving the big dog on his own. His quarters felt empty and dark so he showered and packed some clothes then called Val Verde, asking Jasper to pick him up, planning to stay over

since he expected a late night of preparation. Soon the chauffeur, with

Ludington's pearl grey Mercedes Roadster pulled up. Paco walked out with

Ranger on his heels. Looking into the dog's pleading eyes, he strapped the

suitcase on the back and then lifted the collie into the jump seat. 'There are dogs

at Val Verde', he reasoned. Printise was a cat person with several Siamese that he

treated like children, even dressing them up for occasions. This may cause

concern, but Ranger was not interested in cats having grown up with them on

the Ranch. He knew to avoid eye contact at all times remembering the painful

deep scratches on his long sensitive nose when he was a pup.

Paco and Ranger walked into the kitchen causing the cats to leap onto the top of

the tall icebox. This set Chef Printise off. Morphing into his female persona, he

began crying out in a panicky high voice. "Paco, oh my God, Paco what is that?

A lion? Will it bite? It will eat my babies!" Then, Ranger, minding his Master's

bidding, nested himself in a corner as was his habit in the kitchen and Printise

began to soften. Thinking it best to simply change the subject Paco donned an

apron and said, "What do we do now Chef? We are finalists!" This refocused

Printise right away and the great artist, the gifted man who won the day, returned and began calling out orders in his deepest commanding voice, much like the one he used that thrilled the tourists in the Theatre of Apollo. They began the hard work it would take to win the Medallion d'Oro.

Late that night Ludington came to the kitchen and drawing Paco aside said, "I have an offer for you. It is time to select the final pieces for your portfolio submission to the Academia. We need to send this to Florence by the end of September if you intend to start in January. I have a guesthouse on the far side of the property bordering Il Fureidis. It has a large garage attached that I believe is empty and would work well as a studio. Java Sir's staff is always accommodating and if you give them compensation some would certainly agree to model. I would be very pleased and your big dog is welcome too. I can ask Jasper to take you there and try it out tonight." Paco who was very lonely at the Quien Sabe without Madonna agreed right away, thinking a move out of the garden house studio before the rains began a good idea. And so it was that Paco and Ranger jumped in the middle of a big iron bed covered with pillows and multi patterned Indian coverlets. He was so tired he did not even explore the space.

Early the next morning Paco arose and a little groggy took Ranger outside knowing it was important to find him some bushes. They were on the outskirts of the estate where the landscape was completely natural. Handsome oaks stood around on the softly rounded hills like people and there was a rocky streambed below only showing a modest flow of rippling water. The dog relieved himself often making his mark on the foliage then went to the creek for a long satisfying drink. Paco sat on a large boulder enchanted by the entire setting when out of seemingly nowhere the figure of his little temptress from Il Fureidis stood before him. She put her hand on his mouth wanting him to listen to what she needed to say. "Paco I have a very, very sad thing to tell you now. I have wanted to love you for many, many months but I must say with all possible regret that I may not kiss you again. I may not touch you again either. I am to be married". And with that big tears rolled down her smooth brown cheeks from those huge black eyes with a very pale yellow where the white should be. She continued, "My Father, the great Sepehr Jafar Javeed Foroohar, your Java Sir, has selected a boy who I do not know and he will arrive soon from India. And so you see I must never, never love you again." Paco realized she had taken their little sport in the broom closet seriously while he had not given it a second thought. He needed to show some sensitivity but also agree completely that they would not touch again. This he did sincerely and as Ranger came up to inspect the girl Paco explained he would be staying in the guest house and asked her name never knowing it before. "I am Perichercher but you must call me Peri. And who will take care of your lovely big dog?" She had a voice like little bells with the singsong sound common to the Indians, always enriched by a hint of the British. Paco did not know who would care for Ranger and as he looked at her with question she cried out, "Oh let me, let me, I can watch to see that he comes to no harm. I am caring for a very sick lady who loves animals and I think this dog might make her happy?" Satisfied with this idea he instructed Ranger to follow the girl, something he did with great interest, mesmerized by the scent on the hem of her long skirt as they walked away together.

Spirited by the apparent positive turns of fate that brought him to such exciting new opportunities, he reported to the kitchen finding Chef Printise ready to pack and head for the Biltmore on day one of the grand competition. Carefully padding the Deco mirror they planned to use as a platter and then loading all the baskets of ingredients that covered the entire floor of Ludington's big touring car, they were off. Arriving at the Biltmore they checked in, unpacked and secured everything in their designated kitchen. An excited Miss Penny arrived with Oren and all four found a table in the bar to wait for the moment when they were allowed to begin. Star found the Newspaper, as always. He began to read a story about the competition the day before and the shocking disturbance cause by a disgruntled Chef who was, miracle of miracles, not mentioned by name, probably with due respect to the charitable Hill Baron of Piranhurst who employed him. There were photos of the final twelve with Chef Printice looking like a movie actor, beaming with a big toothy smile. One interesting paragraph described the legendary Maxim's Chef La Mer's spectacular smoked Trout Quenelles in Potage Parmentier and how it shocked the onlookers when he was not included in the finalists. Now this drew big interest from Prentise, Paco and Penny who did not even realize the great Chef was not among the twelve. Oren read on, "The dish was spectacular in presentation and won all the percentage possible for that feature but it is whispered that the Great Escoffier himself found a tiny bone in one perfectly formed egg shaped dumpling with an elegant caviar topping and this was the reason for his elimination."

"You can see my Darling Paco that even the mightiest can fall on their face if they allow anything to be less than perfect", Printise warned, really a little stunned and frightened himself. The article ended with a big story about Chef

Omeyer, the Biltmore's Bertie, and now he was one of the probable winners along with Chef Maurice Grevillet, Delmonico's, NY and Chef Molina, of The International Club, NY. The Chef they targeted to win it all was Chef Oscar Tschirky, The Waldorf, NY, who was a protégée of Chef Escoffier. Penny nudged Oren under the table hoping he would stop reading the details that were making them so nervous.

The Contest now formally opened with a big audience already gathering and the Chamber Orchestra playing. All twelve Chefs lined up, each in front of a kitchen, looking impressive in their whites and tall matching toques. The Judges filed in and then the most honored Chef Judge, the Maestro Escoffier, walked in slowly with the flag bearers. All were waiting breathless for the whistle that would mark the start. A signal was given for the Commis and Coaches to take their places and to the amazement of a cheering crowd and Paco who followed him out, Chef La Mer, the favorite who lost out due to a tiny fish bone, walked proudly to Chef de Vielmond's kitchen to act as Coach. Knowing he was Velly's American mentor when he first came to work in the New York version of Maxim's gave Paco a little satisfied feeling. In his heart of hearts he knew that the greatest talent on the floor that day was Chef Velly for sure.

There was a ten-minute wait between the start times for each chef, allowing the service to the Judges to be spaced out a little and Chef Printise was in 9th place. That meant there would be a little over an hour of anxious waiting before they could begin but it also gave Paco a chance to see the others working. Immediately the Brilliance of the first culinary artist emerged with Chef Peter Wan, from the greatest Hotel in San Francisco, the fabulous St. Francis. The original Chef who made the restaurant's fine dinning legendary was Victor Hirtzler who learned to cook in Strasbourg, France, and then for royal courts across Europe. According to Hirtzler, he had created a dish for King Carlos I of Portugal, called La Mousse Faisan Lucullus, a mousse of Bavarian pheasant's breast and woodcock flavored with truffles, and a sauce of cognac, Madeira and champagne. The dish was so expensive, and the King ate it so frequently, that he bankrupted Portugal twice and was assassinated in 1908.

Hirtzler fled to America becoming the brilliant mentor of Peter Wan who was half Chinese and grew up in San Francisco. Common knowledge had it that he was the son of a woman abducted by the Tong who died in childbirth. He was rescued as an infant and restored to his prominent family who supported him with every opportunity, sending him to France for a culinary education. Wan became a celebrity Chef creating spectacular productions, in his half French-half Chinese style, for the Hollywood set. He prepared parties for Charlie Chaplin, Douglas Fairbanks, Mary Pickford, cowboy star Tom Mix, Mabel Normand, Fatty Arbuckle, and directors D.W. Griffith and Cecil B. DeMille, constantly making news that was reported on the gossipy society pages. Even at the competition there was a sizable loud fan club waving a banner that said, "WAN WILL WIN".

Each of the Chefs must announce the menu for their platter so the audience turned quiet as Peter Wan described his creation. "I will prepare for you today a seafood pastiche of seared yellowtail accompanied by sautéed mussels, clams, shrimp, red onion and cilantro in cloudberry consume, fried calamari, four crispy garden vegetables on jasmine tea scented rice pillows with hoisin, sweet & sour, and ginger scallion dipping sauces". This was followed by a polite round of applause.

Next up was Chef Maurice Grevillet renowned Executive Chef for the Los Angeles Ambassador Hotel who became famous for his signature dish, a dramatic presentation of lobster served in a crunchy vermicelli cage on white porto sauce and pea pomponette. For the contest he added risotto fennel balls, wild mushroom confit and a bitter orange marmalade jell. This sounded intriguing and even caused one or two of the Judges to lift their eyebrows with anticipation.

Chef Francoise De Vielmond, Il Brolino, came next. Velly's menu was sleek and sophisticated calling for the most difficult techniques known. He asked Chef La Mer, his famous coach, to announce the dishes because his French accent was so heavy and hard to understand. The Platter promised to be a work of art. Chef Velly's main attraction was a Checkerboard of Steamed Sole and Salmon sitting on a sliver of black truffle and sauce Bonnefoy, a white Bordelaise. This dish promised a memorable image with it's intricate basket weave presentation in creamy white and pale pink. For sides he planned caramelized black cod mignonette, artichoke canapé with sauce coquille and golden caviar garnish. There would be peas in spring onion custard topped by parsnip chips and graceful little pea pod tendrils. Finally Chef Velly added celery root puree and torched blanched almonds.

Five more Chefs announced their menus and began their platters including

Chef Bertie who ended up with a main dish of colossal Santa Barbara prawns

and lobster tail with several sauces. One of his sides was a fancy version of

pomme frites; cut very long and thin, making a sensational spiky presentation

standing up in black paper cylinders lined with lacy doilies. This last item was

something he served often in the Biltmore's premier restaurant, "The Golden

Marlin", and Paco knew immediately it would be eye-catching for the Judges.

Finally it was Chef Printise who took the microphone and described his platter.

He decided to go a little tropical since at the Biltmore the Judges would be

almost sitting on the beach. His main entre was langoustine nuggets and grilled

pineapple on small skewers with a buttery mango-orange, caramelized onion,

and coriander sauce. The sides were candied smoked eel, crab in mint and green

apple sauce, (something everyone adored from the Mio Cuore dinner party), a

tabouli timbale, grapefruit, argan oil, and blanched endive served standing with a

spicy tangerine shallot sauce. Printise and Paco had practiced the techniques and

especially worked on the theatrical way they used their knives. They planned

every little detail of the way each item would be served and placed on the big

Deco mirror. They found ten small plain crystal glasses or plates for each side dish that would be placed in four rows. For the centerpiece, they planned to

elevate ten skewers of lobster on a spectacular cut crystal Deco style bowl placed

upside down. The entire creation would be judiciously decorated with orchids

and little strands of jasmine. 'Leave it to the Chef for a big dramatic statement

but, remember something that Velly said, there could be purists among the older

Judges who may not like an excessive display" thought Paco.

Three more followed finishing with Chef Oscar Tschirky of the Waldorf in

Manhattan. Working too hard for even a glance at this famous culinary star who

was touted to win the entire competition, Printise, Paco and Penny would have

to hear the details later from Ludington and Oren who had settled into the

audience. Chef Oscar announced the menu for his platter and there were

"oooo's" and "ahhh's" as he described each dish. "Today I will have for your

approval an entree of halibut rolled and stuffed with morel fricassee kissed by

rosemary, and for the side dishes a classic gratin Dauphinois, mille-feuille of

marinated salmon with fresh herbs, pancetta wrapped tuna & melon, avocado

and orange on escarole with pimento shallot and tarragon vinaigrette."

The competition became heated, really heated. There were several small fires that needed to be doused along with a surprising turn of events that sadly ushered the big loveable Chef Bertie out of the race. His Commis, a regular sous chef in his kitchen at the Biltmore accidentally had a serious knife wound that spilled blood over the giant prawns as he was cleaning them and one of the monitors saw it happen. The whistle was blown and the team, after serious consideration by the Judges, was demanded to leave the kitchen immediately. The crowd, many locals included, set up a fierce outburst with boos and general sounds of complaint. Undaunted, the popular Chef with his big pink cheeks plumped and smiling waved goodbye with a sporty gesture and slowly left the ballroom, off to go to work in his big hotel kitchen where he was always number one.

It started five hours to the minute that the first chef to begin became the first chef to present their platter for photos and audience appreciation and then bring it to the table where the servers made the individual plates for each Judge. So Peter Wan was first and received a tremendous ovation as his yellowtail, artistically ornamented by a festoon of cilantro laced with exotic looking orchids, was carried to the table. This was surrounded by small plum colored lacquer bowls of his cloudberry consume presenting various shellfish and a red onion ring garni. All this was esthetically placed on a very large deep red lacquer platter that gleamed in places with lucky Chinese characters in gold. His crispy vegetables on jasmine tea scented rice pillows were exquisite and dotted with a surround of the sauces. And so the Judges began the long process that would finally proclaim the greatest Chef in America.

Going by audience reaction, the big favorite so far was Chef Velly with his jaw-dropping presentation that featured the checkerboard of sole and salmon. This spectacular entre was so elegantly produced that the first sight of his platter caused a hush among the on-lookers before they exploded into a standing ovation.

Four more Chefs presented and then it was time for Chef Printise and Paco to carry out their masterpiece. Astonishing as it seemed to them the audience went wild, banging drums and someone shouting "Bravo, bravo". For the first time they saw many pennants emblazoned with "Chef Printise" waving and a big banner appeared up on the back row that Paco realized was carried by the Val Verde garden staff. It read, "CHEF PRINTISE OUR CHAMPION".

Encouraged by all this approval Printise and Paco made a very dramatic display of the magnificent mirrored platter that was exploding with brilliance, reflecting the lights from a crystal chandelier and the flashes of the photographer's cameras in the ceiling. 'Now if only the dishes taste as great as they look', thought Paco, nervously coordinating the hand over to the serving table and the opinions of the Judges.

The team of three were now released to join the audience were they found a delighted Ludington with Oren and Jasper holding seats. Printise winked at Ludington saying, "Loved the pennants and the banner Darling." Oren whispered, "We paid the drummer twenty dollars." They all felt high with expectation, as the event appeared to be going very, very well. Finally the great Chef Oscar of the Waldorf, sitting in the most handicapped position, going last, brought forth what could be the winner of the day. First, he too chose a mirrored plateau. Large and oval he served his halibut rolls in the center of a very tall crystal pedestal that was lifted high above a bouquet of flowering rosemary and other decorative herbs with small flowers tied together by a powder blue silk ribbon that was wired in place to stand up and create a simulated Baroque medallion. His ten servings of Dauphinois, whipped potatoes, were placed in small cut crystal goblets with a pastry nib that created little castles. Salmon was rolled into ten tiny swirls filled with caviar. Then little packages of the pancetta wrapped tuna & melon were tied with celery strings. Perfect slices of avocado fanned out on ten small crystal plates topped with perfectly supremed slices of orange, a pimento-laced vinaigrette and the addition of small beautifully created orange peel roses, each made from a single strip carved from a single fruit. The overall vision was stunning and the crowd knew it was possibly the winner. Printise looked at Paco with his eyebrows a mile high, spirits a little dashed, obviously thinking they were up against a powerful opponent.

With that it was over for the day and although the Biltmore staff would clean the kitchens, Chef Printise asked Paco and Jasper to retrieve the knives and the mirrored platter. As the two entered their kitchen and stood possibly unobserved they noticed an Asian in black walk by with a nefarious attitude. Paco, thinking he looked strangely like the men recently encountered during the kidnap, stood high on the sink where he could actually see into the surrounding kitchens including the one belonging to Chef Oscar on the far end. The dark figure was in there. He opened the icebox and did some unknown thing then left rapidly. 'This was weird' concluded Paco, but Jasper motioned to him for help with the platter and during the hassle it took to carry everything to the car he totally forgot about the incident.

It was twilight by the time Paco had shared a happy dinner, noticing that Prentise drank far more than his share of the excellent vintage Mumms Ludington pulled out to celebrate a job well done. He had opted to walk through the estate grounds to his quarters, a refreshing little journey through the manicured and sculpture ornamented gardens to the natural landscape that marked his part of Val Verde. Striding up the pathway to his quant wood frame cottage with a big front porch he could make out the image of Ranger sitting on the top step with a turbaned person, apparently restraining him, along side. Coming closer the dog was released and the person introduced himself, "Salutations Sahib, my name is Sorush, I have come at the wishes of Miss Perichercher who has instructed me to watch over the giant dog and guard you through the night." Ranger bounded up to him, jingling with little bells attached to a paisley bandeau tied around his neck. He looked unusually fluffy, his hair feathering out like the collar of a lion. Then landing big front paws on his chest, the collie gave his face a cheery thorough wash with his long pink tongue.

Paco thanked the man but explained he did not need a guard. Hoping he was understood, and bowing to each other several times over, he just turned and entered the little house. He really never had time to look carefully at the place and as he lit the only lamp he could make out a small kitchen in the far corner, a large bookcase filled to the brim and a roll-top desk on the opposite wall. The big iron bed was sitting almost in the middle of the room on a magnificent Persian carpet and at the other end there was a mammoth stone fireplace. Everything seemed very clean and decorated with a hint of Indian style that was further expressed by the distinct scent of patchouli, a perfume he recognized as warm sweet and pungent all at the same time.

Paco felt good here. He inhaled deeply and sensed the comfort that the little cottage would provide. He massaged his aching body, so over worked and exhausted by the events of the day. Entering the bathroom with it's big old iron tub and vintage plumbing he filled the bath and treated himself to a long soaking with Ranger sitting in the corner mildly amused. He dried off with an enormous cotton sheet, the only thing there, and just leaped into the big bed, a collie dog nestling in behind him. Paco slept soundly until almost dawn when he awoke from a vivid sensual dream. He only remembered the ending. He recalled the heart-stopping figure of Lillian standing over him with her long blond hair brushing his bare chest; he could smell roses and the heat of her body pulling him to consciousness. He sat up rubbing his eyes and looked out toward the front door that had been left open with only the screen door closed. He could see Ranger outside sitting on the porch so grabbing the sheet he wrapped up and walked out to the steps. Everything was still and the light was just beginning to filter in through the limbs of a giant oak that created a glorious canopy. All was peaceful but it seemed curious that Ranger was now standing a little way down the front path looking out in the distance with his tail wagging as if he was greeting a friend.

Now it was probably only five in the morning but knowing it was impossible to go back to sleep he planned to make a little coffee and check out everything in the bookcase. Turning to walk in he noticed a big heap of something leaned against the house at the far end of the porch. Looking closer he recognized the turban of Sorush now unwound and serving as a cover. It completely hid the man's entire sleeping body, apparently in a sitting position with knees up as a headrest. Paco, slightly annoyed, resisted the urge to ask him to leave and finding

coffee among plenty of provisions he began to examine the books.

Finding numerous brown notebooks he opened one and read the name

"Krishnamurti". This was the famous Philosopher who had his learning center

in Ojai, a small town nearby, and he recently made news. Oren Star read aloud

about it one morning from his special chair at a tiny table in front of the great

marble soda fountain at Diehls. The story, as Paco remembered it, was that the

man had headed an international organization and, after years of its existence,

he dissolved the order several weeks ago. It was a society that proclaimed the

coming of a world teacher and many believed this man was the one. The news

article went on to explain that Krishnamurti professed to have undergone a

profound spiritual awakening that changed his entire outlook on life. He

believed he found a new understanding of his own spiritual mission as a

Teacher. This awakening was achieved by something he called "the process" and

required days of existing in a dreamlike state refusing food or water.

All this was passing through Paco's mind as he flipped through the hand written

pages. One journal entry marked January 9, 1929 read: "On the death of my beloved brother I suffered, but I set about to free myself from everything that bound me, till in the end I became united with the Beloved, I entered into the sea of liberation, and established that liberation within me".

Another entry was as follows: "I could not have said last year, as I can say now, that I am the Teacher; for had I said it then it would have been insincere, it would have been untrue . . . But now I can say it. I have become one with the Beloved. I have been made simple. I have become glorified because of Him, and because of Him I can help. My purpose is not to create discussions on authority, on manifestations in the personality of Krishnamurti, but to give the waters that shall wash away your sorrows, your petty tyrannies, your limitations, so that you will be free, so that you will eventually join that ocean where there is no limitation, where there is the Beloved".

Paco put away the documents and watched Sorush, turban back in place on his head with a stylish knot, making tea and some kind of cinnamon scented porridge that he soon served to Paco with a bow and a captivating smile. For Ranger, pulled from the icebox, there was a lamb stew with lentils and big chunks of carrot. This pleased the dog who ate everything with ten gulps in seconds. Paco was now very intrigued by what he found in the bookcase and it occurred to him that this Persian servant might know something about Krishnamurti. "Sorush, did you know the man who wrote the books? Was he living here?" Paco was fishing.

Sorush replied, "Oh yes Sahib, I did serve the great one, the most blessed Teacher. He came here often to do his process and it was I who watched very, very carefully to see that he was safely crossing back and forth into his dreamland. This is a secret place for him and I am the guardian of his documents. Now he is traveling and he may not return for many months." This left Paco completely stunned sitting with mouth open as Jasper came bursting in urging Paco to dress and come quickly, the big touring car was leaving for the contest. So clothes rapidly pulled on he headed out for the final day of challenge for the title of Best Chef in America. On the way out Sorush took hold of the scarf around Rangers neck and said, "Come mighty lion and I will give you your morning brushing and massage."

Back at the Biltmore ballroom, stocking their kitchen and placing the brilliant mirrored platter on the counter, Chef Printise and Paco quietly reviewed their game plan. When Miss Penny arrived they carefully discussed the cooking times that would be critical and take several watches to track. The audience was filtering in slowly, a quartet playing a lite piece in the background. An announcer began the salutations and introduced Escoffier, then as if a replay of his prior appearances, with the flag bearers on either side, he walked to his commanding place at the head of the table to resounding applause. The rest of the Judges filed in and the eleven chefs, minus Bertie who had been disqualified, each took their place standing in front of their respective kitchens. The shrill whistle blew and it was Chef Peter Wan who started first with an enthusiastic band of fans cheering him on, some chanting, "Wan will win", over and over.

The other chefs were not allowed to begin cooking since there was a wait period between the start times for each one. The teams who would be waiting for a while sat in a lounge area or just walked around experiencing the event. It would be a little over an hour before Chef Printise and his team would begin so Paco strolled about meeting friends and checking out the menus from the competition printed in a new program. Just reading through the dishes gave him a queasy feeling knowing they were in for a tough ride.

Paco noticed Chef Oscar, the big star from the Waldorf, and his team carrying

in provisions. The monitors watched to see that they did not start cooking but

after several moments there was a loud commotion erupting in the kitchen.

Other monitors were called over and the competition staff arrived. Something

had happened and Paco flashed on the man he saw late the night before who

appeared to be sneaking into Chef Oscar's icebox. Moving as close as he could

he heard the words, "Everything is spoiled, all the veal and foie gras, my rabbits

and the caviar are missing, the vegetables and fresh herbs are limp and useless.

We cannot go on? The ice in the bottom of the box has been removed! This is

sabotage! Call the police! We are ruined!" Oscar and his Commis, arms waving

wildly clearly furious, were threatening to go for the knives. Word of this

disaster spread around the crowd and the buzz grew to a small roar. The

announcer came to the microphone and tried to calm the on-lookers, "Your

attention please, Ladies and Gentlemen, there has been an incident that we are

rushing to resolve. The competition continues and we will bring further

information to you promptly. Now please enjoy the show."

Paco felt a little shaky from this development and found Chef Printise standing

with Miss Penny and Jasper. He had to share what was bothering him and asked

Jasper if he had a good look at the oriental man they saw in Chef Oscar's kitchen the evening before getting a negative response. The little team hurried to their kitchen asking for entrance from the monitor and then checked out everything. Nodding with relief they knew it was all there. The ice had kept everything fresh. Only minutes later the announcement came, Chef Oscar of the Waldorf, the man everyone thought was winning so far had been forced to withdraw along with Chef Maurice Grevillet of the Los Angeles Ambassador who had taken suddenly ill.

Concerned now that three competitors were counted out, and possibly it was more than a coincidence that they were considered by many to be the strongest contenders, Paco had a fleeting thought about Chef Velly, thinking he was now the probable champion. 'Could he be in danger?' Maybe it was his recent experience with men in black that caused his concern. Looking down the way he saw Velly, his powerful arms passionately chopping something in his kitchen and he felt relieved. Just minutes later the whistle for Chef Printise to start blew. Now they had five hours to create the winning meat platter and hopefully the coveted Medallion d'Oro.

They began preparing the veal and chicken stock needed for the Duck a la Greco. Artful chopping and detailed creation of clever garnishes took so much time since they needed ten identical samples of each item. Paco set the pine nuts aside in a sauté pan waiting for the time when he would lightly warm them, keeping them white to create a decorative pattern as a finish on the duck. Careful attention to the preparation of their prime stalks of white asparagus and the trimming of clementine segments would follow. Dressing for the lettuce salad with fancy herbs, the very thin slices of onion to sauté in rich honey wine sauce and the potatoes for the Greek style gratin must be done with precision, every serving perfectly matching. All eyes would be on the visual presentation of the platter and uniformity was a key feature.

The giant ballroom was boisterous almost drowning out the pianist playing Chopin selections. There were bars at either end serving non-alcoholic drinks that would be secretly spiked by many flasks carried in the pockets and handbags of the crowd. People milled around the room, leaving periodically to have lunch, and continually observed the action in each kitchen that by three in the afternoon began drawing to a frenetic conclusion.

The audience was finally asked to take their seats for service to the judges. The excitement was mounting. The flag waving started with vigor and fans eager to encourage their favorite shouted out names. The person with the big drum made an appearance and long banners were showing up. The atmosphere was turning buoyant as the first chef, Peter Wan, was motioned to present his platter. His menu was announced and Paco's heart sank a little when he heard the entre was a rosette of roasted duck with white truffle cherry sauce. His work was excellent, served on the same large lacquered tray with the gold Chinese characters. The dumplings were served in porcelain soupspoons. He made ten tiny servings of froie gras with roasted cepes and sunchoke puree on mushroom cups. Next a warm salad of Brussels sprout leaves, pear and Duchilly hazelnut, presented on ten matching maple leaves. And finally chilled pink grapefruit, elderflower and fennel jelly topped with amazing pink button chrysanthemums carved from watermelon, revealed later as a special talent of his Chinese Commis. Wan's platter received a big ovation with a chant "Wan will win" and lots of red and black pennants with his name in gold waving madly.

Chef Printise and Paco were finalizing the platter with the placement of the dishes but could not resist looking at the work of the others as they passed by. Next up was Chef Velly carrying out a magnificent platter, but Paco who knew him so well could see that his old friend was white, not with his usual dark coloring and bright red cheeks. Even his dark eyes that normally sparkled with energy looked dull and empty. Something was wrong and as the spectacular presentation was placed on the serving table Velly fell to the floor. The crowd groaned as medical personnel came with a stretcher and carried him out, then turned to cheers and a standing ovation for the masterpiece that lay before them on the large white porcelain platter. In the center high atop a tower of many, many layered leaves of frilly edged chartreuse green cabbage, interspersed with a tiny garni of thyme and violets, was a ring of ten stuffed confit of duck legs,

French cut, the bones created a stunning crown touched on the tips with gold

leaf. Quail cakes under little crystal domes stood in a straight line. Wild

mushroom duxelle and caramelized pear had been rolled in individual pastries,

baked to golden perfection and fastened by tall toothpicks, the tops dipped into

dark chocolate then studded with little dark red berries. Ten tiny bite sized

boats beautifully cut out of cucumber rind looked like sculptures. They ferried

morsels of fine fromage siting on thin strips of black truffles in an apricot sea of

creme fraiche garnished with ultra crispy spikes of duck skin. It was clearly a

work of art and given Chef Velly's immense talent each dish would thrill the

pallets of the experts.

Four more chefs presented then it was time for Printise and Paco to carry out the dazzling Deco mirror skillfully displaying their culinary best. The Duck a la Greco was done in ten bite-sized Napoleons, the meat layered between crispy sheets of fillo dough that topped the inverted crystal bowl in the center of the platter. Each one was decorated with teardrop shapes made from black olive that closely matched the pine nuts creating a very chic geometric pattern. The white asparagus was served in ten small altogether matching bundles wrapped with the curls of bright orange Mimolette and finished with clementine segments. Bitter lettuce salad was formed into ten rings then placed on matching rings of sautéed sweet onions in honey. The Greek style gratin of potatoes looked savory with a buttery glaze and a single pressed mint leaf on each of ten small rectangular cakes. The fans made a resounding roar, the drummer went wild and Chef Printise, red faced from the heat was in his glory, curly blond hair feathering out from the humidity and his big white perfect teeth centered in a monstrous smile. Paco was holding up his end almost blinded by the flash bulbs popping and spotlights dancing around the huge oval room causing the chandeliers to cast little rainbows over everyone. They laid the big-mirrored platter on the service table and stepped back releasing their ardent labors to a row of gentlemen looking severe and discriminating.

Paco was thinking the Judges may have even saturated their taste buds by this time but the relief from finishing well was so liberating they rushed to the sidelines joining Ludington, Penny and Oren Star standing nearby. They began to hug, spinning around and other friends piled on forming a group including Mama Genet, Fayola, Chef Victore, Savadore even Corliss and her new boy friend. The congratulations were pouring in as they walked to the restaurant, waiting for the final ceremony to grant the top three winners their copper, silver and gold medallions. These prizes would include cash rewards and round trip tickets plus lodging for the World culinary contest, the Medallion d'Oro Internationale later on in France.

A little before five the great gold and black Biltmore ballroom with it's fabulous chandeliers was filled to capacity by a mob throbbing from excitement. The orchestra played and the spotlights swept around the huge oval space. The Chefs with their Commis and Coach standing behind them were all lined up. Judges were introduced and the Great Chef Escoffier was awarded a lifetime Grand Judge medal. Then it was time to announce the winners with third place first. So many holding their breath made for a sudden silence. "And the winner of the

Copper Medallion d'Oro goes to…" he waited for seconds to add drama, "Chef

Printise Yonkopolis!"

The sound was deafening and there was a modest cloud of confetti released from

the top row of the grandstand. Printise gathered Paco and Penny up in his big

arms lifting them off their feet, whirling around and around. They were really

stunned, secretly thinking they didn't have a chance. The hoopla was over

quickly and again there was a sudden silence. The announcer continued, "And

now, the second place award goes too…" a little wait, "Chef Peter Wan". This

brought on even louder celebrating and his fans began the familiar chant, "Wan

will win! Wan will win!" The Chef bowed politely but it was apparent he was disappointed. His team looked down at the floor and because they displayed

such a lack of joy the revelry ended fast. So the silence resumed and the spirit in

the room floated, suspended in air, everyone poised to cheer on the gold medal

winner, the greatest Chef in America. The announcer began, "We have the

great honor to award the Medalion d'Oro, Americane 1929, to..." now a long

wait making the crowd buzz a little with exasperation. "Chef Francoise De

Vielmond!" Paco was extatic! It was Velly! The wonderful, wonderful Velly

who deserved it so much! Then looking down the line he realized the Chef was

not there? The room had exploded with jubilation with all the lights flashing

and a big burst of confetti sailing around more for the finale of the event than

the first place winner. The Chefs were given the precious medals hanging from

handsome striped ribbons that Escoffier himself placed around their necks.

When it came to Chef Velly's turn his able Commis accepted the award looking

dazed and humble. For Paco it was an unbelievable moment and he missed

Madonna thinking she would have loved this almost more than he did.

Everyone began to leave as Paco and Jasper packed up everything from the

kitchen. They needed several trips and on one of them, out in the parking lot,

they passed some reporters surrounding Chef Peter Wan. Flash bulbs burst and the Chef said, "Gentlemen, this is for publication, I fully intend to file an appeal for a complete review of the judging since the rules of the contest specifically state that the competitors must be attending in person and illness or accident is a cause for immediate disqualification." This made Paco's mouth drop wide open. 'What a ridiculous idea', Paco thought, 'Velly was finished with his platter when he passed out. Where is he anyway? Chef Wan is a sore looser!' Looking a little closer at him he was thinking back to the man who was in Chef Oscar's refrigerator. 'There is something familiar about Wan's face? It was so dark and I really could not get a good look at the man's features? '

All this was still churning around in his mind as they drove home, packed to the rafters with equipment, the platter and food, so much food that when they arrived at Val Verdi Ludington declared, "Let's start the party! Printise call everyone! We will eat the spoils of war and Jasper get out the Mumms!" Within the hour the big terrace was filled with all the local friends and neighbors who considered a good party their life's work. Hot Jazz from Louis Armstrong floated out from the record player and each guest was getting high on a variety of mood lifters. Paco, dizzy and homesick, found the phone in a little office off of the kitchen. He fumbled through his wallet and found the card with numbers for Mia Cuore. Placing a call through the operator it was a long wait before Zio answered in a deep voice. "Good evening, may I help you?" his Italian accent thicker than remembered.

"Yes, Zio, it's me Paco. Is my Mother there?" The old butler was surprised and fumbled for an answer. "No young Master, she has gone on holiday with your Father. They are not coming back for three weeks. When the Captain calls I will give him a message." Sad and empty, Paco simply said thank you and hung up not even caring where they went without letting him know. It was times like this his brain always conjured up the delicious vision of Charmaine and it occurred to him she would know where Velly was. He dialed the number. "Hi, it's me. We won third place? I still can't believe it. Where is Velly? He won the gold you know? I want to see you." Listening intently eyes widening he replied, "Yes, yes, right away, I'm at Val Verde. I'll be waiting at the front gate."

Chapter 15: A Final Delivery, Lillian and Acceptance

The morning after the great Biltmore extravaganza found everyone in their

typical place at Diehls. The newspapers were filled with photos and stories

including one headline that read, "Medallion d'Oro Inquiry Ordered" with a

sub-heading, "Winner May Be Disqualified". Paco clipped some pictures

showing himself with a jubilant Chef Printise and Penny accepting the Copper

Medal to send to Madonna at Mio Cuore. He included the story about the inquiry and a long note telling her of his fears, describing what he witnessed, and that the intruder who was fiddling around in the icebox looked like the ones who held them captive. His Mother knew Chef Velly very well since he came on occasions to the Quien Sabe to cook for famous guests and he disclosed that the great man appeared to be in grave danger.

Paco was thinking back over recent events and the shocking experience he had the night before. 'I could talk to the Captain about all this and not worry Madonna? After all, if my suspicions are right and the Tong or some part of the Chinese underground sabotaged Chef Oscar and possibly the others, Oakley would know how to find out. Just putting two and two together I know that the one person who would benefit from the disqualification of the leading contenders would naturally be Chef Wan. As a matter of fact it was Wan', Paco reasoned, 'who was talking to the reporters in the parking lot. Was he so desperate to win that he paid the Chinese syndicate to rig the outcome? Should I involve the Captain?' Paco asked himself this question because a part of him, even now, doubted the complete integrity of his Father.

On the night before, Paco only waited moments before Charmaine in her sexy little yellow roadster swooped by to pick him up. Vaulting into the seat he could see that her brilliant golden eyes were red rimmed and swollen apparently from crying so he held her darling face in his big hands and tenderly kissed each one. "What has happened? Are you crying because Velly is in the Hospital? Is it so serious?"

"Yes Paco it is serious but I'm heartsick over something else. You know how much I love to be with you? It is really the only thing that makes my life bearable and now it's coming to an end. Paco, Edwin, my monster of a husband ordered me to pack. We are leaving tomorrow for New York and then to live in Bermuda, permanently?" She began to weep uncontrollably, "We are shipping everything there? He says he is closing up Il Brolino? He may even sell it? Oh Paco, I hate Bermuda!"

The two drove to St. Francis Hospital, really speechless, and found Chef Velly unconscious, attended to by a nurse and hooked up to medical monitors. It was shocking to see. They asked about his condition without any response. The look of Velly's face, so still and white, was completely unlike him. The deep scar that reminded him every day of the terrible wrong committed by his vicious

brother was minimized. All this gave him a strangely serene presence. They sat

quietly for a long time, hopeful to have a chance to see the Doctor, then without

any success Charmaine kissed him gently on the forehead and they left, not

knowing what else to do.

In the corridor, on the way out, the looming figure of Chef Fredo came

anxiously toward them. Paco explained they knew nothing about Velly's

condition and that it looked very grave. This fired off a vicious tirade from the

big crazy Austrian who now fostered a deep hatred for the entire Medallion

d'Oro event that had embarrassed him to the core. Fredo, clearly overwrought

with worry over his close friend Velly, who provided the unending creative

hostility he loved so much, intended to make it his business to track down the

truth. Fredo ended with, "And Paco, oh my Gott! Chef Maurice Grevillet, the

one from the Ambassador is dead! When I asked for the Chef at the front desk

they sent me to Grevillet's room by mistake and the man's wife said it was

poison! Paco! He was murdered! And now Chef Velly? Oh my dear man." He

was becoming frantic, "Get the authorities! Paco we must save Velly and see he

keeps his gold medal! Call the police!" This last demand brought forth a man who was sitting on a chair until now unnoticed at the door to Chef Velly's room.

Showing his badge the detective asked, " What do you know about the incidents at the cooking contest?" Chef Fredo, with his heavy German accent, went into a long breathless re-telling of the facts, as he knew them, with plenty of wild accusations thrown in, whereupon the Officer said. "May I have your name? I will give you my card and ask that you call to make an appointment to come in and give a statement." Then he turned to Paco and Charmaine. "Do you know anything about this situation?" And Paco, thinking quickly it was best to stay out of the picture for now, shook his head. The two walked on leaving Fredo to revisit all his suspicions, way up in the face of a weary Policeman, who was by now trying hard to get rid of him.

The two lovers sat in the car in front of Val Verde's big iron gates. There was such a defeated view of things now on both their parts that they couldn't find much left to say. She was leaving the next day maybe never to return and he was hoping to be in Florence, Italy by January. Although they had been in a playful physical relationship for months, their affair had only turned consciously intimate recently. Now it was love wanting to bloom. They only parted with

tenderness, heavyhearted victims of circumstance, vowing over and over to meet

in an unimaginable future time.

It was quite a walk back to his little cottage on the other side of the estate.

Passing the mansion he could hear that the party inside was still raging. Moving

along he came to the large Persian water garden. Along side was the guesthouse

with a tower, the place where he had experienced the vivid hallucination,

brought on, he thought, by the contents of Printise's little pipe. Turning a

corner and taking another look he was dumbfounded! It was like his dream.

There was Lillian standing on the same balcony glowing like an angel in the

moonlight. 'I'm not smoking anything right now' He thought. 'Could this be

true? Was it really her?' Paco found a good vantage point and just sat down on

the ground looking up for a long time. She was singing, really chanting?

Floating in and out of the curtains in a kind of dance, her Indian Sari wrapping

then unwrapping around her. She would bow with palms together, saluting

some unseen source and then with arms outstretched she called out over and

over, "Oh my Beloved, Oh my Beloved." Paco was mesmerized and just

remained seated in utter disbelief. He dared not let her know he was there, fearing discovery would scare her off. Her hair was so long and the color so light it gleamed as she whirled around adding drama to her graceful motions. Finally after one last bow she disappeared into the room behind the curtains and the night sounds came back to nudge Paco into reality. Still astonished he raced to the mansion and finding Ludington talking art with a guest he waited his turn and then declared, "I have seen Lillian Hoover in you guesthouse tower. Do you know about this? Do you know she is here? I though at first I was dreaming but I am sure it was really Lillian!"

Motioning to the bar, Ludington said, not knowing anything of the young man's involvement with the girl, "Have a drink and have a seat. I've wanted to warn you about this and I would also like to plan your studio. Whatever you need I will get it for you. The time is almost here to send the portfolio to Florence." Paco barely heard the last part he was so anxious to know about Lillian. And when Ludington told the whole story including the fact that it was the Captain who saved her, he gained new respect, reassured a little more that his Father was really a good man at heart. After making plans with Jasper to help him move from his garden shed studio at the Quien Sabe to the garage next to the Val Verde cottage and finding his big iron bed already filled with a snoring collie, thoroughly wiped out he lost consciousness.

It was very early on Sunday morning and Ranger was poking Paco with his long nose, wanting to go outside. Wrapping in the sheet they walked out to the front porch where Sorush, at Paco's insistence had created a little pallet and lay sleeping under his turban turned cover. The air was warm but crisp and clean as he followed the big dog down to the stream. He sat on a large rock situated in a strong shaft of sunlight at the waters edge. Lowering the sheet he began soaking up the rays feeling lazy.

After minutes Paco suddenly felt the presence of someone bending over him, blocking the sun. Opening his eyes he was stunned to see her. She was right over him with her long hair draping down almost touching his chest. Lillian's gaze was curious, almost childlike, looking at him, fascinated, as if he was a rare animal. If she had a stick she might have poked him with it just to get his response. Sensing she would bolt and run if he moved, he just laid there as she came very close to his face, hovering only inches away from his lips and then moving down over his body she took a very deep breath, as if trying to inhale his essence. He slowly began to rise and she withdrew with matching speed. There was a change in her expression, possibly recognizing him for an instant and then returning to her strange state that was guileless, wide-eyed like a primitive. Now looking confused she started to move away with Ranger following, tail wagging. Paco called after him but he would not turn back and the two disappeared into the trees heading toward the tower house. He was only wrapped in a sheet so he hurried back to the cottage to dress and then dashed on to find them cavorting together with pleasure around the Persian pool. When she saw him across the water she slowly unwound her sari and showing her splendid lithe ivory body for moments entered the water and floated there appearing weightless.

Paco carefully edged his way around the turquoise pool getting closer and closer without her attempting to flee. All along she was eyeing him suspiciously. In seconds the door to the tower house opened and it was Perichercher who broke the stand off. "Paco, Paco my fine gentleman, you have found us? This is the beautiful lady Aredvi Sura Ana that I told you about. She has made a very good friend of your big dog. They really do love each other. You can see how they play and it is the only thing that has brought her to speak. She calls him Pasha and when he comes to her she caresses him and kisses his forehead. This is a little miracle Paco. She was unable to talk to anyone. We have taken her to the great

Teacher, Krishnamurti in Ojai for an awakening of her spirit. She is being

reborn right now and one day she will be whole." He was wordless watching

Lillian striding out of the water to Peri who was holding her sari and wrapping

her up they disappeared inside with Ranger right behind.

Walking in wonder all the way back to the cottage he found Ludington with

Jasper in the garage where they intended to create a studio. The garden staff was

on the way to remove some stored items and then give the space a good cleaning.

Ludington and Paco discussed the things that he would need. Soon he found

Sorush and Jasper drove the three of them to the Quien Sabe. He needed to

collect all of the paintings, drawings and supplies from the green house deep in

the lush gardens. It seemed like a long time since he had been home. Still a little

dreary with out Madonna he checked his quarters and then directed the two

men down to the studio. Finally done, the big touring car packed, Paco saw

Oneda working with something on his tiny front porch. "I will be living nearby

at Val Verde for awhile so I want you to have the phone number there. I'll be

taking all my work with me to prepare a portfolio that will go to Italy. I'm hoping to study there. Is everyone all right? I think you know Madonna is living near San Francisco and I'm not sure when she may return."

The old sage turned a wise eye on the young man telling him in his soft Japanese accented English, "We are very sorry to see you leave Paco-san, I know about your Mother and we are hearing sad news that the most respected owners of the Quien Sabe will not return this season so it is not necessary to find a new cook. We will be here, Rosalita and her little family and me with mine waiting for your return." Paco smiled at him and looked deep into his eyes that seemed to reflect the Universe. Even though it felt unaccustomed, a little stiff, he hugged the old man, tenderly whispering, "If you need anything from the market just call me. You can count on me. I am coming back."

It was mid September. Paco was showing up early every morning at Diehls and working all day, visiting Lillian each evening, and working on his drawings and paintings every night until very late. The tremors that would eventually almost destroy the country's financial institutions made their first rumblings. The stock market dropped sharply at the beginning of the month but rose again only to drop and rise again. Paco began to realize there was more to Charmaine's sudden move to Bermuda than he thought. He also imagined that the owners of the Quien Sabe cancelled their annual move to California because they were worried about the cost. Other signs kept cropping up, forewarning that hard times were on the way. The orders from all his ultra wealthy clientele at Diehls were strangely tapering off when actually they usually should be picking up, many of the Hill Barons coming to warmer weather for the fall and winter. Even the phone orders were slowing down. Oren Star read the headlines and stories, giving everyone the jitters, predicting a monumental collapse but no one wanted to believe it.

Chef Velly made a miraculous recovery, having teetered on the brink of death for days. The investigation into the Medallion d'Oro, exposing a mysterious disqualification of the two top contenders and the question of murder by poison filled the Newspapers too. Developments sat in limbo for several weeks and then while Paco called Mio Cuore to talk to his Mother he summoned the courage to speak with the Captain and discuss his fear that the entire ordeal had been caused by Chef Wan. He asked if there was any way to know if the Tong had anything to do with it? He voiced his worry that they could still try to eliminate Chef Velly since he was the declared winner and would be sent to

France in November for the Internationale competition in Paris. He explained that Chef Wan who was in second place would be the one to go if anything should happen to Velly. Oakley just remarked, "I will see to it Paco", and it was only a matter of days when the news broke. Wan was arrested along with a trio of known members from the Chinese underground. The case was blown wide open and Chef Velly was again established as the winner, the greatest Chef in America.

The significant day came when Ludington, who had hired a private courier, would complete the selection of Paco's pieces for the portfolio, now planned to arrive in Florence within about two weeks time. The work as a whole made a powerful package. Notable were a number of extremely sensitive anatomical drawings in sepia, umber, charcoal and white Conte crayon done on fine Arches handmade paper that should convince anyone the young man was fully prepared to take on any challenges the Academia would bring. They included three canvases done early on in the little Quien Sabe garden studio depicting the exotic cactus, bird of paradise and flora in the surrounding landscape. His color pallet was exceptional with many variations of gray, green and blue, from Celadon to icy shades of Cerulean and French Aquamarine. There were bright blue patches of sky peeking through and the brilliant touches of crimson and Cadmium orange that described the lilies and bird-like flowers that caused the pictures to vibrate with excitement. As the man took the large package away Ludington said, "Well Paco we will see what we will see. Soon there should be an answer and in any event please understand my man, you deserve to go."

The stock market's rollercoaster ride continued into October as the beginning of the month saw another drop followed by another burst of strength. Then came a day labeled by reporters as "Black Thursday" when a huge dip in stock prices triggered a burst of panic selling so frantic that it overwhelmed the Stock Exchange's ability to keep track of the transactions. The little group at Diehls, sitting by the big marble fountain without even one customer, was glued to the radio, trying to understand what exactly was going on. Wall Street financers were able to reverse the downward plunge only by buying as many shares of stock as they could over the next two days. It was a fleeting victory. Monday's opening bell unleashed a frenzy of selling that soon turned into an uncontrolled panic that continued for the rest of the trading day. The following day, later called "Black Tuesday", October 29th, saw the previous day's panic turn into a disaster of historic proportions.

Oren Star, having read every word the Wall Street Journal could provide, sat on

the glorious patio of the Biltmore getting drunk on shots of Macallan. When

Penny arrived she sat across from him with her dazzling smile, shiny deep

auburn hair, in a lime organdy blouse under a navy suit jacket with smart gold

buttons and a white accordion pleated skirt finished by spectators. She ordered

the first in a succession of frothy peach daiquiris. Both nursing the fact they had

probably lost their small but prized nest eggs, it was not long before the drinks

made them both sentimental and exceedingly romantic, culminating in the

specter of Oren, down on one knee, asking Penny to marry. For an instant she

thought about the fact that she was already married and upon following through

with this it would mean bigamy? It flashed by her consciousness, but she secretly

told herself, 'All that was years ago and a continent away'. Happy and glowing

she simply lowered her eyes and kissing his hand she murmured, "Oh yes,

Darling, yes."

The economy after that night went from bad to worse. Scandalous tragic stories

were passed around and reported daily, vividly describing the loss of fortunes

and property, even suicides, as a result of the Stock Market's crash. In the month that followed, absurd though it seemed, Diehls was forced to close, their cash flow having come to a fatal halt. Paco made one last round of deliveries in the wonderful shiny black truck with the gold lettering that marked the most famous culinary market in the West. He lovingly polished it for the last time and then packed to the gills with all the orders he drove off on his customary route through Montecito. It may have been the artist in him that found such profound pleasure in just looking at the details of the different shaped leaves on a multitude of trees. He noted and memorized the richness of the dense foliage always interspersed with brilliant colored flowers. He daily passed the flashy oranges and fuchsias, and shades thereof, from thousands of bougainvillea that cascaded over rooftops and walls. All along the way he found bright expressions of crimson, cerise, salmon and gold from the roses. An outpouring of annuals like petunias, geraniums and sunflowers formed drifts between breaks in the tall dark green hedgerows. Long passages of lavender or soft purple lantana, with tiny yellow petals and black anthers in each center, graced the by ways.

Twinkling and floating around all this profusion of bewitching botany, besides a grand array of birds, were the bands of butterflies and moths. Paco took great delight in identifying each type, a skill he picked up during a short stint in The

Boy Scouts. He could always see little hyperactive swarms of tiger moths and skippers, orange with black markings or yellow with dark umber edges on their wings. He had caught a wealth of these as a boy, keeping them in a big Mason jar with wholes in the lid until his heart told him to set them free. It was a rare day when he spied a bright iridescent aquamarine blue Morpho Menelaus, resisting the urge to catch and kill it for pinning to his corkboard with mementos. The Painted Ladies flickered, wings splashed by tones like sepia and burnt orange, aqua and ochre, then outlined in black. From time to time the giant Yellow and black Tiger Swallowtail or the white and black Zebra version would fly by radiating a kind of majesty, proclaiming itself King of the gardens. But his favorites had to be the Monarchs with their magical bi-annual flight that migrated right through Santa Barbara. They selected certain groves of eucalyptus as spots for resting between segments of their mysterious journeys from points above Northern California down to Baja, Mexico. There were a number of these places in Montecito like one on the Quien Sabe in a windbreak of ultra-tall Eucalyptus that always wore peels of pastel colored bark on their huge trunks. During the height of the butterflies' travels Paco could see the leaves on these giants heavily laden with thousands of sleeping Monarchs, so many in fact that the limbs actually bent down from the unnatural weight.

The cactus became a passion for him. Paco thought of them as ancient tribes from a strange planet. Grateful for his education provided by Oneda in the landmark succulent gardens of the Quien Sabe, he recognized each one and called them by name.

The sight of a certain congregation of magnificent blue agaves always thrilled him as he climbed the hills to Cima Del Mundo. Walking into Mama Genet's long kitchen, always scented with delicious sultry southern herbs and spices, Fayola ran by hysterical as he put their big order on the sideboard. She was waving around a hammer and hollering, "Somebody get the saw, Miss Latrice is trapped in her room! Paco, we don't hear her cry'in no more? We was having our breakfast and heard the boom! Twas like a little bomb went off. She is jus nutty as a pet coon, that girl! She's got so many cans and boxes of food in there she aint got a place to put her po ole head. Oh you gotta get the girl outta there."

Paco shook the big woman a little, getting her attention, and then ordered, "Go get the gardeners or Gunnar, find Gunnar!" When he rushed down the hallway to find Latrice's room he could hear Mama Genet, begging her to open up the door. "Jus come on over to the door an turn the lock. You can do that for

Mama. Jus talk to Mama." The dear roly-poly little cook was wringing her big hands and wiping her brow with a delicate lace hankie she always had tucked into her ample cleavage. "Mama loves you so much. Please, Tricey, pleeeeease be easy darlin, jus open the door." Paco banged on the door wanting to sound authoritative, hoping that might work. There was no answer and soon Gunnar, giant Swedish wrestler of a man, arrived and once understanding the issue just bashed the door in with brute strength.

Expecting to find Latrice possibly unconscious, there was a gasp when all they could see were stacks of tin cans, every kind of food imaginable, that filled the entryway from floor to ceiling. They attempted to push some of this aside but any access was filled up making it impossible to gain entrance this way. "Go to the window, we gotta go to the window." Mama screamed. So while Paco slowly tried to remove the cans, stacking them along the corridor, the others, Gunnar leading, now with hammer in hand, circled around the house and finding the window broke in. Anxious voices wanting to hear good news were a little relieved when the big Swed announced, "I can see her Mama. She is just sitting on her bed." Back in the hallway Paco had almost cleared a small tunnel that would be expanded and allow Mama in to nurse Latrice back to sanity.

Sometime later Lora Knight insisted on psychiatric treatment after hearing the whole story. They discovered that it was the crash and threat of financial disaster that caused an already traumatized Latrice to take such drastic action for self-preservation.

On his way out of the estate Paco passed the pool where Corliss, bounding over to the truck, told him about her plans to travel through Europe in the months ahead finishing with, "I will always remember the things you did, taking me home on the terrible night of my break-up with Renny. You are a true friend and I am yours always."

The next stop was at his own Quien Sabe where he intended to leave a generous box of canned goods and special jars of pickled seafood that he knew Mrs. Oneda would make into a myriad of Japanese specialties. Rosalita hurried out of the kitchen beckoning him to come in. With a very serious face she presented a Western Union telegram that read as follows.

QUIEN SABE RANCH

MONTECITO, CALIFORNIA

To all interested parties and the staff of the Quien Sabe Ranch

MESSAGE

This is to inform you that the property will be sold. You may stay on unpaid until the final sale. We expect you to find employment elsewhere as soon as possible. Thank you for all your kind services for so many years.

And that was all he needed to drop the paper and fall into Rosalita's big arms, overcome momentarily by yet another bombshell. Vowing to think of a way to help he drove the short distance to Il Brolino. Just knowing that Charmaine was gone made the grand mansion look deserted. With the Chef's usual order in the estate's special monogrammed baskets, he entered the kitchen that stood empty, something he had never seen before. In seconds one of the cooks emerged and directed him to the swimming pool. Paco was still dazed by the telegram and thinking, 'What else can happen', inside he was still worried about Velly's health, after all he almost died from the poisoning. Easily finding the remarkable oval turquoise waters, still and shimmering in the sunlight, Paco could see two figures sitting under an umbrella beside the Palladian style cabana. There a very fit looking Chef Velly relaxed, playing chess, sipping the Master's best champagne, with Chef Fredo who looked anxious, fiercely concentrating on his options to win. Both men brightened by the smiling vision of Paco, they urged him to take a seat.

"Bonjour mon petit frère, sa va? We play chess and drink all the best champagne in the cellar. First, L' Pommard, c'est complete, and now Veuve Clicquot". Chef Velly, waving the familiar orange-labeled bottle around, was obviously inebriated, something Paco never expected to see since he had once been an alcoholic. "Next we drink the Roger Desivry. Join us cher ami, we have le petit celebration, the buse feroce, the huge old dirty bird is gone and he is not coming back! " Velly was referring to the fact that Edwin Ballingford, the mighty Hill Baron and Charmaine's abusive husband, had decided to escape the impending financial disaster by leaving the country, protecting as much money and many assets as possible, finding a safe hideout in Bermuda.

Chef Fredo burst in, complaining in his signature German-English style. Both men often sounded ambiguous, the meaning of their conversation unclear, so Paco depended on body language and today he could see there was big trouble. "Das stinktier, an affenschwanz, that bastard! He leaves Chef Velly here with not one cent! He will eat everything and drink everything and go swimming every day and then sleep in the old fettsact's bed! And he will wear all die kleidung, all his fine suits and der shoes too."

Pouring more champagne Velly was smiling with eyes at half-mast until Fredo came to the part about the suits and shoes at which point he stood abruptly and shouted, "sa shoes? Jamais! Et sa vestements? Jamais! Va te faire voir? What do I care? I leave for Paris in two weeks! Le vestments c'est merde! I go for Medallion d'Oro and I kill my brother! Fils de pute!" Chef Velly was really getting worked up. And now, Fredo, eyes gleaming with excitement, was immediately offended by the Frenchman's negative turn on his effort to champion the cause. He also felt a sharp pain in his heart just hearing the words, "Medallion d'Oro", so, delightfully energized by this, he gleefully put on his verbal battle gear and went to work. "Schlafend! Sleeping, you are sleeping my friend. This dumpfback has done you! You should punch him in die eier! Are you stupid? You will wear the suits! You will wear the shoes! You arschkriecher!" All six foot four of the Austrian was up now and pointing at Velly, demanding even threatening, that he go get the shoes and put them on instantly. At least that is what Paco could surmise given the small amount of words spoken in English.

Something about the word "arschkriecher" ignited a vision so detestable in Chef Velly that he lunged forward and grabbing the huge Chef around the knees that were, on the short Frenchman, about waist high, he forced him backward taking the two of them straight into the pool. Paco could see the water churning with wild flailing of arms as he turned to leave, then walking to the truck, the crazy bellowing insults slowly drifted out of earshot. A warm feeling entered his mind knowing full well the potty old Chefs were happily berserk and completely back to normal.

Casa Bienvenidas, an enormous estate under construction, was always a point of interest on his way to Il Fureidis and Val Verde, his next two stops. Alfred E. Dieterich apparently not affected by the crash had hired a famous architect named Mizner to create a masterpiece. Having lived in Guatemala and traveled Europe his designs were romantic with references to several styles, mixing Spanish elements with Italian and medieval features. The mansion was large with 40 rooms totaling more than 17,000 square feet. The living room alone was more than 1,400 square feet, and a vaulted ceiling was 20 feet tall. Paco knew several men who were carpenters and some cousin's who were completing a long passage of fine stone wall. They told him about a secret passageway constructed behind a bookcase that led to a wine cellar and he thought how silly the idea of Prohibition was. Everyone one he knew had a secret stash of alcohol making it not a secret at all. There was a big movement to put an end to the madness, so many thousands of citizens breaking the law. He thought for a moment of Mio Cuore and how much in love with the beautiful vineyards he really was. He flashed on sitting in the dark wine cellar with the Captain and his heart melted a little more. All this passed through his mind as he drove the delivery truck on it's last round.

The Persians and the Indians who formulated the staff had created a veritable farm on the grounds of Il Fureidis, making it impossible to suffer any of the effects of a plunging economy. They came from regions in the world were this was a way of life and with the continuously running stream that cut across the property, the sublime estate was totally self-contained. Paco really was not filling an order but taking some specialties, his favorite Lokrum from Turkey with plenty of exotic spices, that he knew Java Sir would enjoy, and telling him about the closure of Diehls in person.

The old man sat on a cushion in a corner of the kitchen garden seemingly in meditation. Sitting down cross-legged in front of him, then returning the hand gesture that meant, "the spirit in me embraces the spirit in you", he began, "Java Sir, I am here to say that Diehls is closing it's doors because there are no longer enough customers." Paco looked down tracing a circle in the dirt, "So much has changed in my life. It is also very sad to know that the Quien Sabe, my home for many years will be sold. I have sent my artwork to a school in Italy and if accepted I'll be going there to study. The kind gentleman, your neighbor, who owns Val Verde has promised to pay for this? It is difficult to take so much from him and never be able to pay it back." It was always so easy to pour out his heart to this rare man who seemed to understand eternity.

Java Sir was silent then in his soft voice that was something like singing, "Paco it is possible to give up trying to pay back the people in this world who have given us gifts so precious. A wise man surrenders to the miraculous, saying "thank you", over and over for as long as we live. The great and gracious owner of Il Fureidis has deeded this property to me. It was so astounding that I spent many days searching for a way to repay his generosity but you see there is only my gratitude and I silently tell him 'Thank you' everyday, over and over."

Paco considered this for minutes then admitted, "I am so worried about leaving my home and the people I love."

The old Chef replied, "The ones you have attracted in your life today, are precisely the ones you need in your life at this moment but you see, Paco, today is always changing. Hidden signs are behind all events and if you watch for them they will serve your own flowering. You must find the place inside yourself where not one desire is impossible. Ask for nothing more than inspiration and your path will be blessed."

Standing to leave Paco whispered "Thank you" over and over, and then moved on to Val Verde. He carried the big order brimming with delicacies that Chef Printise requested, knowing it would be the last. Today the Chef had made his eyes up to look something like Cleopatra, black kohl liner and deep blue shadow along with perfectly arched eyebrows, transforming him into his favored alter ego, the Diva. It was always astonishing to see his handsome ultra masculine features changed into the stunning female he created with a little paint and powder. Printise, from the neck up, could have been a leading lady had it not been for his big burly body with muscular calves that looked ridiculous in the mammoth high heels he loved to wear. His voice was feminine and outrageously affected, becoming decidedly British in tone.

"Paco Darling you may put that on the table. I want to properly inspect this order", he said, grabbing at a big tin of caviar and like lightening twisting off the lid. Slowly savoring several heaping teaspoons full, he heaved a giant sigh of relief as if the salty little eggs were a lifesaver, then washed it down with some champagne he had handy on the sideboard. All this time Paco was putting things away and complaining bitterly to Printise about the newest turns of fate that were causing a sharp pain in his head. "Now I have the news that they are selling the Quien Sabe! I no longer have a job! I have no idea where I will find the money for a new place and it is difficult to think that I must ask Ludington put me up and pay for everything if I go to Italy."

Chef Printise, voice lowering to his natural tone, bellowed out, "Are you completely stupid? Are you unconscious? You cannot be serious Darling. You are one of the wealthiest people in the world! Do you really not understand that? An illegal fortune possibly, but nonetheless, you are heir to a gold mine. You little twit! Your Father supplies a thirsty Nation with all the forms of wine and liquor that it craves and that will never stop! I know the Captain will send funds to Ludington for anything you may need, and as for the Quien Sabe? You must call Madonna right now and let her know! She may want to buy it?" Paco stood transfixed and then, a fleeting issue of entitlement passing through his brain, he walked to the little office off of the kitchen and placed a call to Mio Cuore.

All the way to Arcady just remembering the conversation with his Mother and then the Captain lifted his spirits. They promised to come very soon and, "discuss his future" as his Father put it. Paco pulled up to Joannah Prang's large two-story cottage. He brought a big basket of her personal favorites. Expensive luxuries like saffron, cinnamon from Madagascar, and mahlebi, powder from the pit of an African cherry with a hint of almond and rose. She also loved the Indian spices like kalajeera with it's rich nutty flavor, slightly grassy to flavor rice and meat dishes. He included the rose and violet syrups from France that made her delicious cookies so distinctive. With no answer he walked to the back of the house and found her singing out in her splendid vegetable garden that was for Paco a picture to contemplate. The rows of textures and many shades of green were composed of lettuces and cabbage touched with pale orange and rust, beet tops with a lavender tinge, then a long lacy row of carrots and stiff onion stems that looped over on the ends. Tall bamboo sticks formed teepees that supported luscious fat tomatoes.

Down the wide center aisle was a brick walkway that ended in a little wicker teahouse. Over this path she made a series of large arches from willow forming a French style alley that were now, in November, still vine covered with peas and squash. In the summer when she had her famous parties these arches were hung with Japanese paper lanterns and the gazebo's center table was laden with an array of appetizers. Delicious tid-bits like a slice of prosciutto wrapped around a crunchy, slim bread stick or a fresh, slender asparagus spear. Fresh pea pesto slathered on toasted baguettes. Marinated roasted red peppers, artichoke hearts, gherkins, sliced hearts of palm, pickled baby onions, and mushrooms all served from her wonderful hand made pottery in rich deep colors like indigo, forest green, tomato red and mustard yellow.

Joannah's goat Minnie, who always attended her festivities wearing a lei of flowers, also provided the tangy cheese that was shaped into small cylinders then rolled with chives, thyme, dill, black pepper, cumin, paprika, pecans, walnuts, or pistachios. These trays were garnished with all the blooms that dotted her verdant garden. Bright orange calendula and marigolds, little bunches of chamomile and daisies, sweet pepper scented nasturtium and sometimes small beds of clover. To go with this she became notorious for a wicked punch that was mostly citrus juices and ginger beer spiked with mescal.

It was sad for him to think about missing out on the visits with Joannah that in some ways changed his life. She was the one who knew he was an artist for sure. They shared so much visual richness in her books and esthetic knowledge during their conversations. Explaining this would be his last trip, she laughed with her strong arms around him and said, "This is not the last time I will see of you!" He kissed her cheek and left for his next stop at Piranhurst. He simply carried the crates that Chef Fredo had ordered into a spotless kitchen, knowing he was somewhere drying out from the little scuffle in the pool with Chef Velly at Il Brolino, Paco muttering, 'absurd, absurd absurd!'

Arriving at El Mirador, it was a huge surprise to find Chef Victore back in the kitchen working on a grand evening meal with Dulcina, Adiva, and Trella. It was known that The Montecito Inn, Charlie Chaplin's folly, was up for sale and threatening to close, so Victore had no choice but return to his old job. He told Paco of the wild circumstances that caused Chef Pulga to pack up and leave the great estate overnight. The Mistress of the mansion was entertaining guests from Valencia Spain, the region that Juan Pulga always distinguished as his homeland. They discussed in Spanish the specialties from that area exclaiming the Chef's dishes were very different. They made innuendos regarding his accent that they confidently knew was not like theirs. Finally at the dinner table one pompous Spanish gentleman declared after a bite of Chef Pulga's signature tamales, "This cook is from Mexico! I recognize the dish from Barbachano's new Rosarita Beach Hotel." Fearing that his Mistress would know he really was a fake, the Chef paced back and forth in the kitchen. Sulking and in truth psychologically unstable, Pulga burst out of the kitchen and running to the offending guest with a heavy silver tray, bashed him on the head then fled not to be seen again.

Two more stops and Paco's rounds would be finished for the last time. He left a big basket in the kitchen at Miraflores, the glorious estate that was the Country

Club until a new grand development left it vacant. Elegantly transformed into a private residence it was now radiant with handsome details and lovely gardens. These days since John Jefferson was in banking and totally immersed in the crash, Paco could not help but tarry unseen near the terrace where Mary, his refined wife, and all her lady friends were having tea and sharing juicy gossip. One woman was bemoaning the fact that many of their friends who normally arrived from Eastern cities were not coming this year. "What will we do about the Christmas Tea without Margaret and Susannah?" Someone mentioned the strange death of an esteemed city politician, who was found at the bottom of east beach cliffs. They all chimed in on how many of their favorite stores were closing on State Street.

Shaken by the seriousness of all these negative circumstances, Paco made one last stop at Casa Dorinda, enjoying a warm chat with Mrs. Bliss who could cheer up a fence post with her bubbling chatter that promised a better day ahead. A little heartened he drove the fine Diehls Truck to it's place in the back of the store, sadly imagining it would be sold any day now. Hopping on the Indian, speeding toward Val Verde, his thoughts turned to Lillian. These days he, along with Peri and Sorush, cooked tasty little dinners in the tower house kitchen. They dined on a fresh collection of vegetables from the magnificent gardens in neighboring Il Fureidis and it was here that Paco learned so much about creating magical Indian curries.

Paco would play little games with Lillian, encouraging her to take bites while watching her wonderful plump silky lips glisten with a cinnamon and cardamom scented buttery sauce. He desperately wanted to just lick it off, kissing her passionately, loving her deeply but he knew it was taboo. At this point in her recovery from the disastrous kidnap, rape and drugs that changed her life, she imagined herself to be about twelve years old and so innocent and vulnerable Paco was constantly careful not to betray his feelings. They played chase with Ranger and sat on the big rocks flanking the stream, tossing pebbles and giggling over squirrels that scampered through the trees. These moments were sweet relief from a dangerous world for both of them. Lillian's eyes bewitched him, pale grey with dazzling gold and green flecks that gleamed with a rare purity of spirit. This together with her light form and blondness gave her the presence of an angel, opalescent and shimmering in the semi dark. It was pure pleasure for him to simply watch her move. He said good night, leaving Ranger with her as she wanted, then with Sorush went to the cottage. There, for the first time in weeks he forgot his studio work, just bathing and falling into bed he slipped into a soothing blackness.

After the terrible last week of auctions at Diehl's that cleared out the entire store making the interior, once filled to the brim with extravagant goodies from around the world, look small and unimportant, they staged an emotional goodbye party. Saving plenty of libations and expensive gourmet delicacies for the evening, the night unfolded with many stories told of the ridiculous crazy goings-on in the market, leaving them weak with laughter. Salvadore revealed the strange special orders he prepared and secretly delivered to a famous starlet. Val & Paget, Taj and Paula with Esperanza and Chef Victore danced in a circle and then formed a conga line with many of Paco's favorite customers plus more including Chefs Velly and Fredo, Joannah Prang, Gunnar, even Corliss and boyfriend. He stood by as Charlie Chaplin's crowd along with a very drunk Penny and Oren said goodnight. Ludington, Printise and Jasper had waited to take him home. Paco took one long heartsick look back and then letting loose of all the sorrow he dropped his head back on the car's luxurious leather seat, closing his eyes he whispered, 'Thank you, thank you, thank you', over and over.

Events moved on rapidly after this. Paco received word of his acceptance in the Academia del Arte, an admission that he learned much later was never really in question given his money and family status in Italy. Madonna and Oakley arrived shortly after that to celebrate his accomplishment, plan for his move to Florence and a final miracle that left him dazed with joy. Oakley bought the Quien Sabe as a gift for Madonna! On Christmas Day Miss Penny and Oren Star wed in the sublime wood paneled music room with its magnificent vaulted ceiling and remarkable furnishings decorated with fresh pine boughs and a twelve-foot tree. Paco and Chef Printise prepared the buffet. The Quien Sabe was never more beautiful that night. It was a brilliant moment treasured for a lifetime by each member of the party, not one of them imagining what the future had in store.

Several weeks later after his Mother and Father returned to Mio Cuore, leaving him with ardent blessings, plenty of money and important papers of introduction signed by the old Don himself. Paco was busy packing his suitcases with only a few clothes, thinking he would buy more in Florence. He enclosed his favorite sable brushes and a few toiletries. Just as he collapsed on the big iron bed a dark figure entered the room followed by a grave Sorush who whispered,

"Sahib, Paco Sir, the great Teacher Krishnamurdi wishes to reclaim his books and journals." The soft light of a single lamp revealed the face of this spiritual guide that so many followed. He was very dark skinned and had enormous black eyes with strong expressive brows that were now furrowed in concentration as he pulled out all the volumes he wanted from the bookcase. A pure white stiff collarless shirt peeked out of his perfectly tailored black suit. Paco, feeling shy yet not wanting to waste an opportunity to speak with the man who wrote much of the literature that had given him immense pleasure and insight over the past months, quietly said, "I have been so pleased to be able to go through your work, especially the journals." With that their eyes met for the first time. Krishnamurti's expression was fierce with eyes flashing possibly with anger, Paco could not tell, thinking maybe he always looked that way? Realizing he should never have admitted to reading the private manuscripts and not knowing what to say next, he sat waiting for some harsh reprimand but nothing developed. The two men worked for almost an hour, packing up everything in silence. Paco watched from under his cover and in the end they simply left, the revered mentor of many never speaking a single word. Disappointed and weary he fell asleep knowing tomorrow would be his final day and Ludington had planed a small party.

Waking and bathing, looking at himself in the mirror, Paco crinkled his eyes and

smiling ran his fingers through the short dark wet curls that he left natural ever

since his job at Diehls ended. He noticed how mature he looked and there

definitely was an emergence of the Captain's classic profile. His eyes clouded

over and looking down he asked himself, "What am I doing here? Should I be

leaving?" In moments, walking by the book case on his way out he discovered

that a single journal was left behind so he took it to his suitcase and tucked it

into the large inside pocket.

The night was festive and the dinner a spectacular recreation of Chef Printise's

winning meat platter with his remarkable Duck a la Greco, rich in a sauce of

plumbs, Grand Marnier Brandy and black olives, kissed with rosemary and

finished with pine nuts. There was white asparagus, this time of year from a tin,

with mellow orange curls of melted aged mimolette. A bitter lettuce salad with

chives and sautéed sweet onions in honey beside the Chef's Greek cousin's

legendary Chaniotiko Boureki potaoes with mint and Caprino a goat's milk

cheese. For desert Perichercher had created a luscious mound of sweet scented

nut filled rice decorated with many kinds of candied fruits and sparkling dots of

pure gold leaf. The atmosphere was loving and affable, really an intimate sharing of good will and Godspeed to one they all held so dear. Lillian sat

happily on Paco's lap arms draped around his neck, while the others toasted him

over and over with Ludington's best vintage Mumms. And so, drunk but happy

he bid them all a fine farewell and walked to his little cottage alone.

Epilog

Paco was packed and standing with Ludington in the forecourt of Val Verde on a warm yet crisp January morning. Jasper and the big Pierce Arrow Touring car were waiting to take him away. This day would see him travel by train all the way across the country to New York Harbor where he had a ticket for crossing the Atlantic, first class, on Cunard's flag ship The Aquitania. There would be another ship to take him from Southampton in England to Genoa, Italy. From there Oakley arranged to have the old Don's partner, Fillipo Mazzei's grandson Alessandro, meet him. Traveling together to Florence they would find his new studio and he could sign into the Academia. Paco needed plenty of help with his Italian even though he had heard it spoken all his life. This was the plan that thrilled him just moments before and now gave him a pain in the bottom of his belly. Shaking hands with Ludington who appeared uncharacteristically sentimental, he boarded the great automobile. Rolling by the astounding beauty of Val Verde's gardens, ancient sculptures peeking through manicured foliage and tree lined partiers creating mammoth rooms, now dappled with sunshine, he looked out to his right where he could see Ranger dancing along with Lillian.

She was waving and innocently throwing kisses, following along side the car like a child, her long blond hair glimmering with highlights, never realizing he would not be back for a long time. Soon they disappeared from sight. Pulling out of the big front gates, Paco, with head lowered placed one hand over his moist eyes blocking out the last precious images of the Montecito hills he loved so much.

List of Characters

Pacomono Oakley, Delivery boy from Diehl's Market.

Madonna Fazinatos Oakley, Paco's Mother

Pacomio Basinorios Oakley, Paco's Father

The Old Don, Signore Telchide Fazinatos head of the Aroncioni, Paco's possible Grandfather

Carmino, the Captain's first mate

Zio Badare, Butler at Mio Cuore

Quincy & Patrice MacClenny, Diehl's produce department, ex-vaudevillians

Esperanza, Diehls Market Cashier and cosmetics representative

Fortuno Bona Nova, famous baritone & Esperanza's would be Groom

Salvador Rodriguez, Diehl's soda fountain jerk & speak-easy bartender

Libby, Diehl's cook and food server also works at Casa Dorinda

Mac Massini, Diehl's Butcher

Salvador Rodriguez's little brothers, Juan Carlos and Martine

Beatrice Rodriguez, Salvador's wife

Tahj & Paula, Diehl's Market manager and wife

Gana Walska, legendary Diva

Valentino Clemente, Warren Paget, Firemen and Paco's friends

Mr & Mrs Wright, John and Susana, owners of the Quien Sabe

Oneda, Mrs. Oneda, his two children, Quien Sabe Head Gardener

Rosalita, Quien Sabe kitchen & housekeeping staff

Chef De Vielmond, Velly, Il Brolino's Master Chef

Edwin Ballingford, Owner of Il Brolino, wife Charmaine

Mr & Mrs Bothin, Henry & Ellen called Nellie

Chef Wilfredo Henriques, Fredo, Piranhust's Master Chef

Lora Knight, Mistress of Cima Del Mundo

Mama Genet, Fayola & Latrice, Cooks of Cima Del Mundo

Gunnar Vernersen, Lora Knight's Swedish chauffeur

Charles Lindbergh

Corliss Macclelland, Paco's schoolmate

Lilian Hoover, Aredvi Sura Ana, Paco's schoolmate and great love

Amelia Carlyle Addison, Paco's schoolmate

Lionel, Amelia's boyfriend

Frank, Francis Dubois Ralph, friend of Lionel

Rennie, Viscount Renford Combs Fitzroy, Corliss's boyfriend

Oren Star, celebrity romance novelist and Miss Penny's lover

Lolita Armour, Mistress of El Mirador

Miss Penny, Penelope Elise Lavigne, event PR coordinator

Bliss, William & Anna, local patrons

Bernard Hoffman & wife, owners of Casa Santa Cruz

Chef Pulga, Master Chef of El Mirador

Chef Victore, Sous Chef of El Mirador and Head Chef of Montecito Inn

Java Sir - Sepehr Jafar Javeed Foroohar, Master Chef of Il Fureidis

Java Sir's daughter Perichercher ,Peri, of Il Fureidis, care giver for Lillian

Sorush, of Il Fureidis, guard for Paco

Charlie Chaplin, world famous filmmaker

Huguette Clark, heiress

Ludington, owner of Val Verde and Paco's benefactor

Chef Printis Yonkopolis, Master Chef of Val Verde and Ludington's partner

Chef Eugene Plazermine, Old Parsonage, mentor of Chef Printis

Lockwood de Forest Jr., designer of Val Verde's gardens

Jasper, Ludington's chauffeur at Val Verde

George Washington Smith, renowned architect

Mary Craig, renowned architect

Carlton Winslow, renowned architect

Francis Underhill, renowned architect

Bertram Goodhue, renowned architect

Lutah Maria Riggs, renowned architect

Joannah Hartfield Prang, of Arcady, noted ceramicist, Paco's mentor

Chef Phillbert Omeyer, Chef Bertie, executive Chef Biltmore

Auguste Escoffier - Savoy Hotel master judge for Medallion d'Oro

Chef Henri Bassetti of the Ambassador Hotel, competitor Medallion d'Oro

Chef Gus Wasser of the Biltmore, competitor Medallion d'Oro

Chef M. Grevillet, Delmonico's, NYC, competitor Medallion d'Oro

Chef Peter Wan, San Francisco, competitor Medallion d'Oro

Chef Manuel Acurio, from Buenos Aires, Inspirad, NY, Medallion d'Oro

Chef Raymond Olvera, Cafe Madrid, New Orleans, Medallion d'Oro

Chef Alejandro Ruiz, San Francisco, competitor Medallion d'Oro

Chef Sebastian Molina, NY International Club, competitor Medallion d'Oro

Chef Paul Thalamas, Monte Carlo, competitor Medallion d'Oro

Chef Charles Ranhofer (Delmonico's) , competitor Medallion d'Oro

Chef Oscar Tschirky (Waldorf) , competitor Medallion d'Oro

List of Locations

Diehl's

Quien Sabe

Cima Del Mundo

Summerland

Club Sevilla speakeasy

El Mirador

Piranhurst

Il Fureidis

El Paseo

Forbidden Palace

Casa Santa Cruz

The Book Den

Miraflores

Arcady

Biltmore

Portafortuna

Val Verde

Bellesguardo

Santa Barbara Cemetery

Montecito Inn

Il Brolino

The Montecito Club

Mio Cuore

About the Author

Sharon Howard Stockwell is the eighth generation of granddaughters directly descended from Thomas Jefferson.   Born in Santa Barbara, California, she notable as creator of cooking classes featuring Star Chefs & Premiere Cooks at her landmark Masini Adobe in Montecito where she also hosted many winemaker dinners and release parties offering famous vintages from Santa Ynez and the Central Coast.

Stockwell is also known for her top rated Foodie Blogs, "Jefferson's Table", http://jeffersonstable.typepad.com/, that receives thousands of visitors from over 130 countries worldwide and "Foodie Tramp", http://jeffersonstable.typepad.com/foodietramp/, a Restaurant and Resort review format. The cookbook, "From Jefferson's Table", is a classic labor of love that evolved into a description of American style cooking through eight generations with the carefully preserved original recipes that span the first 250 years of our country's remarkable history.

A professional artist and designer with elite marketing expertise for over 35 years, Stockwell has performed assignments for many companies and institutions including, The J.Paul Getty Museum, L.A. County Museum of Art, Mattel, South Coast Plaza, William Sonoma, Geary's, The Wine Merchant, Princess Cruise Lines and The Century Plaza Hotel. An early expert in direct marketing and entrepreneurial business, she has worked as instructor and lecturer in education programs for USC and UCSB. In addition, Stockwell was a partner in the family firm, S. Stockwell & Sons, that created architecture, interior design and murals worldwide, since 1972. Presently residing in the Montecito hills, she is the mother of two artist-architect sons and four grandchildren.

Contact: stockwellstudio@mac.com

15807555R00229

Made in the USA
Charleston, SC
21 November 2012